Secrets Collide

A Bluegrass Brothers Novel

KATHLEEN BROOKS

An original work of Kathleen Brooks.

Secrets Collide copyright @ 2013 by Kathleen Brooks

Cover art provided by Calista Taylor.
http://www.calistataylor.com

ISBN-10: 1492871230
ISBN-13: 9781492871231

BOOKS BY KATHLEEN BROOKS

ACKNOWLEDGMENT

Many thanks to the hilarious Robyn Peterman (Pick up Fashionably Dead to see what I mean!) for her insight and to my Krew for their support.

And thank you to Chris, Lauren, Milo, Marcia, Craig, Pat, Mike, and Doe for all their love and hard work. And for not looking at me funny when I start talking to my characters.

CHAPTER ONE

Gemma Perry gagged as she mistakenly breathed in through her nose. Her muscles were cramping and the smell coming from the dumpster in the small back alley she was hiding in was strong enough to knock out a water buffalo. How did she get herself into this mess? Gemma found herself asking that question a lot recently. Unfortunately, she knew the answer all too well: She hadn't been *serious* like her older sister, Gia.

Nope, she had been bitten with the party bug instead. When Gia made her appearance into the world a full ninety seconds before Gemma, she looked around at the doctor and nurses and decided she had a world to make better. When Gemma came out, she looked around the room and went straight for a drink at the bar. Their time at the University of California at Los Angeles School of Journalism was very much the same.

Her identical twin sister ate only organic food, went running every morning, and never ever used sugar or drank caffeine. Gia had never once stayed out past curfew, gone to a frat party, or called in sick to work. As a result, at the age of thirty, her sister had the body of an eighteen-year-old and a very impressive job as an investigative reporter for

International Press. On the other hand, Gemma, with her more sultry curves, was sitting behind a dumpster in her size ten jeans with a very sugary coffee concoction waiting to get a picture of Hollywood heartthrob Tatum Evans and his married-not-to-him costar, Ginger Coach.

Gemma had finished school on the party program and gotten the perfect job at *Inside Peek* magazine while Gia went to Africa to cover an outbreak of a virus in the jungle. They were night and day, but they loved each other and spoke almost daily. The only time Gemma didn't talk to her sister was when Gia was investigating a big story and didn't have access to a phone or the privacy to talk.

Lately Gemma had been taking stock of her life and felt it was time for a change. She used to tease her sister about being so serious, but Gemma was starting to realize life was more than hiding behind dumpsters. While being an investigative journalist for Hollywood's hottest gossip rag was perfect when she was twenty-one, she felt she had finally outgrown it.

Her job was to hang out at the hot clubs and talk and listen to everyone there. She hit the jackpot when she could work her way into the VIP rooms to hear the industry gossip and investigate it. When she was younger, it was exciting and she was flirty enough to pull it off. But as the years passed, the job was just making her feel old. Hollywood fought age as if it were a disease and Gemma was tired of trying to be an ageless, no wrinkles, size zero knockout in order to flirt her way into the VIP section of that week's hot new club. She was especially tired of hiding in bathrooms and behind dumpsters.

Two weeks ago, she had tried to talk to Gia about a more serious job, but Gia was distracted by a story she was investigating. Gia had only made encouraging noises like *hmm* and *uh-huh*. With no guidance from her sister, Gemma decided to try Gia's way of life and to see how it felt. As a result, her quads where killing her from running, she was suffering from caffeine withdrawal, and there was a very high probability of her hijacking a donut truck.

Gemma took another deep breath through her mouth and gave her large canvas bag a rub. Fred, her small white Maltese, nuzzled her hand in response from the safety of his travel bag. At least her dog was spared the stench of the dumpster. She would give it a couple more minutes and then try to bribe one of the waiters at the restaurant to sneak her in to catch a glimpse of Tatum and Ginger.

One of her informants had called and told her the hunky playboy actor was with his squeaky clean, never-in-the-tabloids costar eating at Oak Hill, the newest, swankiest restaurant in Los Angeles. She'd make a fortune on this photo and storyline if she got it. Her story would be on the front page of *Inside Peek* and she'd get a huge bonus—enough to let her quit and find a better job.

Gemma froze as she heard the back door open slowly. She waited until she heard heels clicking on the pavement before she leaned around the dumpster. Bingo! Tatum and Ginger were locked in a passionate kiss as a black SUV with dark tinted windows approached. She hid her excitement as she snapped pictures of Tatum squeezing Ginger's perfect butt and opening the door of her SUV for her. She switched her camera to video and kept as still as her quivering leg muscles allowed her to.

"Thank you, Tatum. I had a wonderful evening. Edward just doesn't do anything for me anymore," Ginger pouted. Her overly injected lower lip was sticking out in a cute pout as she threw her much, much older director-husband under the bus.

"That should be illegal. Meet me at my place in two hours and I'll show you what a man should be doing for a woman with your body." Gemma tried not to gag as she recorded the illicit affair. Ginger giggled and Tatum slapped her ass as she climbed into her chauffeured car.

Finally the alley was empty and Gemma stood up and stretched her cramped body. Fred poked his little black nose out of the bag and then quickly disappeared again. "Don't worry, we're getting out of here right now." Gemma picked up the bag and hiked it over her shoulder. She needed to get to the office and start researching Tatum and Ginger's love lives.

"One last time, one last time . . ." Gemma repeated as she headed for her parked car. Most of her stories had been celebrity sightings, or inside scoops about which actors were getting parts, getting fired, or heading to rehab. And she hated every word of it. She once submitted a feel-good piece about a Hollywood hottie spending his weekend visiting sick children and watched as her editor tossed the piece into the trash. She had a pile of those stories on her computer but had been told not to bother emailing them to the editor.

Gemma reached her car and placed Fred into his tiny seat belt on the passenger seat of her silver Mazda Miata convertible. She placed her camera gear on the floor by Fred and was about to start the car when a pain like no other gripped her heart. Fear raced through her and Gemma gasped as she fought wave after wave of panic.

She blindly reached for her phone and hit speed dial. Something was wrong with Gia. She didn't know what, but she knew with certainty Gia was in trouble. She had only felt something like this once before when Gia had broken her leg while investigating a story in Iraq almost eight years ago. But the feeling Gemma had then was nothing like what she was experiencing now.

Tears rolled down her cheeks as she listened to the phone ring. "Pick up, Gia. Please pick up," Gemma begged her sister. Gia was here in town—there was no reason for her not to pick up the phone. Gemma hung up and dialed again as she gasped for breath. The feeling of dread smothered her. It enveloped her so much that the outside world disappeared and all she heard was Gia's voicemail picking up. Something was terribly wrong. She didn't know how to explain it; it was just a feeling she knew with certainty.

Gemma pulled into traffic without even looking as she headed for Gia's apartment. Traffic at ten at night was light for L.A. so she was able to speed down highway 101. She didn't hear horns blowing or see middle fingers being raised as she wove in and out of the lanes. Instead, she felt a numbness that scared her more than the pain did.

She hit the exit ramp at ninety miles per hour as she flew toward Gia's apartment. Eight minutes later, she skidded into the underground parking complex and headed straight for Gia's parking space. Her eyes took in all the cars as she slowed to a stop and stared at the empty space. Her heart started beating faster and harder as the panic almost overtook her.

"Hi. This is Gia. I'm not here right now, but I'd love to talk to you. Leave a message," her sister's happy voice rang out as her voicemail picked up again.

"Gia. Call me, please call me. Are you okay? I just need to know you're okay," Gemma cried into the phone. Despair replaced panic as she raced out of the parking garage and back down the 101 to get to Gia's downtown office.

Thirty-five minutes later, Gemma's tennis shoes hit the ground running as she sprinted toward the large glass building. She pushed open the front door and rushed toward the guard sitting behind the information desk in the large lobby. Marble stairs went to one side of the lobby and a shiny bank of silver elevators stood looming behind the information desk.

"Sorry, the offices are closed for the night, ma'am," the guard announced as he stood up. Gemma was sure he was taking in her brunette hair roughly pulled back into a sloppy ponytail and her black peasant top that smelled like garbage with slight confusion since she looked almost identical to her sister.

"I'm looking for my sister. She has to be here. Her name is Gia Perry. Please, can you tell me if she's here?" Gemma begged.

The guard must've seen the panic in her eyes as he softened his voice. "I'm sorry, Gia left almost two hours ago."

"How do you know? She couldn't have. She's not answering her phone and she's not at home. She has to be here."

"She always says good night to me. She's one of the last people to leave and that's when I come on shift for the night.

She told me to have a good night and tell my wife congratulations on our kid's high school graduation. Look," the guard paused, "why don't you go to her apartment? I'm sure she just went to run errands after work."

Gemma nodded. She couldn't speak but offered him a wobbly smile. She turned back to the front of the building preparing to leave when she remembered the parking garage. "Can I check the parking garage for her car? It would just make me feel better."

The guard looked around, unsure of how to handle her request. "Please. I just have a feeling something happened to her and she always answers the phone. Please," Gemma pleaded. She knew she looked crazy, but she had to know.

"Okay. I'll pull up her parking space number. Let me lock the doors and we'll go down."

"Thank you," Gemma sighed. She didn't know what to expect. Maybe an empty spot and Gia's abandoned cell phone. That would explain why her sister hadn't answered the phone.

The guard locked the doors and he and Gemma headed to the bank of elevators in silence. He pushed a button and they descended into the garage as instrumental music played in the background. The metallic doors opened and she stepped out into the dark garage.

"It's this way," he said as he started counting off the parking spaces.

"Oh no!" Tears gathered in her eyes as she looked at her sister's black Lexus sedan parked in Gia's reserved spot. "Where is my sister?"

An hour later, Gemma sat crying at the well-worn desk of Detective Peter Greene. "There has to be something you can do."

"I'm sorry, Ms. Perry, but your sister has only been out of touch for four hours and there's no evidence she's even missing. How do you know she didn't just go home with a coworker for a one-nighter?" the young and overworked detective asked as gently as he could.

"My sister would never date a coworker. It's against the rules and Gia doesn't break the rules. Please, can't you just take a report?" The young detective pushed back his dark brown hair and glanced at the clock. Hanging her head in defeat, Gemma reached for her purse. It was almost eleven at night and clearly the detective just wanted to get home.

"Okay, give me her name again," he said calmly as he pulled up a form on his computer.

"Gia Eleanor Perry. She's thirty years old. Five-feet-seven and a hundred thirty-five pounds. She has short brown hair and green eyes just a shade lighter than mine. She's my identical twin and she was last seen leaving the International Press office downtown. Thank you. Thank you for believing me." Gemma dried her tears and answered Detective Greene's questions with a sense of relief. She didn't know what else she could do for her sister, but at least she was doing something.

"What about your parents?"

"They passed away a few years ago. They didn't think they would ever have kids, but surprise—my mom got pregnant when she was forty-six."

"That's all we need, Ms. Perry. I'm sending this out to my officers on the street and I'll call you soon to give you an update," Detective Greene said as he printed off a picture of Gia that she had just emailed him from her phone.

Gemma stood up and slung the big purse containing Fred over her shoulder. As if sensing something bad was going on, Fred had stayed silent in the bag for the past hour. Every now and then, Gemma would reach in to pet him and he would reassuringly lick her hand as if to comfort her. "Thank you, Detective Greene. Thank you so much."

Gemma walked past the rows of empty dented metal desks and a few of the other on-duty detectives as she made her way through two swinging double doors and out into the small lobby on the third floor of the police station. She pulled out her phone and dialed her sister as she waited for the elevator. "Hi. This is Gia. I'm not here right now, but I'd love to talk to you. Leave a message."

"I love you," Gemma whispered into the phone as she stepped onto the elevator. The dirty doors closed as her feelings of hope disappeared.

Gemma stood outside the police station and stared at the cars driving by. She really didn't know what to do or where to go. Should she go home and wait for the police to call? Should she go to Gia's apartment and wait for her to come home? Deciding she couldn't stand there forever, she started walking across the busy parking lot toward her car.

7

"Ms. Perry!" Gemma turned around and found Detective Greene running toward her. Oh, thank goodness! If they found her already, then Gia must've just been out. She was sure Gia would fuss at her for making such a big deal over a couple of hours, but she didn't care if that meant her twin was safe and sound.

"You found her, didn't you? I guess I did overreact." Gemma gave a little grin and a shrug of her shoulders in embarrassment. "Where was she? How mad is she for having the whole police force out looking for her?" she asked with a shaky smile.

Detective Greene didn't smile back and Gia then realized what she had known for the past couple hours . . . her sister was dead. Tears streamed down her face. She felt as if she'd been punched in the stomach as waves of nausea hit her over and over again. Detective Greene put an arm around her as she started to collapse. "I'm sorry to ask you this, but I need you to look at a picture." Detective Greene held out his cell phone and showed Gemma the image on the screen. "Is this your sister?"

The tears dried instantly as a shocked Gemma stared at the image of her sister on Detective Greene's phone. She looked as if she were sleeping, except for the fact she was lying on a patch of dirt and her face had no color to it. "Yes, that's Gia," was all Gemma was able to say until the twisting of her stomach was so much that she leaned over and threw up while Detective Greene kept a supportive hand on her back.

"What happened?" Gemma asked, wiping her mouth as Detective Greene helped her stand upright.

"We think she was mugged. Her purse is missing. She was found behind the parking garage at International Press. We're looking at security cameras now. I'm on my way over there and I'll come by in the morning to talk." Detective Greene waited for Gemma to nod before he asked, "Can I have an officer take you home?"

"No, thank you. I'd rather be alone right now," Gemma murmured as she stared slightly off into space. Her world seemed over; she didn't even know what she was supposed to do next.

Detective Greene pulled out a card and handed it to her. "Call me anytime. Please take your time getting home. I really would feel better if you let one of my officers drive you home."

Gemma looked up into his worried faced and gave him a weak smile. "I'll be fine. Thank you so much, just please take care of my sister and find whoever did this."

"I will," Detective Greene promised. "And I'll have a patrol car check in on you soon, okay?"

Gemma nodded and then walked to her car in a daze. She was conscious of Detective Greene being picked up by an unmarked car as he looked back at her one more time. She pulled Fred out of the bag and held him tight to her chest as she sat in the driver's seat, letting the tears flow freely as her body was wracked with sobs.

CHAPTER TWO

$\mathcal{G}$emma pulled into her sister's parking space at the apartment complex and stared at the cement wall. There was a crack running along some of the blocks and she followed it until it ended. Gemma debated leaving, but she didn't know where else to go. Her home would seem so empty. She had needed to feel her sister again so she found herself driving to Gia's apartment. But she stayed in her car, hesitant to go upstairs. The pain would be too much to bear.

Gemma knew she didn't need to wait for Detective Greene to tell her when her sister died. She had known the second it had happened. She had felt it. She had lived it right here in her own car. Gemma had felt the pain, the fear, and finally the moment her sister could no longer fight. That's why she was here and that was why she needed to find the courage to go upstairs. She needed to feel a connection to her twin again to help with the anguish washing over her.

"Come on, Fred," she said softly as she put her windblown dog back into the large bag.

Gemma felt as if she were in a nightmare as she made her way to the elevator and pressed the eleventh floor. It didn't seem real. The walls blurred and she couldn't focus on anything but the red elevator numbers as they ticked off the passing floors. When the doors opened, she pulled out her keys and headed to the end of the hall to her sister's apartment. She heard every *clink* of the key as she pushed it into the lock.

"What the hell?" Gemma turned the handle. The door was unlocked. Suddenly she remembered that Gia was mugged and her purse taken. The killers would have her address and her keys. What if they were still here? Anger like she had never felt filled her as she shoved the door open. "Come out, you bastards!" she yelled into the apartment as her pulse throbbed in expectation.

Her breathing quickened as she hurried through the apartment, turning on lights and flinging open doors, but luckily, there was no one there. She set her bag down on her sister's couch and Fred popped his head out and looked around as Gemma sat next to him on the white couch. She grabbed the dark blue decorative pillow and pulled it to her, hugging it while rocking as tears flooded her eyes once again. When she smelled her sister's flowery lotion on the pillow, it felt as if she had been punched in the stomach. Fred jumped out of the bag and rested his head on her leg in silent support.

"It'll be okay, buddy," she choked out. She wiped her eyes and held on tight to the pillow as she looked around the room. It was then she noticed that her sister's usually spotless place was a complete mess.

"Looks like those assholes were already here." She shook her head, feeling violated at the thought of those killers pawing through her sister's things.

Gemma pulled out her cell phone and dug around the back pocket of her jeans for Detective Greene's number.

"This is Greene," his gruff voice rang out over the phone.

"Detective, this is Gemma Perry. I'm at my sister's apartment and it's been ransacked. It's a mess. My sister would've been so upset," she trailed off.

"I thought that might be the case. I've already sent an officer over to secure the premises. Try not to touch anything.

Use a tissue or a glove. We want to be able to get fingerprints," Detective Greene instructed. "Can you tell me what was taken?"

"Um, her computer is gone." Gemma walked around growing more and more confused. "But that's all."

"That's all? TV and jewelry still there?" he asked, perplexed.

Gemma walked into the bedroom and opened the jewelry case sitting on the dresser. "That's all I can tell is missing. Jewelry and other valuables are still here."

"Your sister was an investigative reporter; did she ever investigate dangerous people?"

"All the time . . . do you think this was planned?" Gemma asked as her heart stilled. She instinctively went to the door and looked into the empty hall as if the killers might be there waiting to be caught. She shut and locked the door and set the security chain before going back into her sister's bedroom.

"I'm beginning to think that. The crime scene screams professionals. Who would want your sister dead?"

"I don't know. She was working on something, but she didn't tell me what. Hold on. She has a drawer filled with flash drives for storing her research and notes." Gemma hurried from the bedroom, down the narrow hall, and back into the living room. Gia's desk was on the far side near the kitchen, overlooking the fire escape.

Using a tissue, Gemma opened the top right drawer and looked in. "Empty. All her flash drives are gone."

"I'll be there in thirty minutes," Detective Greene said as Gemma heard the sound of a car being started.

"Okay. I'll sit tight."

The boss watched his right-hand man, Sergei Klimov, look up from the reporter's computer and curse in what had to be Russian. "That *suka* had nothing on her computer," Sergei yelled as he threw the laptop into the wall. The screen cracked and broke when it fell onto the floor.

"Tell me you've found something on those flash drives," he growled. He felt his anger radiating from his thin frame. This was why he hired help like Sergei and all the other little minions.

They were supposed to take care of these things for him. That's why he was the boss.

He knew a man like Sergei held power simply because of his physical strength—and the fact he was a psychopath.

While he himself stood only five-feet-eight inches or so and probably weighed half of what Sergei did, there was no way Sergei would ever cross him. While he may not look physically intimidating, he was quite possibly the most powerful man on the planet.

He could overthrow a dictator, a president, or even an entire royal family with a flick of his manicured hand. With one press of the button on his phone, a country could be bombed or a satellite shot down. Of course, people had to pay heavily for him to issue those orders.

At any given time, he was orchestrating arms deals with rebels, pirates, and warlords while running a highly profitable sex-trafficking ring. His men ran the black market for guns, weapons, and stolen goods. He had just sold *The Portrait of a Young Man* by Raphael on the black market for $100,000,000 to a private art collector in France. The portrait, rumored to be a self-portrait of Raphael dating back to the sixteenth century, had been stolen from Poland by the Nazis during World War II. While the Polish ministry had been on a wild goose chase for decades all through Europe trying to locate it, he had broken into an old bank vault in Austria and had stolen it for himself.

He had more money than many nations and more people of power in his pocket than all of the lobbyists in D.C. He had done it all by himself, too. The idea started when he was just a child, sitting in his room thinking, while his mother *worked.*

His mother had been a prostitute. He realized it by the time he was five. Men had come in and out of their small row house in New Jersey day after day. She was beautiful and they gave her things. They even gave him things. Later his mother had told him her body was marketable and she was going to use that to her advantage. She had her eyes set on the governor of New Jersey and a better life for her family.

She wasn't shy about the fact that his father was her high school sweetheart who had died in Vietnam along with so many other men. She later told him that her heart had died that day and the only way to put food on the table was to use her body. She started off small, with city council members and influential merchants. They received free groceries and a bus pass that month.

By the end of the year, she was the mistress to the governor and her son was starting first grade in the best private school in the state. But, she hadn't stopped there. She moved on to senators and eventually the vice president of the United States. All the while, the boy had listened and learned. These men had real power and he learned by listening to them talk on the phone when they visited his mother. Sometimes they held meetings at his mother's new condo, and he'd be able to stealthily observe, study, and discover the secrets of the game. For his eighth birthday, his mother gave him a camera and he had realized a new way to get the power he had been dreaming of.

But soon it was over. By the time he finished his freshman year of high school, his mother had grown older and had been tossed aside. At the end of that year, the principal had approached him in the private school's library and told him he wouldn't be able to continue in the fall. His scholarship was no longer being funded.

His classmates had laughed as he ran out of the school that day. They all knew who he was and why he was there. But now that he no longer had the governor's protection, he was fair game. They had cursed him and called his mother names as he packed up his locker.

His mother had saved money for his college, which he thought he could use to finish high school. But before the next school year started, she became depressed. She felt weak and helpless. Her youth and beauty had been her identity and now it was gone. She slowly turned to drugs and by August, the money was gone and his mother was lost to heroin.

He had begged the school for a scholarship, but they said no. They had admitted him as a favor in the first place, and now no money would be coming his way. It was then he decided to take the power away from those who had hurt his mother. He had hurried home and had opened the small suitcase he'd hidden under his bed. Opening it up, he'd stared at the pictures he had taken over the years. The first had been his most powerful—his mother and the vice president having sex.

They hadn't even known he was there. He was supposed to have been at chess practice but had skipped it. He knew it had been wrong to take the pictures, but he had been compelled. He had sneaked past Secret Service agents sitting in the lobby of the condo building while he pretended to be a Russian spy. He was on a mission to get the *evidence* to prove the Russians were building nuclear weapons. As part of his game, he quietly turned the large round knob and pushed open the front door to his condo. All he could see was his mother's hair hanging down her back as she moaned from the top of the dining room table. The vice president's face was looking right at the camera, except his eyes had been closed in ecstasy.

Looking at it now he felt the power in it. The vice president was running for the presidency, and this photo would destroy him. With a smile, he put the picture in his backpack and hopped on the bus for the nation's capital.

That had been the beginning of his career. It had only grown since then. Every time he brought one more person of power down to their knees, he thought about those boys who had bullied him when he had been told to leave school.

When he was sixteen, his mother had died from a drug overdose. While he had tried to save her, she was too far lost in the haze of drugs. Instead of going to live with some aunt he had never met, he used his skills to follow street dealers until he identified mid-level management in the local drug trade. He used them to track down the head of the area's cartel. He gathered evidence and turned it all over to the police. When the ring began to collapse, he stepped in and quickly took over.

The street thugs vying for the head job were just too stupid to run it so he made a deal with the toughest thug. The thug would use the physical force necessary for the takeover, just like Sergei was doing for him now. When college started two years later, he handed over power to the thug for a steady twenty percent of all profit.

In college, he fell in love with art and discovered the very profitable side of the black market. After graduating, he'd mastered theft, forgery, weapons, and more. He used his connections to gather evidence and then blackmailed his way to the top. He'd been untouched, unthwarted, and unscathed for all this time—until his dog-fighting ring in Keeneston, Kentucky, was busted last year.

Now he couldn't sleep. He could hear those boys from high school taunting him when he closed his eyes at night. He feared losing the power and control he'd worked so hard to gain. He cursed and realized he'd zoned out again. He'd been doing that a lot since he stopped sleeping. His men had just botched an assignment and that meant they were in trouble, he thought as he unbuttoned his suit coat to expose the .38 at his waist.

"The flash drives appear to be full of notes, but nothing of importance to you. Research on a corrupt Washington senator taking bribes from lobbyists, some coverage from the Iraq war, a bunch of notes on the political upheaval and human rights violations in the Democratic Republic of Congo . . . nothing about guns or sex or anyone associated with you," the young man told him as he held his breath and tried to keep his eyes on the boss. But, his fear was visible every time he glanced away from him.

"Are you sure this woman has anything to do with us?"

The boss felt his heart squeeze as his man questioned him. It was hard to breathe as the mocking voices of his classmates filled his head. He whipped around, shot the man who dared question him, and then breathed as the voices quieted. "I know she has info on us. Go back to her apartment and search again," he yelled. The room cleared and he was left alone with a dead man and his thoughts, once again.

Gemma sat back down on the sofa to wait. She closed her eyes as images of Gia and herself as kids floated into view. She smiled as she remembered their secret hiding place in the attic where they'd go to play and speak in twin. It was their special world.

"Look, Gemma. I made this box in art class. We can put all our treasures in it and keep it forever," Gia said excitedly after school in the third grade as she showed off a pink wooden box with a bright purple flower on the top.

Gemma's eyes popped open and she sat up so fast Fred almost fell off her lap. "The box!" Frantically Gemma started looking around. Had she seen it when she walked through the apartment? No, she hadn't.

"It's got to be here," she mumbled excitedly as she started pushing aside books and looking in drawers. She felt her blood rushing through her body, suddenly knowing she *had* to find that box.

She stopped in the middle of the apartment and looked around desperately. It was here, but where? Gemma wandered around again with her head held back, looking at the ceiling and into every nook and cranny. She screamed for joy when she found what she was looking for in the hallway coat closet.

An unseen force urged her to hurry as Gemma grabbed coats and threw them to the ground. She scrambled into the back of the tight closet and ran her hand along the wall.

Hidden in the far back corner behind the coats was a small panel painted the same color as the rest of the closet. She pried it open with her nails, not caring when they broke off in her quest.

She tossed the panel to the ground, reached inside the dark space, and pulled out the faded box with Gia and Gemma written on each side of the purple flower. Under the box were three notebooks with a symbol on the bottom of them that she recognized.

Carrying them quickly to the couch, Gemma set everything down on the coffee table and stared at the box. She reached a shaky hand toward the flimsy clasp but froze when she heard a key being inserted into the door. Fred began to growl and she scooped him up along with the box and notebooks, shoving them both into the bag. Police officers didn't have a key to the apartment, but the person who killed her sister did and she wasn't going to be next.

Her eyes were frantically searching for a way out when they landed on the window behind the desk. The doorknob turned and the door opened a couple of inches before the security chain engaged.

"What the . . ." she heard a man's voice curse.

Gemma leaped onto the desk, turned the bolt, and threw open the window as the man put his shoulder to the door. She heard the chain pop as she clambered onto the fire escape. She didn't wait to see who came through the door. In her mind she knew she should get a description for the police, but her fight-or-flight instincts took over and screamed at her to run.

She heard the men yell and jump onto her sister's desk as she gripped the rails and raced down the tiny metal stairs. Windows started opening as she beat her way downward. The men were gaining and when she glanced up, she saw they were able to take the stairs two at a time.

Neighbors yelled and threatened to call the police. Gemma was concentrating so much on the steep stairs she couldn't yell for help. In actuality, she was so scared she didn't think she could form words to call for help. Her only hope was that the police were nearby.

She rounded the third floor and looked frantically around for more stairs. She glanced behind her and saw the feet of two men above her. The stairs ended but she saw the sign to pull the lever for the emergency ladder. With a loud *creak,* the sound of metal grating against metal reverberated off the surrounding buildings and the ladder slid to the ground.

Hiking her bag further up her shoulder, she turned around and looked into the eyes of the scariest man she'd ever seen. His head was shaved and the lights from the apartments gleamed off his dome. But it was his eyes that scared her the most. They were a menacing black that sent shivers down her spine. A small scar ran the length of his cheek, adding to his dangerous appearance.

Gemma panicked as she felt her foot slip off the step below her. She gripped the side of the ladder with her sweaty hands as she painfully plummeted to the pavement. Her feet hit with a resounding force, felt through her entire body, and caused her to let go of the ladder. She stumbled backward and straight into a solid wall of muscle.

CHAPTER THREE

*C*y Davies felt his feet pounding the stairs in the darkened stairwell. He controlled his breathing as the sound of gunfire bounced off the cement walls around him. Straight ahead, the locked door to the roof stood in his way. He just needed to get through it.

His expensive Italian leather shoes slid across the floor as he skidded to a stop in front of the door. He looked behind him as a new round of gunfire erupted. Not wasting any more time, he brought his knee up, lashed out with his foot, and was rewarded with the sound of wood splintering as the door flew open.

He chanced a quick glance behind even though it cost him precious seconds. The shadowed form of a man burst forth from the shadows. Cy grabbed the gun hidden beneath his suit coat and fired a shot down the stairwell before sprinting through the door and into the late afternoon sunlight.

His eyes adjusted quickly as he ran across the graveled rooftop. The crack of a gunshot made him duck his head and dive behind the air conditioning unit before returning fire. He looked around the rooftop and saw the tall buildings of downtown L.A. surrounding him on all sides but one. There was his escape—the shorter bank building across the alley from the business center. He had to make the jump.

He stuck his arm around the side of the air conditioner and fired blindly before shoving the gun back into his holster and sprinting toward the edge of the building. He breathed in deep through his nose to control his heart rate and the adrenaline surging through his body.

He slid to a stop as he looked over the edge of the building. Cy was twenty-six floors up and it looked as if the bank building was two or three stories below. What worried him was the distance across. Below him, cars were so small and people looked like ants. Having heard the gunfire, people were standing at the far end of the street with their heads leaning back. He couldn't worry about them. He looked across the wide alley and took another deep breath. It was now or never.

He turned around, jogged back a good way, and then turned back toward the edge of the building. He pushed off in a full sprint. His arms sliced through the air as they pumped, urging his body to go faster and faster. If he didn't have enough speed, he wouldn't make it over the alley.

He kept his eyes on the building behind the one he intended to land on in order to gauge where he needed to aim his jump, since he wouldn't be able to see the shorter building until he hit the edge. He stretched his stride and released the adrenaline he had been trying to control. The extra burst prevented him from hesitating when his foot landed on the lip of the building.

Cy reached for the sky and then swung his arms downward as he leapt off the building without a second thought. It was if he were in slow motion. He felt his feet leave the solid rooftop below him as he soared into the air. It was both somehow freeing and oppressive at the same time, as the adrenaline pounded through his body.

By bringing his knees up and propelling his arms, Cy was able to keep the momentum going a little longer. He didn't chance a look down, knowing it would throw him off balance. Instead he kept his eyes on his landing spot. His body pushed through the hot summer air as he angled through the sky. He felt his body starting to lose momentum just as he cleared the building from above and knew the first part was over. He had made the distance and now he needed to land without breaking anything.

Cy raised his arms above his head as he fell the rest of the way through the air. Exhaling as his feet connected with a solid surface once again, he bent his knees and dipped his left shoulder, causing the momentum from the jump to be shifted forward. He felt the rooftop connect with his shoulder as he rolled over and leapt back up onto his feet. Looking down he dusted off the dirt from his navy blue suit and smiled. He had done it.

"Cut," the voice boomed over the bullhorn. Cy walked over the thick blue foam pads he had just landed on and peered over the edge of the building at the director. "Great job, Cy. Now get down here."

"As you wish, boss," Cy yelled through cupped hands.

"Don't do it, Cy," Jarrod warned.

"What are you going to do, fire me?" Cy laughed at the head stunt coordinator in charge of the safety of all the stunts.

"You're crazy, you know that?" Jarrod complained, knowing today was the last day of shooting for the movie.

"Aren't we all?" Cy asked with a grin as he fell backward with his arms outstretched off the building.

Cy hit the large rectangular inflatable sitting between the building just four seconds later. The air whooshed out at his impact and he laughed as crewmen started deflating the safety measure.

"You son of a bitch, you scared me half to death," his director shouted as he offered his hand to Cy. Cy grabbed his boss's hand and pulled himself free of the inflatable.

"I had to get my retirement party started," Cy laughed as he patted Douglas's back. "What better way? I would've hated to waste that jump."

"Are you sure you want to retire?" Doug asked. "I have a great end-of-the-world movie that I'm going to start filming next. I could use someone with your talents on the set."

"I'm sure. These past ten years have been great, but I'm ready to go home." Cy thought of his family and felt his heart constrict a little. It seemed as if every time they had needed him, he had been on location.

"Then turn your badge and gun in to the prop man," Douglas grinned as he adjusted the yellow L.A. Lakers hat over his balding head. He whipped out his bullhorn and faced the crew who were busy cleaning up from the day. "Cy's retirement party tonight at seven at Molly's. I'm buying the first round."

Cy sat back on the wooden bar stool and tapped his fingers on the large bar at Molly's. Douglas was chatting with the executive producer while the lead actress, Pepper Warner, sashayed her way toward him. Her surgically perfect breasts didn't bounce, though the black see-through shirt and the red leather pants hugged every inch of her lithe body.

"You're much too sexy to retire. That makes you sound like an old fuddy-duddy and you've proven you're anything but that." Pepper winked as she ran a perfectly manicured red nail down his chest.

"Thanks, Pep. But I have a farm and a bunch of family waiting for me back home. I'm eager to get back and spend some quality time with them. The shooting schedule has kept me so busy, I haven't been home since Christmas."

"I might just have to come and see this farm that holds greater lure than Hollywood," Pepper teased as she leaned against the bar, showing off her greatest asset, because it sure wasn't her acting.

"Anytime." Cy picked up his glass and shot the last swallow of bourbon as he thought about his brothers letting him try it for the first time in the barn before they went off to join the Army. Cy hadn't been old enough when his three older brothers—Miles, Marshall, and Cade—had signed up after 9/11, but he had spent the whole night with them talking about the family and what they were about to get into.

Pepper leaned over and gave him a peck on the cheek. "I'll text you some reasons to come back. You'll be missing L.A. so much that you'll be back in six months."

Cy smiled, but he knew he was done. But that didn't mean he didn't enjoy watching Pepper's perfect posterior making its way out the door. "I'm going to miss you too, Cy. " The soft voice came from beside him.

"I'm going to miss you, too, Taylor." Cy slung his arm over the young actress's shoulder. "Do you have everything packed?"

"Yes. Promise you'll call me? I've never done anything like this and I'm actually really nervous." Taylor Jefferies shoved her hands into the back pockets of her skinny jeans and nibbled on her bottom lip.

"You'll be fine. No one knows your actual last name and if you dye your signature blonde hair, no one will recognize you. Just pay attention to your teachers and have fun." Cy squeezed her shoulder. "College is the best time of your life."

Taylor raised a perfectly sculpted eyebrow. "Better than the Oscar I won last year?"

"Better. You know why?" Cy waited for her to shake her head. "Because you get to learn things and discover who you are, not just who a director tells you to be. And you get to make friends—real friends who don't care if you eat carbs or don't wear makeup."

"I'm going to miss you, Uncle Cy. It seems like just yesterday you taught me how to do my own stunts."

Cy smiled. He still remembered the little eight-year-old girl on the movie set standing at the edge of the tree house looking down at the mats with tears in her eyes. Her parents were yelling at her to jump as the director was throwing his clipboard and anything else he could get his hands on. But Taylor was frozen in place. It was her first stunt and Cy calmly walked over to her and introduced himself. He made a joke and she cracked a smile. Climbing up the small rope ladder, he showed her how to jump and promised he'd catch her. She had jumped and started a ten-year career that resulted in many awards.

She had emancipated herself at sixteen after her parents stole over $3,000,000 from her. Cy had spent every day with her at the lawyer's office and then in court. Taylor bought a house not far from him. He taught her how to cook, how to clean her house, and then how to drive. Sadly, she had become more like his little sister than Paige, his real little sister. And that was one of the reasons he was retiring. His own little sister had a baby, and he was tired of being an absentee brother and uncle.

"I know, squirt. Give me a call when you get settled. You're going to school on the other side of the country from your parents, which I know is why you chose it, but know that I'm just three hours away if you need a place to crash for a weekend."

"Thanks. Happy retirement." Taylor kissed Cy's cheek and he grabbed her up in a big hug.

"Talk to you soon, squirt."

"Hey, Davidson. You need a ride home?" Douglas shouted from across the bar.

"Nah. It's not too far, I'll just walk." Cy tossed a hundred-dollar bill on the bar and walked out into the warm air. He had moved to L.A. a little over ten years ago and he still hadn't gotten used to the smell of the air. But now he was finally going home for good.

Cy shoved his hands into the pockets of his jeans and bent his head down as he navigated his way through clusters of men and women making their way to bars. He was going back to his apartment and getting his things ready to be shipped to Keeneston in the next few days. It couldn't come soon enough. He was tired of the grind, the women, the hotels, the directors—the whole thing. What he really wanted was to go back home, take over his part of the farm from his youngest brother, Pierce, and maybe open a small dirt track for race cars and motorcycles.

He stopped after a couple blocks and looked around. If he cut through this side street he could shave off ten minutes.

The sooner he got packed, the sooner he could get home to see his family.

Cy turned down the alley and passed the backside of apartment building after apartment building. Shouting snapped him out of his thoughts and he looked up to see a beautiful woman hurling herself down the fire escape at breakneck speed. A little way above her two men chased after her.

Instinct kicked him into gear. Sprinting toward the emergency ladder, Cy looked for a way to get the ladder down. The only way was three stories above him. The woman was going to have to make it that far by herself, but as soon as she released that lever, he'd be there to help her.

"Come on, come on, pull the lever," Cy whispered impatiently as he watched her jump off the stairs and onto the landing.

After what seemed like an eternity, she pulled the lever and the ladder started sliding down to the ground. The woman turned and grabbed the side of the ladder, but when she looked up at the men chasing her, her foot missed the next step and slipped. Cy watched helplessly as the woman slid all the way down the ladder, her body hitting against it as she held onto the outside rails with all her might.

Jumping to action, Cy held out his arms preparing to catch the falling woman. She came down the ladder with such uncontrolled speed that he had to jump back or risk getting knocked out by her flailing feet.

She hit the pavement hard and stumbled backward, right into his chest. "Good evening. May I be of assistance?" he asked with a smile, completely out of place compared to the woman's terror-filled face. Instead of answering, the woman screamed and stomped her foot on his. "Umph! Look, lady, I'm a good guy. Now get behind me." Cy shoved her behind him and charged the man coming down the ladder.

Reaching up, he grabbed hold of the man's legs and yanked hard. The man's chin slammed into the metal step and snapped back. Cy saw a circular tattoo on the underside of his wrist as he fell back with blood trickling from his mouth. The impact of his body hitting the ground was enough to knock him out.

"This doesn't concern you. Walk away before you die for this girl," the man with the shaved head said with a slight Russian accent from the top of the ladder. He knew Cy held the advantage and didn't go any farther down.

"Or what, you'll come down here and kill me? Then come on, baldy." Cy put his hands on his hips and stared up at the man.

"I won't have to come down there." The man pushed back his coat, exposing a gun.

"Well, shit." Cy leaped back, grabbed the trembling woman by her arm, and shoved her down the street. A bullet hit the brick building just in front of them and Cy shoved her into a narrow alley between two apartment buildings. "Who are you, lady?"

"Gemma. Gemma Perry. Who are you? Er . . . and thank you for saving me. That doesn't seem like enough of a thank-you, though. You did save my life. What do I say to that?" Gemma rambled nervously between gasps of air as they zigzagged between buildings.

Cy couldn't help but grin as he slowed to a stop, hiding behind a dumpster. "A thank-you is good enough. What kind of gentleman would I be if I didn't help a woman in distress? I'd never be allowed back home if my ma found out." Cy held out his hand. "I'm Cy Davidson. It's nice to meet you, even under the circumstances."

Gemma shook his hand, staring in bewilderment as their hands intertwined. His wasn't even shaking. Hers on the other hand were a sweaty, trembling mess. "You're not even shaking." She looked up into his hazel eyes. Green flecks, the same shade as hers, were woven in between bits of gold.

From what she could tell by his short hair, it was a dark blond with a bit of auburn in it. His shoulders seemed to go on for miles and the way he looked in a t-shirt and jeans was ridiculous.

"I'm a stuntman. Or I was. Today was my last day. I'm retired. I kinda live for the adrenaline rush. Getting shot at wasn't anything compared to leaping a building like I did a couple of hours ago. What about you, Gemma?"

"Ugh. It figures you're Hollywood. At least your teeth aren't capped." Cy chuckled at this spitfire in front of him. She came up to his chin and he had the strongest desire to wrap his arms around her and protect her. He didn't know why, because in all honesty, she was a mess. Her shirt was partially untucked from her jeans. Her shiny brunette hair stuck out in every direction and she smelled quite bad. But beneath that were full breasts, a narrow waist, and curvy hips that caused images of her naked and on top of him to fly through his mind.

"And what do you do, Gemma? Is your job why these guys were chasing you?" Cy asked.

"I'm an investigative reporter for *Inside Peek* magazine. Sadly, this is the second time tonight I've hidden behind a dumpster." Gemma took a breath and tried to keep herself together. "And those men were after me because of my sister. They murdered her earlier this evening and I have something they want," she said with a death grip on her shoulder bag.

"I am so sorry, honey. I can't imagine losing one of my brothers or my sister." Gemma held her breath as the huge man with the slight southern accent enveloped her in a hug. Fred chose that moment to stick his head out and make himself known with a whine. "Oh, please tell me the dog isn't the witness to the crime and the only one able to ID the killers?"

Gemma shot him a look that told him to eat shit, but he only laughed and grabbed Fred. "Wait. He doesn't know you . . ." Gemma's worried words trailed off as she watched Fred attack the man's stubbled chin with kisses.

"Aren't you a sweet puppy?" Cy cooed. "Now, why don't you tell me more about your sister and what those guys are after?"

Who was this man? Gemma didn't know, but for now he was better than her sister's killers. "Umm. I'm supposed to meet the police. A detective was on his way when they broke in. If you could just get me to him, that's all I need." Gemma didn't know why, but she was suddenly protective of all her information. What if he was one of them? He kinda looked like them—big and scary when fighting.

Cy chuckled again. "You're thinking I'm one of them, aren't you?"

"No," Gemma denied instantly, but then Cy raised just one eyebrow. "Okay, yes. But, my dog likes you, so I guess you can't be too bad."

"I'm not bad at anything, honey," Cy said with a wink.

Gemma groaned. She escaped a killer but landed with a cocky stuntman. What was next? Being served by a dance crew?

"So, you were going to tell me about your sister," he prompted.

"My twin sister is . . . was . . . Gia Perry."

"The international reporter? She broke some huge stories. She must've stumbled onto something big. Is that what you have?" Cy asked.

"Yes, that's Gia. She was working on something. I don't know what, though. I didn't have time to look. And I certainly am not doing this in the middle of an alley. Now, please, take me to Detective Greene." Gemma looked around nervously.

"Sure." Cy pulled out his cell phone and she started feeling anxious. She felt time ticking and all she wanted to do was get to Detective Greene and hide out in the police station until these men were caught. "Let me just make a quick call."

"A call? To whom?" Gemma asked suspiciously.

"I'm in Hollywood. I have connections all over the place. Let me just check out this Detective Greene and make sure he's clean."

"Okay, that's pretty smart," Gemma said as she nodded her head while Cy walked off a short way to make his call. If only this would end, maybe she could be free of the pressure strangling her heart.

CHAPTER FOUR

$\mathcal{C}$y turned and gave Gemma a reassuring smile as he dialed the phone.

"Happy retirement. Are you calling so late to rub it in that you're drunk and with some starlet?" his boss's gruff voice laughed over the phone.

"Nope. But I did have this cute little number quite literally run into me. In fact, that's why I'm calling. I'm walking home from the bar when I hear shouting. I check it out and look up onto the side of an apartment building where a woman is running down the fire escape with two professionals behind her," Cy told his boss.

"Did you get a good look at them?" he asked, the teasing having left his voice.

"Sure did. Got a real good look at a tattoo one of them had on his wrist as well."

"I'll be damned . . ."

"You'll be more than that. Her twin sister was murdered this evening and she's holding the reason why in her purse. Her sister is Gia Perry."

"Holy shit. Where are you? I'll send St. John to pick her up."

"St. John? He's just a pup. No, I got her."

"You're retired."

"And you can postpone that request with a push of a button." Cy wasn't going to yield. No one was going near Gemma but him.

31

"I have a better idea. You'll like it; it's off the books. Take Gemma somewhere with you and keep her safe. I'll assign the case to St. John and if anyone is looking in the files, all they'll find is a note about her being in a safe house. They'll find you soon, though."

"I know."

"There'll be a jet waiting for you at LAX. I'll call around and find a private air strip for you to land on so we can keep this off the books."

"No problem. I know just the place," Cy smiled.

Gemma watched Cy as he made his phone call. Fred licked her hand as she kept glancing around. Something wasn't right. She couldn't put her finger on it, but something was off with him.

He hung up the phone and she could see him take a deep breath. Did that mean Detective Greene couldn't be trusted? "What did they say about Detective Greene?" Gemma asked as soon as he started walking toward her.

"Gemma, those men who are after you are very bad men," Cy started.

"I think that's rather obvious, don't you?" She was starting to lose her patience. He was hiding something and she wanted to know what it was right now.

"They are professional killers. They won't stop until you're dead and whatever evidence you have is destroyed. I need you to come with me." He was so serious that Gemma just nodded.

"No. Wait. How do you know that? Where are we going? To the police?" Gemma fired off her questions as they came to her.

"They are part of a dangerous international criminal ring. The tattoo I saw gave them away. It was a Roman numeral X. I'm going to take you to my hometown in Kentucky. A plane is waiting for us at LAX right now," Cy

grabbed her elbow and started pulling her down the alley.

"You think I'm going to get on a plane with you and fly across the country to Kentucky? I don't think so, bud. I don't know you, and you certainly aren't a stuntman," Gemma said as she dug in her heels to slow him down.

"You're right about one of those things. I'm not just a stunt-man. I'm CIA and I'm taking you into protective custody.

No one can know where you are. Not your friends, family, or even the police. These men will be coming after you and I'm try-ing to give us as much time as possible to find a way to stop them. Now, we have a plane to catch."

"Do you think I'm an idiot? I don't see a badge. I don't know anything about you. CIA, my ass. What are you, some kind of undercover spy pretending to be a stuntman? Please, that's so Hollywood." Gemma laughed as she started to get angry with her rescuer. These tales were just too much.

"Actually, yes. That's exactly it. Now, we need to move."

"I don't think so." Gemma pulled back. There was no way she was putting her life in the hands of a total stranger.

Bam! The sound of a bullet lodging into the brick building next to her had her diving for Cy's outreached hand.

"What do you think now, honey?" he yelled back as he dragged her down the alley, bullets flying around them.

Cy maneuvered through the web of alleys and side streets as he tried to lose the member of *Ten*. Gemma had stopped protest-ing . . . for now. As he ran, his mind went back. It seemed ages ago that Cy began this journey.

As a teenager, he had been forced to sit back and watch his three brothers head off to the Army when all he had wanted was to join them. He was about to turn eighteen, but his oldest brother, Miles, had begged him to stay and watch over the fam-ily. Their younger sister, Paige, was just about to turn sixteen and their youngest brother, Pierce, was two years younger than that. And so Cy had stuck around.

In high school, Cy had been a nerd. He knew it. He took pleasure in outsmarting his older brothers—not an easy task for sure. He had developed muscles his senior year, but he wasn't anything compared to his older brothers. He'd had a couple of girlfriends, but not the head cheerleader like Miles dated. And he didn't have girls chasing after him like

Marshall. But when his brothers left, he had taken his responsibility as the guardian brother very seriously. He took over all three of his brothers' chores on their parents' large farm. He tossed hay bales, mowed pastures, and then one day he decided it was time to try riding his dad's old bronco.

Cy had been bucked off, but he had gotten back on. The horse jarred every bone in his body and his ass was sore for a week, but it was worth it. The adrenaline rush made him feel alive and he sought it out time and time again. During the summers, he competed on the local bronco-riding circuit and brought Pierce along to watch. Then he had gotten into dirt track racing. He built a car, handed off some of his chores to Pierce, who had gotten old enough to handle the responsibility, and hit the dirt track at night. He was on spring break with his friends when he fell in love with bungee jumping and rappelling. He knew he was becoming an adrenaline junkie, but he loved every moment. It prevented him from worrying about what was happening to his brothers and it got him girls. What else could a twenty-year-old guy want?

Upon returning from spring break his senior year, he took an aptitude test in his psychology class. Two days later, his professor called him into his office and discussed the possibility of a job with the CIA. "Over ten thousand apply, but I have an in with the agency. They'll be on campus next week for the job fair and I want you to meet with the head of recruitment. If he likes you, then you'll need to take a drug test, lie detector test, and another psych evaluation," his professor had said.

"You seem to know a lot. Are you CIA?" Cy had asked.

His professor smiled. "That instinct is part of why I'm recommending you to the agency," he smiled, never answering the question directly. "And with the results of this aptitude test, I'm recommending you for covert status. Someone will be in touch." And he was dismissed just like that.

The next week Cy had a meeting with the recruitment agent. A full background report sat in a folder in front of the man who looked nothing like CIA. His hair was long and he was in jeans and a button-up shirt. "I see you like a lot of action; racing, riding, jumping . . . all while never being arrested." The man hadn't bothered to look up while he pushed aside the rather thick folder he had on Cy and pulled out another one. "Are Miles, Marshall, and Cade Davies your brothers?"

Cy had just smiled. "I think you already know the answer to that question."

The man looked up and took into account Cy's cocky smile and relaxed posture. "I do. I also know about your brothers' top-secret clearances. Did you?"

That had Cy sitting up. "What do they need top-secret clearance for in the Army?" Cy had paused and then smirked again. "Because they're not in the Army anymore. Figures. What are they, Special Ops?"

"You're quick. Let's take a drug test and then I'll meet you back here in ten minutes for a lie detector test."

Cy had passed both tests. He hadn't liked the prying questions into his life, but he had answered them. He was then sent home. Two days later, a man showed up taking a survey and asked his mother all kinds of questions. He'd then given her a new crock pot. He heard his neighbors say the same thing. That night he got a call from Miles.

"What the hell is going on?"

"What do you mean, Miles?"

"I got pulled in from the field to talk to some douche in a suit asking all kinds of questions about you and the family."

"I could ask you the same thing. How's the Army?"

"How'd you find out? No, wait. Don't answer that. It was the douche in the suit in the middle of the freakin' desert—or one of his buddies. Who's recruiting you?"

"CIA. They want me for covert ops."

"Are you going to do it?"

"Yes. Y'all have had your chance to make a difference. Now I want mine. Paige is in college and Pierce is about to graduate high school and has accepted a scholarship to the University of Kentucky."

Miles had been quiet for a moment. "Be safe. It takes a lot out of you to be someone you're not. You won't be able to tell anyone what you do. I'll try to tame the questions on the home front, but you have to promise me something."

"What?"

"If you ever need anything, you call me. I have enough security clearances to cut through red tape. Besides, red tape be damned. If my brother needs me, then I'll be there."

Cy had almost choked up. He and Miles hadn't been the closest of brothers because of age, but he had known down to his core Miles would be there for him. "Thank you. I'd like that."

Upon gradating from UK, he immediately went to Virginia. He graduated top in his class from the academy. After his covert training at The Farm, he was shipped to L.A. to begin his undercover work. Due to his penchant for doing dangerous things, the CIA had gotten him hired as a stuntman on an action movie that needed a driver. There was a scene where he was racing a car on the ice in Siberia. The director had been so impressed he'd asked what else he could do.

It turned out it was quite lucrative to be a little crazy. The more insane stunts you did, the higher the pay. Of course, while he was in Siberia, he was tasked with chatting up the local extras for gossip on the area. Being from Keeneston was a huge benefit. Small town gossip has always been an international pastime. Cy began telling stories of his hometown and, soon enough, the locals were telling theirs.

One of which turned out to be a secret research lab for the military that the U.S. hadn't known about.

As the years went by, he became more and more specialized in his skills for the CIA. He could get into any VIP club anywhere in the world thanks to being in the movies and having a leading actress on his arm for the night. He taped conversations, stole incriminating papers, planted bugs, and much more.

Miles had called him almost two years ago. "Marshall is in trouble. There's this dog-fighting ring in Keeneston. We don't know much more, and while these can be localized problems, sometimes they're just a small part of a much bigger picture."

Cy had gotten all the information he could and then called Marshall to casually investigate further. When he found out drugs and guns were also involved, he took it to his boss. After Paul Russell, the local man who was running for Congress, mysteriously died in an abandoned part of D.C., Cy's boss told him to look into it officially.

He sent the pictures and description of Russell's death through the system, triggering the Department of Homeland Security and NSA to call his boss and chew him out for stepping on their turf.

"Those pricks over at DHS and NSA want you to back off. Apparently this Sergei character is a real badass. Well, you know who's best at catching a badass?" Cy's boss at the CIA had asked. "Another badass. I'm not backing off and I told them that, so don't screw this up."

Boxes arrived at his home in L.A. the next day. Bombings, murders, gun trades—all accredited to Sergei and his band of misfits. They all worked for a man the agency called Mr. X. Each of his troops, except Sergei, was marked with a Roman numeral ten tattoo under his wrist, the same tattoo he had just seen on the man on the fire escape . . . and the same tattoo missing from the wrist of the man who had fired at them. It was missing because Sergei was a mercenary.

His only loyalty was to money.

Cy had never before gotten this close to Sergei and he itched to capture him but not with Gemma holding his hand as they ran through the night. Instead of taking Sergei down, Cy was going to go into hiding. The only question that remained was whether Sergei knew as much about Cy as Cy knew about Sergei?

CHAPTER FIVE

$\mathcal{G}$emma held onto Cy's large, strong hand tightly as she followed him. He was running through alley after alley until she had no idea where they were. She was thankful she'd started running for exercise or she'd be bent over throwing up by now.

She looked up his arm and to the back of his head as he confidently ran on. He was very handsome, maybe just a bit scary due to his mysterious side. The question was, should she trust him or not? He made a pretty compelling argument for why she should go with him. Cy was dangerous looking in that sexy sort of way. The man who was after them was dangerous in an I'm-going-to-kill-you way.

Gemma finally looked around and realized they were close to the posh part of downtown. "Where are we going?"

"To my apartment. I need to get some things."

"I'm not going up to your place with you? Are you crazy? I still haven't decided if you're an axe murderer or not." Cy was so the type of man her mom had warned her about. Sexy, confident, and he probably had a motorcycle, too.

Cy just laughed. It was a low deep rumble that had her biting her lip. He was definitely the man her mother had warned her about. "That's fine. You'll be safe downstairs," he answered as he slowed to a walk.

Gemma looked down at her sweaty shirt and ran a hand through her damp hair. Hotshot over there didn't even have a bead of sweat on his body. "What's downstairs?"

"A club. The bouncer inside can watch you."

"You live above a club?"

"Yeah. I'm not home much, so the bouncers look after the place when I'm gone and I help them out sometimes when they need it. Works out pretty well," Cy explained.

They rounded the corner and Gemma stopped in her tracks. A long line of young women in sky-high heels and short to non-existent skirts stood around as they talked and applied makeup. Cars and vans belonging to paparazzi lined the street and flash bulbs brightened the night sky. "This isn't just a club, this is the freaking Le Vue. It's the hottest and hardest club to get into. Trust me, I know. I tried more than once to get into that VIP section."

"Yeah, well, I guess you didn't have the right connections." Cy's cocky smile reappeared and Gemma rolled her eyes.

Oh, she had made it in, but it hadn't been easy and she didn't know the number of people she flashed in her trashy getup. But it had been worth it. She had gotten information about one of the giant movie companies paying off the most respected review critic in the industry. During her investigation, she discovered that the movie companies bought almost all of his reviews, even though he touted himself as completely independent.

"Squeeee!"

Gemma cringed at the high-pitched screech and Fred popped his head out of the bag and growled at the woman in knee-high leather boots and a micro-mini running over to him.

"Cy!" The woman flipped her long hair over her shoulder and threw herself on him. Her bright red lips left a perfect imprint on his cheek as the flashbulbs from the paparazzi went wild. Wait, Gemma knew who that was. That was the actress from the summer's big chick flick, *Summer Island.*

"Hey, Autumn," Gemma heard Cy say. Autumn Hayes moved to block Gemma out now.

"I heard you were leaving L.A. for some Podunk town in the South. Want a going-away present?" Autumn dropped her voice when she asked her question and Gemma felt a little annoyed, somewhat jealous, and totally dumpy as she stood in her damp shirt, jeans, and trashed hair. Not to mention the woman with her exposed back and long tan legs was a knockout, rich, and famous. How could anyone not feel self-conscious being ignored by that?

"Actually, Gemma and I were on our way up to my place for a bit. But, thank you. If you're ever in Podunk, let me know."

"Gemma who? Is she that new actress on that action movie you just finished?" Autumn put her hands on her hips and looked around the crowd.

Cy leaned around Autumn and grabbed Gemma's hand. "This is Gemma. It was nice seeing you again." Gemma let Cy drag her past the stunned starlet and through the VIP entrance. He ducked behind the bar and into the kitchen before stopping. "Do you want to stay here or go up with me?"

Well, if Autumn Hayes was about to go upstairs with him, it couldn't be that bad, right? "I'll go up with you. Then we can go to my place."

"I'll be quick. You'll need to be too." Cy unlocked the door and walked through a large open living room filled with dark leather furniture and continued toward his bedroom. "You can grab a drink from the fridge if you want," he called from the depths of his room.

Gemma looked around at the spotless, state-of-the-art apartment in confusion. Bachelors she knew didn't live like this. Of course, the bachelors she knew were still stuck thinking they were in college. Some boys just never want to grow up and move past that phase of their lives. She set down her bag and Fred jumped out, trotting straight to Cy's bedroom. Guess he made his choice; now it was time for

Gemma to do the same. The question was whether she should trust Cy Davidson enough to put her life in his hands.

Cy threw his clothes into a large suitcase as Fred sat on the bed watching him. He was trying to give Gemma enough time to make up her mind. He hoped she would decide to go with him or he'd have to take the situation into his own hands. No matter what she thought, he was going to do everything he could to keep her safe.

He walked into his bathroom and pulled out his Swiss army knife and began to chip away at the grout between the large white tiles behind the door. He wiggled the knife under the tile and lifted it to expose a safe. Cy entered his code on the keypad and then placed his thumb on the scanner. The safe's lock released and he opened the heavy door. He pulled out his agency-issued Glock, his weapon of choice, and his documentation proving him an employee of the CIA. He also pulled out his spare credit cards and passport under his cover name, Cy Davidson, as well as his real ones.

Raising his t-shirt, he placed the gun at the small of his back and shoved the rest of the documents into his bag. He only had one picture in his whole apartment. On his nightstand was a picture of his family. He wrapped it in a shirt and put it in the bag before zipping it. The owner of the club was going to ship everything else to him in a couple of days.

It was time to find out if Gemma had made up her mind. "Let's go see what your mommy decided." Cy grabbed his bag and scooped Fred up in his arm. He walked into the living room and found Gemma looking out the tinted windows on the far side of the room.

"I can't go," Gemma said distantly. "My sister needs to be buried with all the love, respect, and honor that she deserves. I can't leave her in some city morgue."

"Gemma, listen to me. I'll have someone from the agency claim your sister. She'll be with U.S. heroes and can then be buried at a time and place of your choosing. But if I don't get you away from here right now, I'm afraid you'll join her. These are professionals and they won't quit until you're dead. I can protect you. Please, come with me." Cy looked down and saw that he was holding her hands in his as he willed her to understand the seriousness of the situation.

Gemma took a deep breath, her hands shook in his. "Thank you for taking care of my sister. That means so much to me. I'll go with you," she paused, "on two conditions." Gemma squeezed his hands. Her dark green eyes snapped in determination. "First, you agree to tell me everything. Nothing but the truth. No secrets and no hiding anything from me. Second, you promise you'll find the men who are responsible for my sister's death and bring them to justice. I want them dead, but justice is what my sister would've wanted."

"Deal. Let's go get your stuff."

Cy drove his red F-type Jaguar convertible around the block twice. There didn't seem to be anything unusual outside the six-story apartment complex, so he pulled into a spot to the right of the entrance.

"Can you see your apartment from here?" he asked as he put the car in park.

"Yes. The light's off and everything looks okay, I guess," Gemma said hesitantly as her eyes darted to every shadow surrounding the building.

"Okay, let's go." Cy pushed open his door and walked around to Gemma's side. No one was shooting at him so he took that as a good sign as he opened her door.

They headed into the small lobby and he waited as she grabbed her mail in the bank of boxes before pushing the elevator button.

"Fourth floor," Gemma told him as she got in. The soft classical music filled the small space as they rode up to her floor. "Bach."

"Beethoven."

Dammit, he was right. She could never get the right composers. The door opened and she stepped out and turned right. She walked the length of the hall to the end unit.

"Is this it?" Cy asked as they came to a stop in front of her door.

"No. I just stopped here for fun." Gemma put her key in and hid her smile when she heard Cy snicker. Most people didn't appreciate her smartass side.

Gemma opened her door and felt the cool air condition-ing hit her. Cy's hand gently wrapped around her wrist and squeezed, silently urging her behind him. It was only then that she noticed he had a gun in his hand. Gemma watched as he efficiently went through her small apartment checking all the rooms. It sure looked like he was a professional. Of course, he could just be a really good actor. The town was full of them, after all.

"It's all clear. Pack whatever you need. You have five minutes and then we need to be out of here."

Gemma rolled her eyes as Cy went to the window and looked down at the front entrance of the building. He looked so big in her small place. He seemed to fill it, and it wasn't his height or his wide shoulders. He just possessed an aura about him that radiated confident male.

Gemma grabbed some food for Fred, his leash, and a bowl and stuffed them into a tote bag. She poured out the milk from her fridge and headed back to her small bedroom. The bed filled most of it and she couldn't resist sitting down for a minute. Gia had helped her pick out the comforter. Tears welled in her eyes. It felt as if everything she knew was being ripped away—her sis-ter, her apartment, and her comforter—everything.

"It'll be okay. I promise, I'll keep you safe and find out who did this." She heard his low voice drift over her as she looked up and found Cy leaning against her door watching her.

"It'll never be okay. Everything has been taken from me. What do I have left?" Gemma turned her head, not wanting Cy to see her tears.

"You have everything left. It hurts now and it'll always hurt. But if your sister was anything like mine, then she'd want you to experience life, love, and kids. Let me help you find these men and bring them to justice for your sister. I'll show you just how much you have left."

Gemma felt the tears flow down her cheeks as she listened to him. Her eyes connected with the picture of her and Gia smiling at their last birthday. Cy was right about something. She did have something left—vengeance.

Cy watched as she wiped the tears from her face before turning back to him. With a nod she stood up and promptly bent over to dig under her bed, leaving Cy with a great view of her rear end. With a mental groan, he turned and headed out of the room.

He picked up Fred and started looking at the pictures she had on her mantel as he waited for her to finish packing. It was obvious she was very close to her sister as he looked at pictures of them as kids, teenagers, in college, and more recently.

"Hey." Cy turned toward the bedroom as he heard her voice call out to him. "Can you put all those pictures in this bag? I just need to grab my bathroom stuff and I'll be ready to go."

Cy caught the bag she tossed at him and quickly stuffed the pictures into it. By the time he was finished packing all the pictures from the apartment, Gemma was walking out of the bedroom with a duffel bag over her shoulder. Cy hiked up the bag with the pictures and bent down to pick up Fred who was balancing on his hind legs begging to be held.

"Ready?" he asked.

Gemma tucked her hair behind her ear as she looked around her place one last time. "I'm ready."

Cy opened the door and looked out into the empty hallway. Taking the lead, he walked by the stairs and to the elevator. He pressed the button and waited as the elevator came from the floor above.

He looked at Gemma standing next to him and saw the doorknob from the stairwell turn. "Do any of your neighbors use the stairs?"

"Hmm?" Gemma asked. She had obviously been deep in thought. The barrel of a gun coming out of the slowly opening door answered his question.

"Get back!" Cy shoved Gemma behind him and against the doors of the elevator. He shifted Fred into his left arm and pulled his gun in one movement. The door flew open as the man scanned the hallway.

Cy fired off a shot and hit the doorjamb. The man jumped back but stuck his arm out and fired blindly. Fred growled in Cy's arms as he returned fire. He had Gemma smashed against the elevator doors with his body shielding hers as he tried to keep the man pinned down.

"Come on," he grumbled at the elevator. There was no such luck, though; the stairway door flung open. A man tried to run across the hall for cover while his buddy fired at Cy and Gemma. Cy could feel Gemma's fingers digging into his back as she hid behind him. Every instinct he had was to keep her safe. He had never felt anything so strongly before.

Cy reloaded his gun and fired at the man leaping for cover across the hall. He was satisfied when he heard the man scream out as his shot hit its mark—the man's foot had been carelessly left exposed. The man hiding in the stairwell fired off another shot that had Cy pressing further back against Gemma. The bullet lodged in the wall not far from his head with drywall exploding onto him as he heard Gemma scream.

Suddenly the elevator doors opened and they fell backward into it. Cy scrambled forward and fired some shots back into the hallway as the men sprinted toward them. Gemma banged the Close Door button over and over again as Cy returned fire. Bullets pinged off the metal doors as they slowly closed.

Cy reached over where Gemma was still hitting the button and pushed the number two. Gemma finally stopped and they both sat in silence as the soft classical music played.

"Chopin," Gemma finally said in a shaky voice.

"Handel," Cy grinned as the elevator started its slow descent.

The doors to the second floor opened and Cy slowly looked out. The hallway was clear. "Come on."

"Why are we getting off here? Won't they be in the stairwell?" Gemma asked as she slowly walked out of the elevator.

"Yep. And they'll be in the lobby, too. That's why we're going to send the elevator down to the first floor while we climb out the fire escape in the back of the building. You have experience with those, after all." Cy shot her a smirk as he carried Fred to the window at the end of the hall. With a bit of effort, he got the window open. "Ladies first."

Cy looked back where a pale Gemma stood plastered against the brick building. In one hand she had a suitcase and in the other, Fred's bag. She looked worried, and if he was honest, he was worried, too. He only had seconds before the men inside realized they weren't inside anymore.

His car was parked just a short distance away but the trouble was the man standing next to the black SUV. While he wasn't holding a gun, the bulge of his jacket told Cy the man was definitely armed.

"Okay. We're going to quietly walk to the car. We should be able to get to it without being seen. By that time, it'll be too late for them to get us. Once you get to the car, dive in and keep your head down. Okay?"

"That's the plan? You're a freaking CIA agent and your plan is to just walk over to the car?" Gemma whispered frantically.

"Yeah. You got something better?"

"Running and hiding?"

"Nope. All my supplies are in that car. No matter what, they'll leave someone here as a lookout. Better to get it over with. Just like pulling off a Band-Aid."

"I'm starting to think you enjoy this way too much," Gemma grumbled.

"What? You're not having fun. I thought this was a pretty memorable first date." Cy winked and then grinned as her cheeks flushed and her eyes narrowed. Good. She wasn't shaking with fear anymore. Anger was an emotion he could work with.

"This isn't a date," she hissed.

"You're right. If it were a date, we'd be kissing by now. Come on, let's go." He tucked Fred under his left arm and pulled Gemma close to his side as he walked out of the dark shadows and into the parking lot.

Cy kept his eyes on the man leaning against the SUV. He was looking through the glass doors of the lobby in Gemma's building. Cy's breathing was slow and steady as they approached his car. They were almost home free when a ringing cell phone broke through the silent night air.

Cy shifted his gun to his left hand and reached into his back pocket to silence the phone, but it was too late. The man at the SUV was already screaming out their position. "Come on," Cy yelled, pushing Gemma toward the car as the men ran out of the lobby.

He turned and returned fire as Fred growled, his tiny white paws wrapped against Cy's wrist as he hung on tight. Cy used his remote key to unlock the door and shoved Gemma, bags and all, into the front seat.

"Get down," Cy yelled as he returned fire and ran around the car to the driver's side, leaping over the closed door into his seat. He pushed the Start button to his sports car and let the V8 engine loose as he floored the accelerator.

"Cy! Are you there? Are you okay? Answer me, dammit!" the voice yelled from the car stereo.

Gemma looked around at Cy to see who was talking and saw that Fred had released his grip on Cy's arm and was now curled up in his lap as he drove at break-neck speeds through the streets heading toward the 405 freeway.

"Who's that?" Gemma asked as she held onto the door when Cy took a corner at sixty miles per hour.

"Who are *you?*" the voice shot back. "Cy, now's not the time to be messing around with some bimbo."

"Bimbo? Excuse me, but I'm not a bimbo. I've been chased, shot at, and am now trying to survive this lunatic's driving. If anything, I deserve a freaking medal. So back off," Gemma's shout turned to a scream as Cy shot onto the freeway at well over a hundred miles per hour.

"Didn't realize you're in the car with my brother. You *do* deserve a medal. He forgets he's not a racecar driver anymore . . . or well, maybe he still is. Now, Cy, we need to talk."

"It's okay, Pierce. You can talk with Gemma in the car. Are you okay? You didn't get arrested again, did you?" He took a quick glance at Gemma and almost laughed as her eyes widened before slamming shut as he zoomed around cars and trucks on the freeway.

"I remember. I remember everything. It had nothing to do with me. It was you they were after. They kept asking about you . . . where you were and how to get in touch with you. They were planning on killing me, and then capturing and torturing you when you came home for my funeral," his youngest brother told him in a rush.

Dammit. That changed everything. He was no longer going to have the time he thought he would to capture Mr. X and his gang. They knew where he was and had figured out his real last name. His cover had been blown—dammit!

"I'm on my way home and I'm bringing someone with me. I'll be there by breakfast." A plan was already formulating in his mind as he drove toward LAX.

"What's going on? What are you involved in that someone would go to these lengths to find you?" Pierce asked. Cy could see Gemma turning and looking at him with the same question in her eyes.

"I'll tell you everything when I get there. I'll meet you at the farm."

"Okay. Be safe, bro."

Cy ended the call and took a deep breath.

"What . . ." Gemma started before being cut off by the ringing of his cell phone. The number came up as Unknown and Cy figured it was his boss.

"Is the plane ready?" Cy asked as he answered.

"Yes," the deep, accented Middle Eastern voice answered. "You'll land at the private air field around eight-thirty in the morning. That is, if you can get out of Los Angeles alive."

"Ahmed?"

"Yes."

"How did you get this number?"

"John Wolfe does not have anything on me," Ahmed answered seriously. "Now, you seem to be having some problems with a man I am particularly interested in and I want to offer my services."

"I'd appreciate that. I'll see you at the farm?"

"Yes."

The line went dead and Gemma turned to him. "Who was that?"

"Ahmed. He's like the Secret Service for the Prince of Rahmi. He happens to live in the town we're going to," Cy explained as he turned off the freeway and onto West Century Boulevard heading to the airport. He followed the signs to the private jet field and parked in a reserved spot. His car would be shipped home with the rest of his stuff soon. He didn't know how practical a sports car would be on the farm, but it sure would be fun on those twisting country roads where he grew up.

"This is the CIA's plane. Well, kinda. It was confiscated from a weapons dealer and we're just using it until it's sold at auction. We're flying to the prince's private runway in Kentucky," Cy told her as he handed her Fred and picked up all the bags.

"I got that part. What's the plan after that?" Gemma asked as she looked up the steep stairs leading to the plane.

"I'm still working on it."

"Working on it? You don't have a plan?" Gemma stopped climbing the stairs and looked behind her to glare at Cy.

"I believe the key will be in your sister's notes. I won't be able to develop a plan until I know what we're working with."

"And you think we'll have those resources in Kentucky? We should be staying here and working with the LAPD."

"Oh, don't you worry about resources. You haven't met my brothers yet. Or for that matter, the rest of the town," Cy grinned.

CHAPTER SIX

*C*y leaned back in the light tan leather seat as the plane shot down the runway. Gemma sat next to him with Fred curled up in her lap. As soon as the plane leveled off, Cy turned to her and placed his hand on hers.

"You okay?" he asked, pulling Gemma back to reality. She had been thinking of Christmas when she and Gia were just seven years old. They had been embroiled in a debate over Santa Claus and Gia was determined to prove he existed. They fell asleep at eleven-thirty, but when they woke up the next morning, the cookies had been eaten and a note left by Santa telling them how sisters were the most treasured gift any girl could ever get.

"Yes. Sorry. What?" Gemma blinked her eyes and looked out the window into the dark night sky before looking back at Cy's handsome face. He may be edgy and slightly dangerous looking, especially with his five-o'clock shadow, but the way his warm hand relaxed her made her think he couldn't be all that bad. He did save her life after all—twice.

"If you wouldn't mind, and since you're not too happy with my lack of plans, can we take a look at what was so important that someone is trying to kill you?" Cy looked down at her purse and Gemma similarly looked down at it. Inside was the key to everything, but a force was holding her back.

51

Gemma finally took a deep breath and handed Fred over to Cy. It was time to see what Gia had gotten into. She opened the large bag and pulled out the three notebooks.

"What's that?" Cy asked and pointed at the almost-Greek-looking symbol on the bottom of the cover.

"It means one. We had a secret language." Gemma's eyes misted as she remembered sitting at the dinner table having their secret conversations about school, boys, and how horrible their mom's chicken was—all while their parents looked on in confusion. It was theirs and theirs alone. She couldn't remember when it started; they had just always had it from the time they could talk. Gemma opened the notebook and swallowed hard. The notebook was filled with their language . . . every page and every line.

"What the hell is all that?" Cy asked as he looked at the notebook.

"It's all in our secret language," Gemma said as she shook her head.

"Can you read it?"

"Some of it. It's been over ten years since we talked it, even more since we wrote it. Since high school, I think. It's going to take me a while to go through this and try to remember all the symbols for the alphabet and for certain words." Gemma felt crushed. From what she could see, it meant nothing. She remembered some words for her name and some other random words, but not nearly enough to translate it.

"Don't worry," Cy said as he placed his hand on her knee and gave it a slight squeeze. "You'll remember. I don't know if I'll be able to help, but I'll do whatever it is you need me to do."

Gemma looked up from the notebook and over where Fred had curled up in the crook of Cy's arm and fallen asleep. She felt the pressure of needing to remember the secret language pressing down on her. She needed to think about something else. That's when she remembered the phone call from Cy's brother. "Wait. Didn't your brother say you were in danger at home?"

"I was. That's what I'm trying to figure out—how my cover was blown." Now it was Cy's turn to look distant as Gemma could see him thinking.

"Well, it's not as if you're hiding who you are." Gemma watched as he slowly turned to look at her. "Well, you're not. You gave me your name right away. It would be easy for someone to make a couple of calls to find out where you were born."

"I didn't use my real name."

"Cy isn't your name?" Gemma asked. Who was he then?

"Cy is my name. But my last name isn't Davidson. It's Davies. That simple little switch was easy to remember and enough to hide my identity. The CIA provided me with such a deep background and documents that it would be impossible to trace me back to my real identity. Instead of being from Keeneston, I was from Louisville. There were even yearbooks at the high school with my real high school pictures in them."

"And you have no idea who the people are who were asking about you at home?"

"Oh, I have a very good idea. They're the same guys who are after you."

"Me? Why would they want both you *and* me? That doesn't make sense. Wait. Were you in the alley for a reason tonight?" Gemma buried her head in her hands. "Oh God, you *are* an axe murderer."

"I'm not an axe murderer. The guys who are after you are the same ones after me. See, one of my brothers is the sheriff of Keeneston. He busted a dog-fighting ring recently. When I looked into it, I connected it to a group known for trafficking kidnapped women. When I dug around further, I connected it to a group that sells weapons and everything else on the black market. They're real bad people. I've caught a couple, including a group trying to sell chemical weapons out of Russia just a while ago.

"The only connection I've found is that these men all have a Roman numeral X tattooed on their wrist. The boss man, Mr. X for lack of a better name, has never been caught on camera at any of these fights, trades, or deals. No one knows a name, a description, nothing. But Mr. X is powerful enough to have many connections in governments and law enforcement all over the world." Cy leaned forward and placed his elbows on his knees as Fred crawled over the seat and back onto her lap.

"It sounds as if he has enough power to find out who you are. Could've been someone at the CIA even." Now this was something Gemma could think about. Her investigative reporter side jumped to attention and she wanted to know more.

"Yes. They could have. I think it was Russia, though. With the threat of a weapons sale, I dug around a little more than normal and really pushed some contacts. I must've thrown up a red flag somewhere. I was so worried that the bust wouldn't go down, I beat the other CIA team members to it. They could have followed me afterward and have seen who I was." Cy rubbed his hands over his face as Gemma's thoughts raced forward.

"Then why are we going to the one place they've been looking for you?" Gemma drummed her fingers on her sister's notebook as she thought about the situation.

"They're not there now. Ahmed will have taken care of that. Also, as you've pointed out, my cover is blown and it could've been by one of my own. Keeneston is the only place I can think of where I can trust every single person."

"Who is this Ahmed? And how can you possibly trust the whole town? That's just naïve."

"I might not have mentioned all there was about Ahmed in the car. Yes, he's the prince's head of security. But he's also one of the most feared and respected soldiers and interrogators you'll ever find. Shoot, he's a legend at Langley and he's only a couple of years older than I am. That should tell you something right there."

"And you're trusting this guy?" Gemma knew her eyes were round, but this was just too much.

"Yes. He's very good friends with my family and I've worked with him before. My sister was testifying in a large corruption case and he was guarding the other witnesses. But, he's not the only one there. My older brothers were all in the military and the

town as a whole is the nosiest group of people you've ever met."
Gemma didn't smile along with Cy.

"Then how can you trust a bunch of gossips? I mean, I should
know. I do it for a living."

"They only gossip about what's going on in town. I'm telling
you, the town will be our biggest protector. They have an information network—well, a church phone tree—that is better than
any government agency could ever dream of. The added benefit
of a town so small is that we'll know the second someone who
isn't a resident comes into town."

Cy couldn't help but feel excited to be going home. It had
been too long and there was definitely no one he trusted more
to help him than his family: three brothers in Special Forces, his
sister-in-law, Annie, a former DEA agent, and his brother-in-law,
the head the FBI's Lexington office.

"If you say so. Have you come up with a plan yet?" Gemma
teased.

"Yep. Find them before they kill us." He may have sounded
sarcastic, but that was really his plan. Sometimes simple was best.

"You should get some sleep. It's going to be a long day tomorrow." Cy heard his voice soften as he fought the urge to pull a
blanket over her. She had handled today well, but he knew from
experience it was the quiet of the night when the nightmares
struck.

"You're right." Gemma gave a little smile and pushed her seat
back. The large seats allowed her to roll onto her side and look
out the window. She heard Cy move and then the overhead lights
were turned off.

Gemma closed her eyes, but images of Gia filled her mind.
Of them skiing at Big Bear, at the beach, at graduation, and the
hours they'd just talk on the phone when they first moved into
their own apartments. The emptiness gripped her and she felt
her body shudder. Fred curled closer and snuggled his small
head into her shoulder. When the despair was so strong she felt
as if she'd break, a warm hand touched her back. She leaned
back into its heat and strength as she let the tears come.

"It's okay, Gem." Gia stood next to her as they looked up at their new high school. "I won't let anything happen to you. You're in good hands." Gia reached down and held her hand. Gemma didn't want to admit it, but starting at the new school scared her to death. But she didn't have to admit it, her sister just knew.

The memory brought a sense of comfort to her as she let Cy rub gentle circles on her back. Gemma's tears dried up and slowly her eyes closed as Gia talked to her through her dreams.

***

Sergei watched the boss pace back and forth in front of the huge floor-to-ceiling windows in his penthouse. He was in one of his moods. His boss ignored everyone in the room while he talked to himself.

"They'll find you, just like that bitch did," his boss mumbled as he turned around to pace the long length of the opulent living room once again. "No, they won't. I haven't been caught yet." He turned again on his heel. "Sergei!"

"Right here, sir." Sergei stepped forward as his boss returned to reality.

"Are they watching us?"

"Who, sir?" Sergei tried not to roll his eyes. It meant a lot more work for him when his boss was in this mood.

"You know who. Sweep the place for bugs and then find that damn woman. I need those flash drives. I know they exist. I know it," his boss yelled as he slammed his hand on the shiny glass coffee table. "Ready the jet. I'm going back to Virginia."

"Yes, sir." Sergei knew he'd also have to sweep the massive mansion in McLean, Virginia, right outside

Washington, D.C., before his boss even set foot inside. His paranoia was growing worse. Failing to retrieve that damn reporter's research had pushed his boss over the edge.

His boss disappeared into one of his multiple panic rooms in the apartment. He had at least three in every property he owned. He never rented when he was in a new city; he just bought houses through shell corporations. He kept a few of them but sold the ones he wasn't going to visit again. His theory was it was hard to find him when no one knew where he was going to be. The deeds would be signed and paid for in cash and then never recorded until after his business had been resolved and he left town.

"What do we do about that gossip reporter—the sister?" one of his underlings questioned as the other started sweeping the room for bugs, again.

"Find out everything you can about her. And for God's sake, find out who that man was, too. A regular person does not walk around with a gun and have the ability to use it like that."

Sergei took a silent breath and let it out. Detective Greene had been assigned to the case. When they hacked the LAPD, they found that the man who helped the woman wasn't Detective Greene. "The room's clean."

"I know. It was clean an hour ago, too, but sweep the rest of the penthouse anyway." Sergei turned and walked out of the main part of the residence and into the small secure computer room where one of his men was already working on shifting through years of information on Gemma Perry.

Sergei took a seat at one of the desks and started inputting everything he could remember of the man he had come face-to-face with in that alley. He would find him. It might take more time than his boss wanted, but Sergei never gave up on a mission.

CHAPTER SEVEN

The plane hit the runway, rocking Gemma out of a restless sleep. She lifted her head off the window and saw that not only was Cy awake, he had also changed into a new shirt. He had shaved and it looked as if he'd slept well all night. On the other hand, Gemma was a wrinkled mess with her brunette hair sticking out in some places and stuck to her face in others. Right now she didn't care if Cy had saved her, she hated him.

"How do you look so good?" Gemma accused.

"You think I look good?"

Gemma just rolled her eyes. "You know what I mean. You're changed and clean."

Cy's phone beeped and Gemma instinctively looked down at the phone in his hands. If she didn't feel like a hot mess before, then she sure did now after seeing a picture of an actress from the number one movie in the theaters in nothing but panties and a bra with a note asking why he wasn't at her pajama party. Apparently she only wore sexy, mostly see-through underwear to bed.

Cy gave it a quick glance and then deleted it before pointing to the back of the plane. "There's a bathroom and our luggage is back there, too. Do you want to clean up before we get into town?" Cy stood up as the plane slowly taxied to the hangar at the small private airfield outside of Lexington.

Gemma didn't bother to answer as she pushed past Cy, shoved Fred into his arms, and hurried to the back to find her luggage. She was so relieved to change and get cleaned up she didn't even care that she heard Cy chuckle as she slammed the small door to the even smaller bathroom.

Gemma looked into the bathroom and realized what she had thought had been bad hair was a major understatement. Her hair was dirty and there were pieces of unidentified stuff clinging to it. Her face was smeared with dirt, dried sweat, and tear tracks. There were dark circles under her eyes and her normally clear eyes were red, dry, and swollen. Not the image she needed to see after that picture on Cy's phone.

"Can this get any worse?" Gemma asked her reflection as she reached down to pull off her shirt. Her elbow connected to the door as pain shot down her funny bone. "I guess so," she mumbled as she battled her shirt.

Finally, she had managed to toss the shirt onto the floor and turn on the water in the small sink. She looked at the reflection of her jeans and baby-blue push-up bra. She shook her head to clear her thoughts. They were going in twenty different directions at once and she needed all the voices in her head to stop for a while—or at least be narrowed down to just a couple.

She let her hands fill with cold water and splashed it onto her face. The simple act of washing her face invigorated her. Feeling adventurous, she bent over and splashed as much water as she could onto her hair and ran her fingers through it. It was definitely not up to Hollywood standards, but she felt as if she were ready to face whatever was next.

Gemma kept the window to the pickup truck rolled down as the warm air dried her wet hair. Fred enjoyed sticking his head out and letting his long white hair blow in the wind. "So, why didn't your friend Ahmed stay around to pick us up?"

"He's probably gathering intelligence," Cy casually replied as he picked up his phone and punched in a number.

Gemma shrugged and looked out at the countryside as they drove along. A beat-up pickup truck was driving through the middle of a large fenced pasture, tossing out clumps of hay to the horses eagerly waiting in a line nearby. The morning sky was bright blue and dotted with puffy white clouds. The lack of smog seemed foreign to her as she took in the smells of grass and hay mixed into the country air.

"I'm almost home, Miles. I need your help," Cy spoke into the phone. "Okay. I'll see you in fifteen minutes. It'll be good to see you, too."

She saw a slight smile come over his face and noticed it was different from his Hollywood smile. This one seemed real. The others were sexy in a smoldering way, but this one fit him. It softened his dangerous side and, quite frankly, intrigued her.

"Who's Miles?" Gemma asked as she rolled up the window.

"My oldest brother."

"How many brothers do you have?"

"I have four brothers and one sister. Miles is the oldest. He owns a company that helps family farms secure big contracts. He recently married a girl named Morgan. She's a former lobbyist who's now working as a consultant in Lexington. They're expecting their first child next year. Then there's Marshall. He used to own a private security firm, but now he's the sheriff of Keeneston. His wife is Katelyn. She's a veterinarian and heir to the Jacks Hotel franchise. They're expecting a baby in the fall."

"Oh my God . . . he's married to Katelyn Jacks, the supermodel?" Gemma exclaimed. She had written an article on the dark side of modeling and had wanted to interview Katelyn, but her agent had politely refused, saying that Katelyn was no longer modeling. Apparently she was in vet school.

"Yep. But she's not a model anymore. The only modeling she does is for my sister who designs hats. Anyway, next is Cade. He's a high school biology teacher and the head football coach. He's married to Annie who's a former DEA agent and now a deputy sheriff. They have the cutest daughter, Sophie. I'm next in line. Then Paige, who owns her own girly store and is married to Cole, who's the head of the FBI office in Lexington. They have the most handsome boy, Ryan. Finally, there's Pierce who just invented this amazing Cropbot, which is an agricultural robot. It's so cool. Paige emailed me a demonstration and this thing can do everything. Pierce just got engaged to Tammy who's a receptionist at the law firm in town."

"That's one huge family. And you were right; your family sure does have resources. Your brother-in-law and sister-in-law will be a big help." Gemma felt her spirits buoyed as they turned down yet another small narrow road outlined with black fences and rolling hills. "Your mother must be a saint."

"She is. My parents are wonderful and, for that matter, so is Keeneston. It's not for everyone. Some people can't stand everyone knowing everything. I know I couldn't when I was younger, but now I can't wait to get home and see everyone and sit in the café to hear all the local gossip. The Rose sisters are something to behold." Cy gave his sweet little smile and Gemma bet he didn't even know he was doing it. She couldn't help but feel excited to meet all these people.

"However, over the years they've given me my space when I asked for it and now I miss that connection. I miss having connections with neighbors, walking down the street and waving at everyone who passes by, or stopping to talk to someone on the sidewalk. Mostly, I can't wait to see my niece and nephew. I was there when they were born. It was in the early hours of Christmas and I'll never forget it. They must be so big by now."

Gemma heard the wistfulness in his voice and the way his normally deep and graveled voice softened as he talked about his family. But hearing him talk about his niece and nephew took her by surprise. "*You* like babies? You're like Mr.

CIA kickass agent guy with hot actresses trying to get into your apartment."

"Yeah. That doesn't mean I don't like kids. I love them. I want a whole bunch of them, too."

"Who are you?" Gemma asked again. He was a total contradiction—Hollywood hottie with a dangerous edge, but also a protector and family man. She just couldn't help wondering who the real Cy Davies was.

"We're here."

Gemma turned away from trying to figure him out to look at the large white farmhouse they were approaching. She didn't quite know what to think of the range of cars lined up in the front yard. Pickup trucks, SUVs, a bright red M6, and a shiny black Mercedes S600. If a TV crew jumped out and told her they were filming her for a surprise show, Gemma wouldn't even blink. The whole scene was just too strange.

The door opened and people poured out of the farmhouse. She could identify his mother and father because of the gray streaking their hair, and she spotted Katelyn Jacks standing tall in the back, but the rest were a clump of people hurrying down the wide wood steps toward them.

Cy parked the truck and hurried to open Gemma's door for her. Before she could ask who everyone was, a beautiful woman with shoulder-length brown hair and a miniskirt flung herself into his arms. Jeez, could women not help throwing themselves at him? Okay, who was she kidding? Under different circumstances she would, too, although she doubted she'd be able to get through the line of starlets waiting at his apartment to even get the chance.

Gemma cringed when he placed a kiss on her cheek and set her back on the ground. "Hey, sweetheart. Let me introduce you to Gemma Perry." Cy put his arm around the pretty woman and smiled his genuine smile at her. "Gemma, this is Paige Parker, my sister. And that man over there in the black cowboy hat is her husband, Cole."

"Nice to meet you, ma'am," Cole tipped his hat and came to join them.

"It's so nice to meet you," Paige said. "Usually when Cy comes home, it's to nurse some kind of injury. He's never brought a woman home before." Paige openly checked her out and Gemma suddenly felt even more self-conscious than normal as she felt all eyes on her. She instinctively clutched Fred closer to her.

"And these are my parents, Marcy and Jake Davies." Cy shook his father's hand and then wrapped his mom in a tight hug as she laughed.

Marcy clapped her hands and everyone quieted down. "You must be exhausted from traveling. Let me make this quick and then get you some breakfast while Cy tells us what this is all about." Cy's mother slipped her hand onto Gemma's arm, gave Fred a scratch behind his ears, and propelled them toward the stairs.

"This is Miles and his wife, Morgan." Gemma shook hands and introduced herself to the very tall, serious-looking man and his wife who had the darkest hair she'd ever seen. "And this is Pierce and his fiancée, Tammy." Gemma smiled at the petite blonde practically bounding forward to meet her.

"It's so nice to meet you. We *so* have to talk later. I want to know everything," she whispered to Gemma as her handsome fiancé simply shook his head.

"And this is Cade, his wife, Annie, and their daughter, Sophie," Marcy continued as she marched Gemma closer and closer to the house. The little redhead clung to her mother's red hair and giggled as Gemma said hello to them both. Cade, in a Keeneston High School t-shirt and athletic shorts, smiled down at his wife and daughter after shaking Gemma's hand.

"And here she is," Cy kissed his sister-in-law on the cheek and scooped Sophie up into his arms as she squealed in delight. "That's right, I helped bring you into the world and that makes me your favorite uncle," he cooed.

Annie shot Katelyn a look and they both rolled their eyes, "Yeah, you were a big help all right," Katelyn laughed with her hand resting on a very small baby bump. "Hi. I'm Katelyn Davies and this is my husband, Marshall," she said, gesturing to the man standing next to her with short brown hair and jeans that fit tight around well-muscled legs.

"I know you . . . er, I know of you. I'm an investigative reporter for *Inside Peek*," Gemma said as she shook hands with the tall sleek blonde.

"Oh," Katelyn said slowly as she looked straight at Cy.

"Don't worry, sis, she's not here for you. I take it everyone else is inside?"

"Yes," Cy's father said as he came to stand next to his son. All the brothers had inherited their father's hazel eyes and tall frame while Cy and Pierce seemed to have lighter brown, almost blond hair, like their mother.

"You're almost done with introductions. We'll give you a quiz after breakfast," Cy joked. Gemma just didn't know how many more people she could remember, but she followed Marcy up the steps and into the large living room. There were plenty of chairs and couches to accommodate the whole family.

Pictures of all the kids throughout the years hung on the walls, and pictures of the grandkids were set on tables. On the far side of the room sat a man in jeans with his long legs stretched out in front of him and a baby on his lap. On the far end of the couch was a man in the most amazing black suit she'd ever seen. His black hair was slicked back behind his ears and he had his arm around a very pregnant woman whose dark brown, almost black, hair was tied back in a sleek ponytail. She had obviously been in conversation with another lady in a suit with her auburn hair pulled back into a French twist.

Marcy led her over to the couch first. "This is Mo and his wife, Dani."

"Pleased to meet you," Mo said as he stood and gave a slight bow over her hand. His low, Middle Eastern accent flowed over her and she found herself with a strange desire to curtsy.

"Please excuse me for not getting up, but I am huge. Once you get me down, it takes a crane to get me off the couch again. Hi. I'm Dani." The woman in jeans and a maternity tank top held out one hand to shake while her other rested on her very pregnant belly.

"No worries. Wow, when are you due?" Gemma asked as she shook her hand.

"In about eight weeks."

"Do you know if it's a girl or a boy yet?" Gemma resisted the urge to reach out and rub the perfectly round belly. Okay, she could admit to herself she wanted a baby badly.

"No. We didn't want to know, plus it's a thing in his country. We instructed our doctor to tell us nothing. It's going to be a surprise for us and all of Rahmi," Dani smiled as she rubbed her tummy. Rahmi, what was it about that name that sounded familiar?

"Hi, Mo. Thanks for letting us land at your airport." Cy stuck his hand out and shook Mo's hand.

Airport, Rahmi, prince . . . "You're the Prince and Princess of Rahmi?" Gemma froze as she clapped her hand over her mouth. She didn't mean to say that out loud.

Dani chuckled and Mo gave her an understanding smile. "We are. Although here we're just Dani and Mo. We're enjoying our last week in Kentucky before going to Rahmi for the rest of the year," Mo told her as he sat back down and slipped his arm around his wife's shoulders.

"And I hate that they have to leave next week, but her doctor is forcing them. Something about not flying too late in the pregnancy," the pretty auburn-haired woman pouted playfully.

"The doctor left yesterday, in fact. He wanted to check out the palace and set up a delivery room and a recovery room for the baby. Unfortunately, he has my cell phone number. He's worse than a mother hen," Dani laughed.

Marcy smiled kindly but then got back got to the business of introductions. "This is Kenna Ashton and her husband, Will."

"It's nice to meet you, ma'am," Will said as Kenna smiled.

Cy reached around Gemma and with one large hand scooped the baby into his left arm. Sophie was still goo-gooing in his right. "And this handsome fellow is my nephew, Ryan. He's Paige's and Cole's son, aren't you, big boy?" Cy bounced him happily as both kids laughed gleefully at a man who was suddenly not looking so dark and dangerous anymore.

Cy reluctantly gave the babies back to their parents when he saw Ahmed quietly slip in through the door. Miles pushed himself off the dining room doorframe and quietly headed toward him as well. The silent show of support meant a lot to him.

Over the last twenty minutes, the group had naturally separated. The women were huddling around the couch talking about babies, and Gemma was filling in Paige about the changes to Los Angeles. It had been so many years since Paige had left there after fashion school. Cy practically forgot she had been there the first two years he was there. Of course, L.A. was so huge, he was never in any risk of actually seeing her. But that didn't mean he didn't check up on her.

"Ready?" Miles asked as he stopped next to him.

"I guess. I'm really not looking forward to this. You think Ma's going to be mad?" Cy asked as he shot a glance at his sweet-looking mother.

"Does a one-legged duck swim in circles?"

"You could've just said yes."

"And you've been in L.A. too long," Miles grinned.

Gemma scanned the room and her eyes connected with Cy's. Even at his parents' house, he wasn't really relaxed. Oh, he looked it on the outside—as he was just lounging and talking to his brothers. But she could see his lips were drawn slightly and there was tension around his eyes.

Catching herself daydreaming, Gemma smiled at something Annie said before she continued scanning the room with her investigator's eye. What she realized frightened her slightly. She received the same looks from a number of people there. The room was full of people who were impossible to read, including Cy's mother, Marcy.

A shiver rippled down her back and she knew she was being watched. Gemma casually looked around the room and connected with a pair of cold, almost black, eyes. The man they belonged to stood quietly next to the door. She hadn't even heard him come in. He wore a black suit with a black tie. For a second she thought the shirt was even black, but when he moved out of the shadow she realized it was the deepest red.

His slightly wavy black hair looked as if it had just been cut and was pushed back away from his strong face. It was his eyes that had made Gemma shiver, though. There was no emotion behind them. The mask this man wore weighed him down to a point where she didn't know if the man behind it even existed.

Gemma fought the panic she felt trying to claim her. While looking nothing like the man with the shaved head in L.A., the black suit and dark eyes had her scrambling to escape. She knew the women were looking curiously at her, but she didn't care. She had to get out of there—now.

Miles and Cy turned to where Gemma shot off the couch, her eyes wide with panic. "Does she know Ahmed?" Miles asked.

"No, but she might get him confused with the men after her," Cy whispered before speaking up. "Gemma, come join me. I think it's time to tell everyone why we're here. I also want you to meet Ahmed, the man I talked to on the phone. Remember?" Cy added gently as he reached out for her. He felt her trembling as he brought her against his side to calm her.

"My apologies for startling you, my dear," Ahmed said in a low voice as he slowly approached.

"I feel so silly. It's just that you look, well, you don't look like them. But the black suit and way you were looking at me . . ." Gemma shivered.

"Thick man with a shaved head. Eyes the same color as mine and a scar along his cheek?" Ahmed asked as if he already knew the answer. "Sergei," Ahmed said as Gemma nodded. Obviously interested in Gemma, he asked, "Who are you?"

"I could ask you the same question," Gemma shot back, her fear having subsided. She was surprised when one side of his lips quirked but didn't smile. However, for some silly reason she felt triumphant.

"Son, are you going to tell us what this is all about? I know your mother is over there hoping you'll tell her you're married and have a baby on the way so she can die happy, but I have a feeling it's nothing of the sort. What kind of trouble are you both in?" Jake asked from his chair in the *man corner* of the living room.

Cy had to grin as he saw Gemma flush with embarrassment and his mom shoot his dad *the look*, which only served to tell Cy that his dad had been right. His mom was on a major baby kick.

"I don't really know where to begin or how to even tell you all what's going on," Cy stumbled. It was finally time to come clean, but he didn't know where to start. College? His brothers going off to fight and being left behind? Last week?

"For cripes sake," Miles muttered, "Cy's an undercover agent with the CIA. He's been living in L.A. for the past ten years working as a stuntman for his cover."

The room froze as they all looked at him. "Thanks, Miles."

"No problem. Now get on with it."

Marcy stood up and placed her hands on her hips. "Cyland Dillon Davies, you tell me right now if that was you jumping naked from a window in that movie last year. Oh fiddlesticks, what was the name of it?" Marcy turned to the women around the couch. "You know, the race car driver solves a murder. He's messing around with a married woman and jumps out her window naked when the husband comes home."

"Oh, the movie with that hot guy with the great buns? Turn around, Cy, let's see if it was you," Kenna joked as Will just shook his head.

"Cyland, you tell me right now," Marcy demanded.

"*Blind Turn* was the name of the movie. Yes, it was me." Cy paused before putting his hands on his hips. "That's what you're most concerned about? Out of all Miles just said, you're upset I jumped out of a window?"

"It wasn't jumping out of a window, it was jumping out of a window as naked as the day you were born for all the world to see. What kind of wife are you going to attract running around naked in movies all the time? Not the kind I want in my family, that's for sure."

Cy's phone alerted him to a new text message. He glanced at it quickly and tried to delete it, but it was too late.

"Holy sh . . . shoot," Miles abbreviated after a stern look from his mother. "That's Katrina Poklavich, the Polish supermodel.

What is she doing sending you pictures of herself completely na . . ."

Cy delivered Miles a quick elbow jab to his side. "Nothing," Cy said through gritted teeth, but it was too late. He saw Gemma roll her eyes and his mother toss her hands in a "see" motion.

"Let's talk about me being in the CIA."

"I already know about that. I want to talk about models sending you inappropriate pictures. Isn't that a thing now?" Marcy asked the women again.

"Sexting," Paige said with a huge smile on her face.

"That's right. See, you run around naked for the entire world to see and now you're sexting. What's next? Eloping with a pinup? Oh, Jake, the mother of my grandbaby is going to be a pin-up girl posing naked in some magazine."

"It happens all the time. Shoot, Autumn Hayes wanted a one-night stand with him," Gemma told his family and friends nonchalantly.

Cy was going to kill Miles if he didn't stop laughing. Then he was going to kill Gemma. After dropping that bombshell, she just leaned back and smiled.

"Autumn Hayes and Katrina Poklavich? Damn, I mean, dang. Why didn't I become a stuntman? Or were they throwing themselves at you because you're CIA?" Pierce asked before Tammy swatted him hard against his stomach. "You're right, then I'd never have met the love of my life."

"That's better, hon." Tammy smiled sweetly.

"What do you mean you knew?" Cy asked his mother before turning on his brother. "I can't believe you told her, Miles."

"Oh, pish-posh. Your brother didn't tell me anything. I'm your mother. I know everything. I even knew my own son's bottom was plastered across the big screen. I was at that movie with my quilting club. Oh my, Edna was with us. The whole town is going to know by lunch." Marcy dropped into her chair as if the world was now over.

Cy stood speechless as his brothers grinned and the women bit their lips trying to contain any comments that he could see sitting on their tongues. How had he lost control of this situation?

A sharp whistle pierced the air and all eyes immediately snapped their attention to Jake. "Now, I'd like to hear what's going on. Just hand the phone over to me so we won't get any more interruptions." Cy grimaced as his mother threw a book and nailed his father right on the head.

"At least it wasn't an iron this time," Paige said before breaking out into peals of laughter.

"Dammit! The people who tried to kill Pierce are trying to kill Gemma and me," Cy finally yelled. The room quieted down and Cy let out a breath. He finally had their attention.

Ahmed listened intently. It was exactly what he thought. Sergei. Debate raged inside of him. He could easily manipulate Gemma into becoming bait for Sergei, but she was an innocent and he wasn't like Sergei. He didn't hurt innocents. Besides, if Cy was anything like his records indicated, he wasn't to be messed with. The family all thought Miles was the toughest. But they were all wrong. It was Cy.

The secret file the CIA kept on him read like a spy novel. He took on missions no one else would take and managed to get out without a scratch . . . that is, until Russia. That's where Sergei must've discovered him. Cy had breached a secure laboratory guarded by armed soldiers. He had busted up the sale, arrested the men involved in the trade, secured the weapons, and was in the process of hauling them out of the facility when he was detected. A firefight ensued and he held them off until he set a trap, escaping with the weapons and criminals. The rest of the CIA was stationed five miles away getting ready to breach the facility, but Cy beat them to it. The records quote him as saying he went alone because he "wanted to make sure the job was done right."

Ahmed looked Cy over again as he stood telling his family the events from the last twelve hours. Gemma was quietly shedding tears as Marcy and Paige held her hands. She was innocent, he kept reminding himself, but she might hold the key. He'd just have to work with Cy this time, but he'd make it clear—Sergei was his.

CHAPTER EIGHT

Thwack! Miss Lily Rae Rose slammed her broom down on John Wolfe's balding head. She took advantage of stunning him to race past him down the sidewalk. She might only stand at five-feet two-inches, but she gained four feet with that broom. Enough height to bonk John on the head, she thought as she raced toward the Blossom Café where many regulars were eating lunch.

"Oh no you don't, Lily Rae," John bellowed, his round belly bouncing as he chased after her.

John caught her by the arm and swung her around to attempt a kiss. Men. It worked one time so they think it'll work every time. Lily grabbed hold of his suspenders, rose onto her tippy toes, and kissed him with everything she had. Right when he was leaning forward but before he wrapped his arms around her, Lily shot off down the street again, leaving him standing dazed on the sidewalk.

"Sucker," she called over her shoulder as she ran toward the café. She passed the large windows and arrangements of bright flowers under them. Lily saw people enjoying lunch as she threw open the door and barged into her sisters' restaurant.

The patrons all stopped and stared as she gulped in some air. Her sister, Daisy Mae, halted setting a plate of fried catfish in front of Judge Cooper. Violet Mae stuck her head out of the kitchen to see what was happening.

"Cy Davies is back in town." She had done it. She had beaten John and had gotten the news out first.

The door burst open once again as John entered. "And he's a stuntman in Hollywood," John gasped as the restaurant groaned in response.

"As a cover for being a spy with the CIA," Miss Lily hurriedly yelled out to make sure she beat John.

"YES! Yes, yes, yes." Pam Gilbert leaped up from her chair and did a dance in the middle of the café in her soccer mom attire of khaki capris and a polo shirt. "I won, I can't believe I won." The restaurant groaned again. "I can take the kids to Disney for vacation," Pam squealed as she jumped around some more.

"I thought for sure he was an mixed martial arts fighter," old man Tabby mumbled before digging into his sandwich.

"I thought he was a professional skier," Trey Everett said as he slid into a booth next to some of his friends.

Miss Lily smiled at the dear boy . . . well, man now. Trey was back for the summer after his first year in college. He'd grown two inches and packed on thirty pounds of muscle during his first season playing college football. In fact, he'd done so well, he was transferring to Vanderbilt to play.

Pierce Davies had hired him to work on the farms and Trey jumped at the chance to be back home and train with Will Ashton. Not every kid got to train with an NFL player. But Will and Cade were so proud of him for making it into the Southeastern Conference that they agreed to work with him every day. She didn't even have to guilt Will into it—he'd come up with the idea all on his own.

"Why is he coming home now? Is he injured again?" Miss Daisy asked as she finally gave Judge Cooper his catfish.

"He's in trouble and we need to help him," Miss Lily said with a thump of her broom.

Gemma had been quiet for the last couple hours as the debate raged on. Cy had filled them in on what was happening, and she had answered some questions here and there. Quite honestly, she was still in a state of shock. Cy had a tendency to under-state things. Such as, "My brothers were in the Army" turned out to be "My brothers were Special Forces with high-level security clearances."

"Hey." Cy had broken away from his family and had come over to where she was sitting. "How are you doing?"

"I'm a little in shock, but I'm ready to get to work."

"Good. Then let's get going." Cy nodded toward the door and held out his hand to help her up.

"Go where?"

"To get some lunch and find us a place to stay."

"Us?" Gemma asked as she stood up.

"Yep. Mom's converted the old room I shared with Cade and Pierce into the grandsons' room and Paige's old room into the granddaughters' room. Then she turned Miles and Marshall's room into a scrapbooking room."

"I thought you lived in Keeneston."

"I do. I have two hundred acres of land here, but no house. I plan on building. It's one of my projects for my retirement."

"Retirement? You're what, 33-ish? How can you talk about retiring?"

"Between the CIA and my job in Hollywood, I have enough to live a very comfortable life. But, I wasn't going to just sit at home. Pierce has been taking care of my land for over six years. It's time I take it over."

"So, where are we going to stay then?" Gemma asked. This family was loud, sarcastic, and a little scary, but they were genu-ine and she felt safe. She didn't really want to leave the comfort-able couch and venture back into the real world.

"I have just the place. Come on."

"Maybe he was burned. Is that what it's called?" Daisy Mae asked Judge Cooper as she cleared his dishes.

"Just because I'm a judge doesn't mean I know about spies," Judge Cooper quipped.

"Oh, don't be a sore loser. Your guess of professional bull rider was a good one." Daisy patted him on the shoulder before making her way to the kitchen.

"Well, whatever it is, I want to know about this woman with him," Henry Rooney, the local defense attorney, asked with a smirk.

"You do, do you? And why is that?" Neely Grace asked from her tableful of Keeneston Belles.

Lily cringed. If anyone could keep Henry in line, it was Neely Grace. Not only was she an attorney in Lexington, she'd whipped those snobby Belles into shape faster than a rabbit's nose can twitch. They were now planning a charity event to benefit the arts program at the elementary school.

"Well, I wouldn't want to be negligent for not checking her out," Henry said casually as he took a bite of his pecan pie.

Neely Grace rolled her eyes. "*Miranda* didn't warn me about you."

"*Res ipsa loquitur,* sweetheart. Your hot body speaks for itself. No need to be worried about some new woman in town."

"For the love of the legal system . . . cut that out, you two." Judge Cooper rapped his cup on the table as if it were a gavel and shook his head. "That's just wrong. I'm going back to my chambers."

Henry's mouth opened and Miss Lily thwacked him with her broom. "Bless your heart, don't go there. For all our sakes."

Henry looked up at her and gave her a little wink before blowing Neely Grace a kiss. Oh, he was a cutie, all right, but there was only one man she was worried about fixin' and it wasn't Henry Rooney.

"Henry makes a good point. I haven't heard a thing from the sheriff. I wonder if this has to do with the woman. Maybe she's an international criminal," Deputy Dinky said as he took a sip of iced tea.

"Or maybe it's as simple as a girlfriend," Noodle, Dinky's partner, said.

"I like Dinky's idea. I have twenty on international criminal," Miss Daisy said as she pulled out her ever-present notebook and marked the newest bet.

"I'll put ten on her being a spy from another country that he's turned," Pam said.

"Oh, that's a good one," Miss Daisy murmured as she took the bet.

Cy pulled the truck to a stop a block away from the café. The street was lined with cars. It was lunchtime, and since this was the only place to eat in the town, he knew it was going to be packed. "It's right down there," he told Gemma, pointing to the umbrellas providing shade to the bistro tables on the sidewalk.

"It's a cute town. This is nothing like L.A.," Gemma said as she took in the old façades of Main Street painted in the historic colors of tan, white, dark red, and grayish-blue. Flowers were blooming in the baskets hanging from the old-style lampposts where American flags fluttered in the warm breeze.

"It is. I remember being a teenager and thinking it was horrible. Everyone knew all my business. I couldn't get into too much trouble because someone would tell my mom. And then, of course, everyone had an opinion about who I was dating, what sports I should be playing, or what I should do with my life.

"I left and never thought I'd want to come back. Funny thing happened. About one year after leaving, I started missing the place. By three years out, I missed the place so much I started buying up property just to keep my connection to the town. I knew then my goal was to work hard enough to make it back here," Cy told her as he pushed open the door to the café. He had never told anyone so much about this town. It was part of his secret life he hadn't been able to talk to anyone about and it felt good to tell her about his life, goals, and desires.

Cy walked into the café and stood grinning like a fool. The place had gone silent in a heartbeat. Everyone turned and stared at them with guilty looks all over their faces. Strange how he had actually grown to miss this.

"Were you all talking about us?" He laughed.

"Cy, welcome home, sweetheart." Miss Lily wrapped him up in a tight hug as her sisters hurried over. He gave each Rose sister a kiss on the cheek and shook hands with everyone else from the town. His good friend, Coach Parks, gave him a tight hug as everyone peppered Cy with questions.

Gemma stood slightly behind Cy and watched the scene unfold around her. They had already known he was back in town and needed help. They had already known she was there and, one after another, shook her hand, gave Fred a pat, and introduced themselves to her.

"Cy," she whispered, getting his attention, "how did these people know we were here?"

"I told you they had an information system better than the government's," Cy said with a grin. "Miss Lily, we need a place to stay. Mom's turned my room into a baby's room and Paige rented her apartment out to Bridget."

"Oh, I know, dear. Are you adding to that?" she asked with a quick look to Gemma's belly. Gemma blushed and then for a second time got self-conscious. Why was everyone thinking she was pregnant? Did she look fat or something?

"Nope, sorry," Cy said easily.

"Dang," Miss Lily said under her breath. "Why don't you introduce us to your friend?"

"As many of you have met her already, I'll keep it short. This is Gemma Perry. The same people behind Pierce and Tammy's attempted murder and the dog-fighting ring murdered her sister. We need to keep her safe until we can capture them." Cy paused as he saw the people nod their heads and whisper to each other. "Unfortunately, they're after me, too, because of my time in the CIA."

"So, is she a witness you're trying to protect?" Trey asked from his seat next to his friends.

"Yes, exactly like that," Cy nodded. Gemma looked around in confusion as the café groaned and Trey pumped his fist into the air. "So, Miss Lily, do you have room for us at the bed-and-breakfast?"

"How many rooms?"

"One" Cy said at the same time Gemma said, "Two."

Gemma jumped back as the broom was raised and smashed onto Cy's head. "You rascal. There is no hanky-panky going on at my place. Now, if you promise to behave yourself, I'll show you to your rooms."

"Yes, ma'am." Cy sounded humbled, but Gemma worried that the spark in his eye said he took it more as a challenge. She flushed with excitement or fear; she couldn't tell which one she was more worried about.

Cy thanked Miss Lily as he put his bags down in his room across the hall from Gemma's. A large sitting room stood between her door and his, but Cy wasn't concerned. It couldn't be that hard getting past Miss Lily. After all, Kenna and Will are now married and so are Dani and Mo. The ladies both stayed at Miss Lily's bed-and-breakfast when they first arrived.

Cy started to unpack when his phone rang. "Hey, Miles. What's up?"

"Come on out to my farm. The brothers are getting together for a ride around the property and we thought you'd want to see yours. Also, it'll give us a chance to talk without Ma listening."

"Sounds good. See you in twenty." Cy hung up and dug out his cowboy boots from the bottom of his bag. His worn brown cowboy hat was in the back of his truck. Amazing how giving him those two things and a horse made him truly feel back at home.

Cy slipped on his boots and headed across the sitting room to knock on Gemma's door. He waited as he heard her stumble in her room and curse under her breath.

The door was wrenched open and Gemma stood in nothing but a towel, her hair hanging in waves around her shoulders and her green eyes flashing with annoyance.

"Yes?"

Cy was momentarily stunned by the sight of the swell of her breasts and shapely legs under the fluffy white towel. "Brothers."

"What?"

Cy cleared his throat and tried again. "My brothers are getting ready to ride the property lines. They want to show me what they've done to my farm. I'm going to head out there. There's going to be a deputy outside if you need anything. His name is Noodle. Are you okay with me heading out for a bit?"

Gemma took a deep breath and smiled. "Thanks for letting me know. I have a date with that amazing claw-footed tub and then I thought I'd open Gia's box she left with the notebooks. Have a good time."

"Here." Cy handed a piece of paper to her and was rewarded when the towel slipped a little. "It's my number. Call me if you need anything at all. I'll be back by dinner."

CHAPTER NINE

Cy leaned forward in the saddle and rubbed his horse's sweaty neck as he looked at the massive fields. All of this was his and he was proud of it. His brothers raced to a stop next to him and stared him down.

"Do you always have to race?" Marshall asked. "Do you know how long it's been since I've run a horse that fast?"

"Sorry, old man. I'll make sure we go at a nice canter on the way home for you. Married with a kid on the way and look what happens to you. And you all wonder why I'm still single," Cy teased.

"Ha-ha. You'll see. Don't knock it until you try it. I held out longer than any of you and now I'm kicking myself for waiting so long," Miles told them as he gazed out over the rolling fields dotted with cattle.

"If you got married sooner, you would've ended up with a Belle," Cade said with a mock shudder. "It's just a good thing Morgan came back to town to save you from the summer picnics and charity galas."

"True. And now I'm going to be a father. I still have trouble believing it," Miles said in a wistful way that left Cy feeling slightly jealous.

"I guess I'm the last one standing. You all will have kids and I'll be the strange bachelor uncle wanting their dads to come play poker," Cy laughed as he teased his brothers.

81

"Yeah, right. You just moved into the number-one marriage spot on the list. I'm sure Marianne will have a write-up in the paper this week. You'll be off the market in no time," Pierce predicted.

"I'm not going to feel too sorry for you when all the single women of Keeneston descend upon you either. Not when you're getting text messages from naked supermodels and America's Sweetheart. I still can't believe you were in that movie with her," Cade said as he took off his cowboy hat and wiped his brow.

"Yeah, I guess I can't complain about that," Cy said with a grin.

"Yep, but payback's a bitch and her name is Kandi," Marshall laughed as he slapped Cy on the shoulder.

"Kandi? She's married with like a couple of kids, right?"

"It's never stopped her before," Cade warned.

"What about Gemma?" Miles asked. "She was a little distant, but after what she's gone through in the past twenty-four hours, I can't really blame her for that. And boy, she's a knockout. Curves in all the right places for me."

Cy narrowed his eyes at Miles.

"That she is. And the women all liked her. Tammy thinks she's really nice and has ordered me to have her over to our apartment for dinner," Pierce told him.

"Yep. Katelyn, too."

"And Annie."

"Morgan sent me armed with an invitation for Gemma. You know, you all could've stayed with us. We have plenty of room."

"I know. But y'all have wives and babies on the way. I don't know how much danger I'm going to be in, but I thought I'd be safer in town where someone looking for me would have to get through the Rose sisters, John Wolfe, the PTA, the Belles, and every farmer in the area before finding us," Cy explained.

"Well, you know we're all here if you need us. We have a certain skill set that could come in handy. Well, except Pierce there. All he can do is invent robots," Marshall joked.

"Ha-ha. My robot can kick your ass," Pierce shot back.

"We're just teasing. We couldn't be prouder of you, and you too, Cy. What you've done is very dangerous and I'm sure has saved many lives," Marshall said seriously.

Cy just nodded his head in response. He had saved lives. He'd stopped the bombing of an airplane bound for L.A. He'd broken up the sale of chemical weapons. He'd helped the Swiss secure their banking system to avoid increased hacking activity. Cy had never felt as if he had saved people, though. He was just doing his job. Miles, Marshall, and Cade had been the real heroes and he was just trying to make them proud.

"I'm proud of you, too, bro. Now, what do you think of your land?" Pierce asked.

"It's great. Thanks for buying it for me, Pierce. You picked a great area," Cy said sincerely. Pierce had called him and told him this farm was for sale years ago. Marshall's farm sat on one side and Cade's on the other. It was filled with a mixture of rolling hills, woods, and a small creek.

"I think I want to build the house right over there." Cy pointed to a clearing close to the boundary line with Cade's property. "I can continue running the cattle in this pasture and maybe plant some crops in the fifty acres on the east side of the property."

"Well, welcome home, brother. It's great to have you back. We've missed you," Cade said as he reached over to shake Cy's hand.

***

Gemma pushed the swing with her big toe as she sat with one leg resting on the large porch swing. The bath had been restorative and she had gotten out with a renewed sense of justice. She slipped on a wispy white skirt and a green peasant top before heading downstairs with the notebooks and the box her sister had made.

Not wanting to feel closed in, Gemma had decided the large porch overlooking the street was the perfect place to see what secrets her sister held. With a quick wave to the sheriff's cruiser keeping watch, Gemma looked around the porch for a place to work. The swing had called to her and with a deep breath, she set the box on her lap and opened the lid.

It was filled with pictures—some taken with a telescopic lens, others with a phone or a concealed camera, and a few seemed to be from the police department or other government offices. Gemma flipped through each one as her frustration grew. She didn't know a single person in these pictures.

She fought off a feeling of despair as she dug deeper into the box. Her fingers paused as they came to an old, worn photograph. Gemma stood smiling at the camera with her left front tooth missing. She had a side ponytail sticking out the left side of her head while Gia smiled with a missing right front tooth and a side ponytail on the right side of her head. On the back, Gia had written the word *Twins* and decorated it with hearts. Her feeling of despair fled as she looked under the picture and found a stack of notes they wrote to each other in their twin language.

"That's it," Gemma said to herself as she hurriedly looked through the pile for the one note she knew had to be in there. She remembered writing it and what it said. From there she could start remembering their translation.

She found it stuck in the middle of a bunch of notes. Gemma had written it to Gia, telling her she had missed a math question because Graham Bullock had asked her to the middle school dance and she'd been so excited, she'd forgotten to answer the question on her quiz.

Gemma picked up the notebook marked with the symbol for *One* and started to read as much as she could.

"Hello, dear. You've been at it for hours and I thought you might like something to drink and a snack before dinner." Miss Lily set down a tray with a brownie and a glass of lemonade on it.

"Thank you. I am hungry." Gemma put down the notebook, took a bite of the rich brownie, and moaned. She could get used to the cooking out here.

"What is this you're working on?" Miss Lily asked as she looked at the notebook.

"I need to decipher it for the investigation. My sister took all these notes, but I'm having a real hard time remembering our twin language." Gemma paused as she took another bite of the brownie. "Strange, huh?"

"To have a secret language with your twin? Not at all. Daisy Mae, Violet Fae, and I had one growing up, too. It was great to be able to talk about all the important stuff without our parents knowing what we were saying," Miss Lily winked. "Take, for instance, talking about a hunk of a man with hazel eyes and abs I could wash clothes on."

Gemma blinked and paused with the last bite of brownie halfway to her mouth. "Excuse me?"

"Oh, don't tell me for one second you haven't noticed Cy. You'd have to be dead not to and even then it would be hard."

"Even if I noticed him, it doesn't mean anything. He dates actresses and models. I enjoy food too much to be like them," Gemma popped the last bite of brownie into her mouth as if to emphasize that fact.

"Mmm, hmm. Do you see him married to any of those women? I don't. Men like women who look like women, not ten-year-old boys with inflatable toys on their chests. Trust me, he's noticed. You better make a move before the rest of the town descends upon him." Miss Lily gave her a wink and headed back inside.

Right. Like she had a chance with Cy. But, she did have a chance with some of the notes. Enough that she was able to translate a couple of the photographs. She went through the pile and pulled out the ones she could translate and started writing the translations onto notes and sticking them to the back of the photos. Her trouble lay in the notebooks, though.

Word by word, she slowly made her way through the first ten pages of the notebook. The longer she worked on it, the more it came back, but it was still hard to remember every detail of a language they had developed as children. Determination filled her as she bent her head and went back to work.

Cy parked the truck at Miss Lily's and walked up the pathway to her front porch. Gemma was curled up on the porch swing with two notebooks in her lap. She didn't hear him as he approached so he took a moment to observe her. A lock of her hair had escaped from behind her ear. Unlike so many people he knew in Hollywood, Gemma wore no makeup and didn't seem self-conscious about it. In fact, all he wanted to do was run a finger down her cheek to feel its softness. His brothers' talks of marriage and relationships were messing with him.

"How's it going?" he asked as he stopped in front of her. He saw her jump in surprise as her wide eyes looked up at him.

"You scared me." Gemma took a deep breath and smelled grass, hay, horse, and man. That wasn't something she was used to smelling. Men in L.A. didn't smell like that and it was intoxicating. Images of him shirtless on a horse had her fanning herself with her notebook before she even knew it. Damn Miss Lily for putting those ideas of Cy into her head.

"Sorry. It looks like I'm interrupting. Are you making progress on your sister's notes?"

"Some. Here, take a look at these pictures." Gemma swung her feet to the ground and made room on the swing for him to sit next to her. Cy filled the swing and her heart fluttered when his shoulder pressed against hers.

"This girl is twelve years old and was shipped on a container ship with twenty other girls from the Philippines to Europe as part of a sex trade Gia was investigating. Here are some more." Gemma handed him pictures of young girls of all ages, races, and nationalities.

"They're so young," Cy sighed as he shook his head.

"Gia believed the sex trade was run by a mystery man she called Lucifer. She talked to some of these women. While most wouldn't say anything, some told her of being taken from orphanages and shipped to Europe and the Middle East. Then these . . ." Gemma handed him another couple of pictures. "These women are all Americans taken via interstate trafficking. They are prostitutes who were kidnapped and traded all across the United States. Do you know what they have in common?"

"Besides tragedy? Let me guess, the rings are all run by Lucifer . . . or Mr. X as we call him at the agency."

"That's right. And there's more. He's not a low-level criminal living in the dark. He's very well connected. In her notes, Gia wrote about a man that your Mr. X was preparing to back for Congress. But he bumbled a job and this is what happened to him." Gemma pulled out the three pictures and showed him the first picture of the body that still made her cringe. "This is what happened to him for messing up a dog-fighting ring, see?"

Gemma flipped to the next two pictures showing people at a dog-fight. Cy grabbed the photos and shot to his feet as he stared at the pictures.

"I don't believe it. The dead man is Paul Russell. And this woman here," Cy tapped the picture of the woman in her prim suit taking bets outside of a dog-fighting ring, "that's Nancy Kincaid. These pictures were taken here in Keeneston. This is the dog-fighting ring that Marshall broke up."

"What? Are you sure?"

"Yes. This is the whole reason I started investigating Mr. X. Your sister was looking into the same thing I was, and it got her killed. At the same time, I was being hunted here in

Keeneston. This is good news. Mr. X's organization is taking out anyone looking into them and now they know you are."

Cy stood up and started pacing along the wooden porch.

"How is this good news?"

"It means we're on the right track," Cy shot her a smile, the one she recognized as his Hollywood smile. He could shell out his smiles to the ladies, but they never reached his eyes. Gemma wondered what he would look like when he finally let go and smiled for real.

"You're basically going to sit here and wait for them to kill us? I don't know if I like that idea," Gemma worried. She had just traveled across the country to try to avoid these guys and now it sounded as if Cy was excited that these guys would be coming after them.

Gemma nibbled her bottom lip as Cy slowly came to stand in front of her. "My plan is to have enough evidence to take them down before they get here. When they arrive, we'll be here wait-ing to arrest them."

"That's what my sister probably thought, too. Instead, she got in too deep and they killed her." Gemma looked up into Cy's eyes and wondered what was really happening behind the façade he kept firmly in place.

"I won't let that happen to you," he said softly as he pushed a stray lock of her hair away from her face. Gemma felt her breath catch as his fingers brushed against her cheek. For a moment his eyes softened and she caught a glimpse of the man behind the mask.

The screen door slammed and the spell was broken. "Oh dear. I didn't interrupt anything, did I?" Miss Lily asked inno-cently as her wide eyes blinked. "I just wanted to see if you two were staying for dinner."

"Thank you, but we're going to miss dinner. We're going to see Marshall . . . and his files."

CHAPTER TEN

*C*y was relieved when Gemma sat quietly in the truck watching the farms pass by. He was tired of playing the playboy. The models and actresses had irritated him when he started working in Hollywood, but it was all necessary for his cover. The thing was, he didn't even sleep with them—well, not many of them. He guessed that was what made him so popular with the famous women. They weren't used to having someone say no. Unfortunately, it was an unintended aphrodisiac.

After the first year of undercover work, the acting had turned real. He got used to the secret games and power plays of making movies. He fit in with ease at parties, clubs, and on the set. He was popular, confident, and one of the best at his job. And it didn't hurt that some of Hollywood's hottest starlets took a shine to him.

But then Cade had problems with drugs at the high school and Marshall busted up a dog-fighting ring. That's when he realized he had missed so much in life. Sure, he'd done amazing things and gone to faraway places, but that wasn't really him. It was Cy Davidson who had done those things. All he'd done with the CIA was try to live up to the legacy left to him by the older brothers he had idolized his whole life. He wanted to give back to his country just as they had done.

Somewhere along the way, though, he had lost himself.

Cy had thought as soon as he came home, everything would be as it was; the real Cy Davies would return. But it wasn't happening. He didn't know how to be himself anymore.

"Cy? Cy . . . is everything okay?" Gemma's voice shook him out of his reflections.

"Hmm?"

"Are you okay? I've been trying to ask you a question, but you seemed in another world."

"I'm fine. What did you need?"

"I was wondering what you think Marshall can help us with?" Gemma asked with a concerned tone in her voice.

"I want to see his files. He said he'd call the others and they'd bring everything they have. They found a black book on Nancy and arrested hundreds as a result. I'm hoping some of the names match up with some of those pictures you have. Maybe it can give us a lead to identify Mr. X."

Cy pulled the truck to a stop in front of the farmhouse he used to live in whenever he came back to visit. It looked like his brothers were already there and waiting for him. The grass in the surrounding pasture had just been cut and the smell hung in the air. The large round bales of hay were tightly coiled, waiting to be used to feed the animals through the winter.

"How is Fred with other dogs?" Cy asked when he opened Gemma's door.

"Great. He loves running at the dog park with them, why?"

"You're about to find out," Cy barely had time to say before Katelyn opened the front door and a herd of dogs came running out. Justin, with his bright yellow bow, led the way as Bob, Chuck, and finally Bill ambled out to see them.

"Aw, look how pretty she is," Gemma cooed as she petted Justin.

"Don't say that too loud or he'll get his feelings hurt. His name is Justin. Pierre, the dog groomer, just doesn't

believe me when I tell him no more bows. But the darn things work at keeping the hair out of his eyes," Cade said as he came outside. Justin's big black nose shoved her arm as a way to try to figure out what Fred was.

"Looks like Justin has a mini," Annie joked as she watched Justin's big, hairy tail wag and his brown eyes light with glee when he looked at Fred.

Gemma bent over and placed him on the ground and then screamed and jumped when something cold and wet hit her bottom.

"Sorry about that. Bob likes to goose the women. It's actually rather embarrassing, but it's the least outrageous of his quirks," Marshall said, not looking the least bit embarrassed as Bob trotted over and leapt up onto the porch swing.

"He's not the only one with an embarrassing dog. Paige kicked Chuck and me out of her shop. *Someone* may have gotten into a whole can of refried beans," Cole cringed. Chuck let out a timely fart and thumped his thick tail in response as his ears stuck straight out of the side of his head. Gemma could've sworn Bob rolled his eyes as he moved upwind of Chuck.

"It looks like Fred is doing just fine with the gang. Come on in. I have drinks set up for you all and I'll take the dogs for a walk while you all work . . . if that's okay with you, Gemma?" Katelyn asked.

"That would be great. Thank you," Gemma smiled. Poor Fred had been pretty cooped up the last couple days.

"Excellent. We're off then. Marshall, remember you've got two hours. Your mom wants us all at the farm for dinner. We'll meet you there, won't we, boys?" Fred yipped and danced on his hind legs as Justin's big tongue hung happily out of his mouth. Chuck had already started ambling down the path as Bob grudgingly got off the cushioned chair and followed, keeping an eye out for any wildlife to chase.

Gemma took a seat in between Cy and Marshall on the couch. She'd never felt so small as broad shoulders towered on each side of her. Cole, Cade, and Annie sat on the other side of the table that was piled with papers and pictures.

"Here are all of the files on the dog-fighting case. Here are the mug shots of the people we arrested. And this final stack has the names and whatever information we have on those who were never caught. These names were in the black book we found on Nancy," Marshall explained as he pointed out the papers and pictures on the table.

"I'm a little in the dark here. What is it that you have that relates to this old case?" Annie asked as she leaned forward in her chair.

"My sister Gia is . . . was an investigative reporter for International Press. It appears that she was investigating a man she called Lucifer and who Cy calls Mr. X. This man runs sex, guns, drugs, and more. Cy got wind of him during this dog-fighting case and I just found these pictures that my sister had hidden away." Gemma handed Annie the first picture of Nancy taking bets and handed the picture of Paul Russell's body to Marshall.

Marshall let out a low whistle as he traded photographs with Annie. "So, your sister was here in Keeneston during that dog-fight. And your sister was just killed because of this?"

"And this." Gemma showed the group the pictures of the women and told them what Gia's notes read about the sex trafficking and the dog-fights.

"Damn. I thought this was over. I thought I had cleaned up Keeneston," Marshall cursed as he angrily stood and started pacing.

"This is so much bigger—but it all relates back to this mystery man. How much of our trouble relates back to him?" Cole asked himself as he flipped through the pictures.

"We don't know yet. Obviously what happened with Pierce and Tammy, and then Gia and Gemma, are related to this man. What I think we need to do is dig through those files and see if we can draw more connections."

Cy took the stack of pictures from Gemma and split them up before handing some to everyone. "These are all the pictures we found in Gia's box. They have to be important. Let's look through what you all have and see if we can put any names with these faces."

Gemma was deep in research mode as she tried her best to be her sister. What would Gia think? What would she look for? The blast of text messages hitting Marshall and Cole's phones broke her concentration.

"Crap!" Marshall and Cole both leapt up.

"We're late for dinner." Cole grabbed his black cowboy hat and slid it on as he picked up the notes and pictures he was working on. "Here are the pictures I was able to identify. Mostly they are of mid-level criminals. Some we picked up during the raid and some are still at large. I took notes to tell you everything I know about them."

"Here are mine. I was only able to find the ones we caught in that raid and some were killed. Beyond that, I couldn't find much else," Marshall reported as he handed her his notes and pictures.

"Me too. I'm afraid it's the same as Marshall. If you want, I can run some of these pictures by the DEA office," Annie suggested.

"Let's keep everything in the family right now. If these guys have infiltrated Congress, then I bet they're in law enforcement. We run a picture through the FBI or DEA database and I guarantee an alert will be sent to Mr. X."

Cy picked up the photos he had been going through and held one up. "This guy is a bad guy. He was in Russia as part of the arms deal that went down. He's the one I arrested and he's the one I bet somehow got information on me to Mr. X. Like Cole, I recognize some of these men from wanted posters. But I don't have any specific information on them. Did you find anything?"

Gemma looked down at her notes. They weren't much at all. "Not really. I was trying to find a certain name or something that would be the key, but I didn't see anything like that. I guess that would've been too easy."

"Don't worry about it. Leave the identification of the photos to us. We need you to work on those notebooks. You're the only one who can do that." Cy helped her gather everything and gave her a little nudge. "Don't look so worried. We got a lot done and now you'll be able to relax at my mom's dinner."

***

Cy lied. This was not relaxing. The food was amazing. She had chicken-fried steak smothered in gravy and a side of home-made macaroni and cheese with chunks of country ham in it. The first bite made her alternately groan in delight and shake in fear at what the scale was going to read the next day. For the past month, she'd been living on salad, tofu, and yucky cleansing drinks.

While her stomach wanted to lick the plate, her mind kept flashing to the picture of the barely dressed actress Cy received early that day. She knew she wasn't Cy's type, but she would like to feel she had a fighting chance.

"Dear? Is something the matter with the dinner? Do you want me to make something else?" Marcy asked, her feelings clearly hurt that Gemma wasn't eating.

"Don't worry, Mom. She's just trying to justify eating that many calories. Remember, she's still on California food. Took me months to give in. Give in, Gemma—it's delicious." Katelyn winked as she took a big bite of her food.

Gemma gave in, and it was better than sex. At least the sex she'd had recently. In fact, she was so in love with the food that she didn't even hear the conversation going on around her. When her plate was clean, she looked up and Katelyn gave her a knowing smile.

"You're lucky you're not dating Cy," Annie said.

Gemma looked at her in confusion. Maybe she shouldn't have eaten so eagerly?

"Yep, you're lucky. It would be bad," Cole agreed.

"It definitely wouldn't be an enjoyable dinner for you, to say the least," Morgan added.

"Oh, yeah, it's not fun then," Katelyn smiled sweetly.

"Stop scaring her. It would be so cool if she was dating Cy," Tammy giggled.

Gemma felt glued to her chair. She was stunned. She'd never been warned away from someone so blatantly and was too embarrassed to even be insulted.

"Well, of course we'd love for her to date Cy," Marcy said with a sweet smile. "Don't you dare scare her off." Marcy narrowed her eyes at Pierce and he just grinned wider.

"Who? Me?" he asked innocently.

"And your sister and brothers."

"Us?" they all asked in unison. Gemma was totally confused, but the way their faces all showed mocked innocence had her cracking up.

"Don't try to act like y'all didn't interrogate every date one of you brought home. I was grilled to well-done when I first came to dinner." Cole stared at his brothers-in-law and shook his head.

"I think we all were. Although, I must say Miles and Pierce were the worst. Miles with all his serious questions about our stability and Pierce just shouting out randomness," Annie said to Cole and the other wives.

"Totally agree with you there," Katelyn laughed.

"For me it was Pierce and Marshall," Morgan said with a smile.

"If I recall, y'all handled it like a pro. We're happy to have each and every one of you in our family. Now that we've settled that our sons and daughter are rude interrogators of unsuspecting dates, let's have some dessert," Jake said, putting an end to the discussion.

Paige rolled her eyes. "We weren't *that* bad. Okay, maybe we were. I'll get the pies I made this morning."

"Excellent. I'll go check on the babies in their new room." Marcy shot from the table and disappeared upstairs. Within seconds her voice came over the monitor as she cooed
to the babies.

"We won't see her again," Jake said. "Guys' night to do dishes after dessert. I get her piece since she left the table." Jake grinned and Gemma could see what Cy would look like when he was older. All the brothers shared the hazel eyes and the strong build of their father.

Gemma took a seat in the corner of the living room and let her thoughts take her away again while the women talked weddings and babies. She guessed that was why Gia was so successful and Gemma was still working for a gossip rag. Not that she wasn't good at what she did; she was just a dreamer. This time however, her thoughts made their way back to the same thing—Cy. He worked with ease as he cleared the table. But then he stopped and looked at his phone and reality came crashing in. She could like him and be attracted to him, but that was all it was ever going to be.

"Focus on the case," Gemma murmured.

"What was that?" Paige asked.

"Sorry. I was just thinking of the case." Gemma gave a little smile and hoped they couldn't see her blushing.

"What about the case were you contemplating so hard?" Cy asked smoothly as he came into the living room.

"I'm itching to get back to my sister's notebooks. I know the answers have to be in there."

"Well, I'm all done with my part of the cleaning. Let me take you back and we can get to work. Good night, ladies."

"Good night, Cy." Tammy smiled and looked to Gemma and she realized she hadn't gotten away clean. Someone had noticed her looking at Cy. The question was what Tammy was going to do, if anything.

Miss Lily's porch light was on as they pulled to a stop at the bed and breakfast. Gemma was relieved to see the warm lights of the old house. She'd only been there for the day, but it felt like a retreat.

Cy opened the front door for her and she walked into the large entrance way. These old houses with the wide, sweeping staircases and gorgeous wood detailing just didn't exist in L.A.

At the top of the stairs, Gemma paused at her door to dig for her key. No matter how small a purse she carried, she still couldn't find what she wanted in it. Somehow her tiny purse would turn into a bottomless pit the second she tried to find something.

"Gemma."

She raised her head and saw that Cy stood closer than she thought. He was looking down at her with a look she hadn't seen before. Whatever it was, it was not the normal carefree mask he always wore.

"Yes?"

"I wanted . . . well, I thought . . ." Cy leaned forward and Gemma held her breath as anticipation coursed through her. *Dink-dink.* An incoming text on his cell phone interrupted the moment. Cy barely acknowledged the phone as he pulled it out, but Gemma caught an eyeful.

"Isn't that the lingerie model who just posed nude on the cover of . . . ?"

"Doesn't matter."

Gemma gave a shy smile. Was he really talking about her? *Dink-dink.* Gemma let out a frustrated breath. Every *dink* of that cell phone was a splash of cold water to the face. How stupid did she have to be to think he would want to be with her when *that* was texting and calling him? "And it seems she wants to talk to you. Better answer. Good night, Cy."

Cy wished Gemma had slammed the door. Then he would know that she cared. Instead, Gemma quietly closed and locked her door as Angelina kept calling his phone and he kept sending it to voicemail.

With a sigh, he turned and headed for his room. He may not be taking Angelina's call, but that didn't mean he wasn't going to be making one of his own.

"Hello. Tonight?" Cy said into the phone as he stood by the window looking down to the front yard. "Good. I'll see you then."

Gemma took her time getting ready for bed. She had worked a couple hours on the first notebook as darkness fell outside her window. She took a seat on the window bench and stared at the stars, still unused to seeing them so clearly.

She glanced at the clock and saw it was already close to midnight. Somewhere in the back of her mind she had to admit the reason she hadn't let the exhaustion claim her was hope. Hope she would hear a small tap on the door and open it to find Cy standing there ready to finish what it appeared he wanted to start earlier. Of course, that was just a dream.

Gemma climbed onto the big four-poster bed and slid under the covers. Well, a little dreaming never hurt anyone—so long as you realized it was nothing but a dream. Gemma closed her eyes and dreamt of the kiss she had hoped to receive. The way his lips would dance along hers before taking her mouth possessively and with such eagerness, robbing her breath.

Cy checked his watch and slid on his sneakers before heading out the door. He quietly went down the stairs and unlocked the door. He drove in silence out past the Ashton Farm and turned into the next drive. He gave a nod to the man at the gate who buzzed him in.

He traveled the long drive and passed the dark massive house before turning down a side road and heading farther into the property. A two-story brick Federal house with black shutters stood at the end of the road. Lights warmed the house and made it look like a family home instead of a bachelor pad.

Before he could park, the front door opened and Ahmed walked out to greet him. Next to him a large pit bull stood at attention. "Zoti, go greet our friend," Ahmed said in an unusually relaxed voice. The large dog wagged his tail and
ran over to Cy. He sat down at Cy's feet and raised a paw.

"What a good boy you are," Cy reached out and shook his paw before Zoti caught his face with a lick. "Nice dog, Ahmed. I kinda pictured him attacking me, though, not giving me kisses and wiggling around my legs."

"I thought you of all people would know not to judge something by its appearance. Zoti, alert." Ahmed gave the quiet command and the dog's demeanor changed in a split second.

He was tense and scanning the area and Cy could easily see the well-trained protection dog within.

"Relax. Good boy. Who's a good boy?" Ahmed praised as he rubbed behind Zoti's ears.

"Impressive. I guess you're right. I should've known better." Cy walked up the steps and followed Ahmed into his surprising house. Another assumption he should not have made. He had expected dark and masculine with weapons lying around for some reason. Instead he found a home that was bright and welcoming. The walls were dark beige, the couch was red with navy accents, and the floor was a gleaming honeyed oak. Pictures from around the world were framed and hanging on the walls.

"I'm sure you recognize some of those places," Ahmed said as he handed Cy a beer.

"I do. These are amazing." The pictures played with lights, shadows, and angles in such a way as to captivate the observer.

"Thank you."

"You took these?"

"Judging by appearances again?" Ahmed almost cracked a smile. If he had, Cy would have thought he entered an alternate universe.

"I guess so," Cy turned and took a seat in a chair across from Ahmed, who sat on the couch with Zoti. "So, tell me about Sergei."

CHAPTER ELEVEN

*G*emma cursed under her breath and threw her pen down. She had been working on translating her sister's notebooks for the past three days and was still only getting bits and pieces. She remembered the alphabet Gia used to spell out a name or words that didn't have specific symbols. But it was those symbols that were hanging up her translation.

To make matters worse, she found a flash drive in the bottom of the box. Gemma worked all day yesterday and couldn't even get the thing to open. She tried to think like Gia and tried to crack her password, but she had no luck.

"Oh, bless your heart. It's not going well, is it," Miss Lily stated more than asked. "I just came inside from taking Dinky a snack and thought you might want some iced tea and cookies to help you while you work." Miss Lily set the tray down on the chest of drawers and smiled understandingly at her.

"No. It's not. We grew up talking this language and then we made up this huge written language when she came home with this box. The trouble is, I haven't used it in well over a decade. There were around seventy-five words we had symbols for—all the pronouns and so many adjectives. I just can't finish translating without them."

Gemma paused and took a deep breath. "See, this sentence. *Blank will be at the blank club on blank at eleven.* I'm just glad I remembered the symbols for words like *and* and *the* or I wouldn't even have this much and what I do have does us no good."

"Tell me when you came up with these symbols. Was it at home? Did you do it all at once or over the course of the year?" Miss Lily asked as she handed Gemma a cookie.

"We were upstairs in our secret place. She sat down with this box and we agreed it would hold all our secrets. It was then that Gia suggested we make up a way to write in our secret language so we could pass notes at school. That way, if they were intercepted, no one could read them."

"What then?"

Gemma thought back and envisioned the meeting. "We wrote down all the words we used frequently and then spent the whole night coming up with symbols for them."

"Lordy! How did you remember all of that?"

"We didn't . . ." Gemma paused and her heart started beating quickly. "We didn't! I totally forgot about that. We had a master list that each of us looked over and practiced for weeks until we remembered everything. Then it became second nature. Gia learned it quickly but I had to use the cheat sheet. Once I didn't need it, Gia told me to destroy it so our parents couldn't find it."

"But you didn't, did you?" Miss Lily asked with a grin.

"No, I didn't," Gemma grinned back as she leapt off the bed. She grabbed the bag that Cy had packed with all the pictures from her apartment. "I put it behind a picture of Gia and me."

"Here, let me help you. Which one?"

"I don't know. I'm horrible about stacking pictures in frames. Instead of taking a picture out of the frame when I put a new one in, I just move it behind the new picture. It could be somewhere in any of these. The frame would have to be old, though, so probably a smaller one. Kids don't enlarge photographs." Gemma started prying off the backs of the frames as Miss Lily handed her all the smaller frames.

One after another, Gemma pulled off the backs and sorted through the years of pictures. But there was nothing. "There are three more, dear. Don't lose hope," Miss Lily said reassuringly.

Gemma didn't feel too reassured, though. In fact, she was worried she had thrown out the frame a long time ago. She popped off the back of the silver frame in her hands and pulled out the thick stack of photos underneath. It must be an old frame to have that many photos in it. She turned them over—a picture of her and Gia at the Journalists Award Banquet where Gia won two honors that night was on top. Underneath was a picture of them in their dorm room in their senior year of college, followed by a picture of Gemma and one of her friends at a frat party in their freshman year. Gemma looked further back and found a picture of the two sisters and their friends in high school. Underneath that was an old scrap of white lined paper folded into a rectangle.

With shaking hands, Gemma dropped the remaining pictures and stared at the wrinkled piece of paper. "Well, go on," Miss Lily gently urged.

Gemma opened the paper and stared down at the list written in her sister's handwriting. She had found the key, all thanks to Miss Lily. Without saying a word, Gemma threw her arms around the older lady and hugged her.

"Oh," Miss Lily exclaimed before returning the hug. "There, there. You have a lot of work to get done. Call if you need anything." Miss Lily gave her a smile and headed back downstairs, promising to return with more snacks as the day went on.

Gemma picked up the first notebook again and, with renewed determination, went to work translating. It was time to discover what her sister had left for her to find.

***

Cy tossed the cards on the table and scooped in the pot. He enjoyed wiping that smug smile off Marshall's face. His

phone vibrated again and Pierce grabbed it before he could.

"Really? A socialite? So boring compared to the America's Sweetheart who called you an hour ago," Pierce complained as he tossed the phone back to the table, ignoring the dark look Cy tossed him.

"Sorry to be late," Ahmed said as he walked into Mo's study and took a seat next to Mo. "What did I miss?"

"Besides the who's who of Hollywood calling my brother wanting to know where he is and offering to send planes to Kentucky to rescue him from the boredom of retirement?" Cade sniped.

Ahmed simply raised an eyebrow at Cade and then looked at Cy.

"I've gotten through about half of the unknown pictures and have been able to identify them. They're mostly arms dealers, some higher-level foreign politicians, and known operators on the black market," Cy snapped as he dealt the next hand. He tried to take a deep breath, but it felt as if his undercover life was smothering him. He was lost in the lies of his job.

His phone vibrated again and Cy bit back a curse as Pierce grabbed it again. "Oh, this one I bet he takes," Pierce teased as Cy yanked the phone out of his brother's hand.

"Gemma? Is everything okay?"

"I'm sorry to interrupt poker night, but I found something," Gemma squealed. She sounded so excited and proud that Cy couldn't help but smile. The tension coiling around his heart eased slightly. Immediately his brothers snickered.

"No problem at all. I'll be right there." Cy hung up and glared at his brothers and his friends. "Really? You're a prince and you're laughing at me?"

"I am sorry, but it's so obvious you're completely out of your element," Mo said while sounding not at all apologetic.

"Did you hear his voice?" Cole asked.

"I did. He's a goner," Miles said as he tossed a chip onto the table.

"I noticed whose phone call he didn't take while he leapt to get Gemma's call," Cade teased as he placed his bet.

"Please. She has nothing on Gemma," Cy folded and stood up from the table.

"Except she's the highest-paid actress in the world," Pierce snickered.

"Gemma's real; she's not. Gemma's also funny and braver than her any day. Miss Actress threw such a hissy fit when she had to pick up a snake for a scene, but Gemma . . . Gemma didn't even scream when she was being chased and shot at by those thugs," Cy told them. He respected Gemma and he trusted her. That's more than he could say for any of the other women in Hollywood.

"Let's cut to the chase here," Miles said as he won the hand, "you like her. Why aren't you with her?"

Cy looked down at his feet. It was embarrassing. "I don't think she likes me. She doesn't find ways to touch me. She doesn't bat her eyes at me. She doesn't try to find ways to spend time together," Cy shrugged. "Doesn't that just beat all? I finally find someone I like and she's not interested." The tightness returned around his heart and Cy felt his jaw tighten. He was lost again to the smothering feeling of his life.

"Well, she called you, didn't she?" Marshall offered.

"Yeah, to tell me she found something. She's been locked in her room for the past three days. I'm glad she sounded so excited. She's been too hard on herself for not being able to contribute more."

"Well, what are we waiting for? Let's see what's she found." Cole stood up and the rest of the table followed.

Gemma was pacing the length of the front porch when she saw the line of cars pull up to the curb. Apparently poker night had moved to the bed-and-breakfast.

"Oh my. I better put more cookies in the oven and get more snacks ready."

Gemma whipped around and saw a tuft of white hair hurrying inside. She hadn't realized Miss Lily had been standing there.

Cy's truck was the first to park and she had to stop herself from running down the path in her excitement. She had worked all afternoon and evening on the first notebook, just finished it, and found a lead.

Miles walked up the yard with his brothers, Mo, Ahmed, and Cole. "I hope you don't mind that we all came. We were eager to hear what you had found."

"No, not at all. Let's go into the sitting room. There's enough room for everyone there," Gemma replied.

Cy opened the door and Gemma gave him a smile. She had finally done something to help her sister and she could barely stop herself from jumping around.

"Did you find Mr. X?" Cy asked, standing next to her while everyone else sat down.

"No. But I did find something big. You know how I told you Paul Russell was going to pursue a seat in Congress to further Mr. X's purposes?" She waited until everyone nodded. "Well, Gia found out who had been in that position before. And it's huge. He totally got busted for a huge corruption/prostitution/murder thing a couple of years ago. Not only did I discover who it was, I found out he's still alive and which prison he's in."

Cy had a sinking feeling he knew who it was. "Holy shit," he cursed under his breath. Everyone stopped and looked at him pointedly. They had all been thinking it, too. "Senator Bruce."

"How did you know?" Gemma asked, upset that they knew her big discovery.

"Kenna, Dani, and Paige were the key witnesses in the trial of the men found guilty of those crimes. I was there as Paige's bodyguard. Senator Bruce's daughter is Will Ashton's ex-wife and Kenna was the eyewitness to the crime that brought them all down. Bruce took a plea to avoid the death penalty and has never said a word about his involvement. We know nothing more than that," Cy told her.

"Yes, very uncharacteristically he hasn't said a word about the crimes. Most people in his position write a tell-all book or sit down with a prime-time reporter to cry about a bad childhood or something that makes them appear the victim. But now it makes sense." Cole was now sharing the same excitement she felt.

"How so?" Pierce asked as he picked up a cookie Miss Lily offered.

"If he was in the pocket of Mr. X, then he knows a single word would wind up getting him killed. He's hoping Mr. X uses his influence to get him out of jail. But now we have leverage." Gemma had never seen the cool lawman so animated in her short time in Keeneston, and his excitement was contagious.

"How so?" Gemma asked.

"Bruce was indicted on twenty-three counts of murder. He agreed to a deal: life in prison. As you read, the case involved prostitutes the men murdered and then Bruce's bodyguards dumped. How much do you want to bet he got those prostitutes from Mr. X? I'm willing to bet it all," Cole grinned and Gemma thought that Paige was a very lucky lady.

"Ah. I know where you're going with this." Cy smiled and this time Gemma saw the real Cy. She was so wrapped up in the way his eyes shone with excitement and his lips quirked a little higher on one side that she almost missed his explanation. "We pay Bruce a visit and ask him about Mr. X. If he resists, then we'll have a way to make him talk."

"What's that?" Gemma asked. She wasn't following, but it appeared all the men understood.

"Death," Cy answered cryptically. "Mo, can we borrow your plane. We have an inmate to visit."

"It'll be at the airport in an hour. I let my eldest brother and his wife borrow it. They are flying in from *in vitro* treatments in New York City," Mo told them.

"And you're okay with that?" Cade asked.

"Most definitely. It may be selfish, but I wish for them to have an heir so my children can be raised here in Keeneston and have the childhood I never had—a real one."

Gemma felt for him. While Mo stood regally, the hope and desire rang in his voice.

"Well then, I wish them luck. Thank you for the use of your plane." Cy shook his hand and Mo smiled at him.

"You are very welcome. Call me if you need anything else. I always love talking to bureaucrats." Mo turned from Cy to

Gemma. "Good luck, my dear. I hope you find the justice you seek."

Gemma thanked him and watched Mo, Miles, Marshall, Cade, and Pierce head home while Ahmed and Cy stood quietly to the side as Cole placed a phone call to the penitentiary in Jonesville, Virginia. She thought about what Mo said. Justice. It consumed her. No matter what she had to do, she would find justice for her sister.

CHAPTER TWELVE

$\mathcal{G}$emma looked up at the penitentiary and shuddered. The depressing cement prison towered over her. She felt Cy slip his arm around her as if sensing her distress. It was the middle of the night as they were led through the front entrance and buzzed in past the visitors' waiting room. A tired-looking older man, salt-and-pepper hair still mussed from his pillow, stood waiting for them.

"Agent Parker?" the man asked as he eyed Gemma, Ahmed, and Cy suspiciously.

"I'm Parker. You must be Warden Cummings. Thank you for seeing us so late at night." Cole strode forward as Gemma and the rest of the group stopped.

"I wasn't expecting anyone else . . ." the warden started before a cold look from Ahmed stopped him. Gemma looked at the easy smile Cole flashed the warden and wondered how he was going to explain a reporter, a spy, and a whatever-Ahmed-was to him.

"Is Senator Bruce ready for us?" Cole asked, not bothering to answer the question.

"One of my guards has gone to get him out of solitary. Let me take you to the interview room. The guard will bring the senator to you there." The warden gave one last look to Ahmed and Cy where they stood on each side of Gemma before leading them down a long network of halls.

Gemma's sandals tapped the floor along with Cole's cowboy boots, but Cy and Ahmed's thick boots traveled silently as they navigated the halls. Gemma stuck close to Cy in the darkened hallway but he had changed. In fact, all of them had. They all appeared relaxed, but their bodies radiated tension as their eyes took in every detail.

Finally the warden led them into a small room with a thick metal door and bars on the one small window against the far wall. A metal table with three chairs sat in the middle of the room. The table had a metal ring on it and there was one on the floor below the chair for chaining prisoners if necessary.

Cy and Cole took a seat on one side of the metal table while Ahmed led Gemma to the far side of the room. He crossed his arms over his expansive chest and didn't take his eyes off the door. Gemma hadn't learned all about Ahmed yet, but she knew enough to know she was safe with him and Senator Bruce definitely wasn't.

The door opened and a white-haired man in an orange jumpsuit was pushed through. "Here he is, Warden," the guard said as he looked curiously around the room.

"Parker? What are you doing here?" the senator spat.

"Thank you, gentlemen. We'll tap on the door when we're done here." Cole ignored Senator Bruce and didn't say a word until the warden and guard had left.

Gemma's heart was pounding as she watched the scene unfold from the corner. Cole and Cy looked calm. Ahmed was so still. How could they stand it? She wanted to fire off question after question as she paced the room.

"How are you doing in here, Mr. Bruce?" Cole asked as he leaned back in his seat.

"It's *Senator*," he growled as he narrowed his eyes at Cole.

"Not anymore. Now it's *inmate*," Cy smirked and Gemma's eyes widened. It wasn't the same man. Cy's face was cold and dangerous. Gemma fought the ridiculous feeling of needing to hide from him.

"Who the hell are you?"

"The man who has some questions for you."

"Sorry, I don't answer questions. Now get lost. I'm going back to bed."

Cy shrugged. "Sure. We can let you go back to bed. While you're sleeping, I'll go to the papers and tell them I had a great chat with you all about the man who supplied the women to you at those poker games in New York," Cy said casually.

Senator Bruce's face turned white as he dropped into the empty chair. Cy leaned forward, placed his elbows on the table, and looked Bruce right in the eye.

"See, we've put it all together. We know all about the sex trade, the guns, the drugs, and even Sergei." Cy paused and then drilled Bruce with his gaze. "And we know that you'll be dead in a heartbeat if they think you talked."

"I'll be dead either way now. They'll know you were here. They'll know I was alone in this room with you and that will be enough. I'll be dead by the morning, thanks to you." Gemma almost felt sorry for him. Almost.

"Then you might as well talk," Cy responded without a hint of sympathy in his hard voice.

"To some asshole I don't even know. No. I want to talk to my daughter. I won't say a word to you until I talk to Whitney and know that she's alive and safe." Bruce crossed his arms over his chest and stared at Cy and Cole who just sat staring back. Gemma could hardy stand still as she watched the standoff.

"And, if we let you talk to Whitney, you'll answer all of our questions?" Cole asked.

"Yes. If you promise she'll be safe until it's all over."

"Deal," Cole said as he pulled out his cell phone.

Ahmed stepped forward and put a quiet hand on Cole's shoulder and handed him a phone he had in his pocket. "It's untraceable."

"Who is this guy?" Bruce said incredulously as he looked Ahmed over.

Gemma leaned forward so she wouldn't miss the answer, but Ahmed simply smiled a thin, terrifying smile before stepping back. Cole went to work calling the U.S. Marshal's office and organized a patch through to Whitney's witness protection location through a series of secure lines.

As Bruce took the phone from Cole, Ahmed leaned back and handed Gemma a pen and a pocket notebook. "Write down everything he says."

Gemma started scribbling as she heard Bruce's voice go soft when he talked to his daughter for the first time in years. She tried not to cry. If Bruce was right, then this could be the last time he ever talked to his daughter. How could everyone stand listening and show no emotion whatsoever?

Fifteen minutes later, Bruce hung up the phone and handed it back to Cole. "Thank you."

"You're welcome. Look, Bruce. You help us; we'll help you. We'll take you with us and change your name, your look, and put you in a prison where no one will find you," Cole told him. Gemma felt relieved. She knew the former senator was a criminal, but it was different seeing a defeated old man sitting in front of her, completely broken.

"Sure you will. Or you'll try. It may even protect me for a couple of weeks, but they'll find me eventually." Bruce took a deep breath. "What do you want to know?"

"Who did you report to?" Cy asked.

"I didn't have his name. It was the same man for years and then came Sergei. I only knew his name through my work on the Foreign Affairs Committee. But, my main contact was thin and bookish. He had a goatee."

"How did you get in contact with him?"

"I had a number." Bruce motioned for a pen and paper and wrote it down along with an address. "This is where I'd sometimes meet him."

"Was he the boss?" Cy asked as he pushed the paper over for Cole to view.

"No, but he was close to him. I only met the boss once but never saw him. He was in a limo and rolled down the window only enough for me to hear him."

"How many women did they supply you with and where did they get them?" Cole interjected.

"I pled guilty to twenty-three counts," Bruce shrugged.

"I'm not going to charge you. I'm just trying to find out how the cycle worked and maybe a common location. Besides, as you said, you're a dead man," Cole said so harshly that Gemma shivered. "Why don't you just start at the beginning? When did you meet the boss?"

Bruce took a breath and Gemma could see he was debating what he should tell them. But then the look of utter hopelessness came across his face and he focused on the back wall. "It was twenty years ago. I was a local attorney who had just won a big case in North Carolina when I decided to run for Congress. A man approached me with promises of a big supporter. So I went to this meeting. It was in a deserted sawmill. A limo pulled up and the window came down three inches or so.

"The man inside asked if I wanted a blank check. He'd pay for every election and reelection. I asked what the rub was and he just laughed. He told me information was the rub. That, and every now and then he would need support for certain legislation. The driver of the car got out and handed me a check for $5,000,000. I stupidly agreed.

"The first year, I was only contacted a couple of times, but more importantly, I was introduced to very important and influential people. The second year, I was appointed chairman of the Foreign Affairs Committee and that's when the phone calls started, needing information or telling me which countries I needed to push for sanctions." Bruce took a breath and shook his head as if clearing his thoughts.

"It never occurred to you that this was above your normal Washington corruption?" Cy asked.

"At the start of my second term, the requests became more frequent and more intrusive. He wanted me to plant bugs in other congressional offices and embassies. One of those embassies was blown up three months later."

"Why didn't you stop? Turn him into the FBI?" Cole leaned forward and laced his fingers together.

"I thought about it. But the money started coming. He knew my weakness—gambling. The money came with private invitations to big-stake games. He funded my gambling for years. He collected all my markers and I knew it. But I couldn't stop. I could try to pawn it off as an addiction, but it wasn't. I was just having too much fun. I was being flown to Monaco for a weekend of gambling with some of the richest and most powerful men in the world. I didn't want to give it up, so I kept accepting the cash that showed up at my house every two weeks and decided to do whatever the hell I felt like doing."

Gemma gasped and Ahmed nudged her. She hadn't been expecting that. She had been expecting the sob story about a gambling addiction. But what he had was a power addiction. He tasted power, rubbed against it every day, and wanted more and more.

This time, Cy leaned forward. "When did the women start?"

"Ah, the women. I loved poker night," Bruce said wistfully. "A small group of us started that almost ten years ago. The boss set up the first one. There was Judge LeMaster, an ambassador to Syria, a British ministry official, and me. The goatee man came with a submissive woman one night dressed in nothing but a big red bow. He said she was a gift to the winner. That's when they started. We met every month. Sometimes it was the same group and sometimes others came, but always an equally powerful group. A new woman was dropped off each time."

"But why kill them?" Gemma silently nodded in response to Cy's question. She wanted to know the answer, too.

"At first, we just dumped them in a bad part of town and left them. But then one night, we got a woman who had been a stripper before she was taken from the club. The damn bitch was stripping to put herself through law school. She knew who we all were and wouldn't shut up about it. We had no choice. I shot her and dumped her in some alley. It was just a precaution after that. I talked to the goatee man and he said he'd fix it. Two days later, I was attacked on the floor of the Congress. That afternoon, four men showed up and said they were my security detail. I didn't question them—no one did. They were real handy in cleaning up my messes from then on. I knew where they came from and knew they wouldn't be squeamish so I didn't bother being a gentleman any longer," Bruce sneered with what Gemma could only describe as joy.

"How many?" Cy simply asked.

"Too many to possibly count. Strippers, escorts . . . who knows where they all came from? Some spoke English, some didn't. It didn't really matter." Bruce shrugged.

"And you never investigated your boss? Never tried to learn about him?" Cole asked in mock amazement.

"Sure I did. The only reason I've lived so long here is because I found out one juicy bit of gossip that could ID him. See, you asked me the wrong questions. You asked if I'd met him. You never asked if I knew his identity."

Gemma jumped as the alarm above her head sounded. The door was thrown open by a concerned-looking warden. "I see my time has come early. Who knew women would be all our downfalls?" Bruce said as he stood.

"There's a riot. Somehow the prisoners got loose. I've got to get you all to safety." The warden grabbed Bruce and waited for the group to stand up.

"Who is he, Bruce?" Cy demanded as he burst from his seat.

"He's . . ." In one quick motion, Warden Cummings slashed Bruce's throat.

Gemma stood frozen as she watched Bruce's body fall to the floor, blood gushing from his neck. Ahmed shoved her back as Cy rocketed himself across the table and onto Warden Cummings. Cole was by Bruce's side with his hand pressed against his throat trying to slow the bleeding.

"Do something," she screamed as Cy and Cummings wrestled on the floor.

"Come on," Ahmed grabbed her wrist and pulled her toward the door.

"We can't leave them." Ahmed didn't say anything as he shoved her behind the door and went to Cole's side first. Cole shook his head and stood up just as Cy delivered a staggering blow to Warden Cummings. The warden's head slammed back against the concrete floor, stopping his fighting.

Cy stood up and looked down on him. "Why?"

"I got a letter with a picture of my wife and daughter at the playground two hours after Bruce was imprisoned here. I was told to call a number if anyone came to see him and I'd be given instructions. If I didn't follow them, they'd kill my family slowly," Cummings said as he slowly sat up. "Tell them I love them."

Before Cy could move, the warden reached out and grabbed the guard's gun and shot himself. Gemma choked back a sob as she stared at the destruction in the room. Then the sound of gunfire snapped her back to reality. The prison was rioting and they were not safe.

"We have to get out of here. Cy and I will take point. Cole, make sure she gets out of here alive." Ahmed and Cy pulled out guns from everywhere.

Cole looked down at his service weapon. "Well, I sure feel inadequate," he said in such a dry voice that Gemma actually let out a nervous laugh in the middle of all this chaos.

Ahmed pushed out the door first, followed by Cy. The interview hallway was empty, but the sounds of the riot were growing closer as they hurried toward the exit. Pounding erupted beside them as they passed the visitors' section. It sounded as if the prisoners were trying to knock down the strong door separating the meeting area from the hallway leading to the cells.

With a final bang, the door was pried open and men rushed through it, past the small tables, to another door leading to the hallway where Gemma and her group were. Cole pushed Gemma, forcing her to start running again, but when she turned back toward the entrance, she froze as she faced a wall of guards in riot gear.

"FBI," Cole shouted as he raised his badge. "Let us through."

Cy pushed forward toward the guards but it was too late. The visitors' door crashed opened and they were now caught between the prisoners and the guards in the middle of the wide hallway. The prisoners smiled as they saw Gemma, and Cy felt his heart turn to ice. No way were they getting their hands on her. With a quick glance, he looked back and saw that Cole had shoved her behind him and was backing her up toward the guards.

Cy turned to Ahmed who gave him a barely visible nod and raised his weapon. The prisoner who was leading the riot stopped and smiled at him. The tattoos covering his neck moved as he swallowed. "Hand over the girl and get out of the way, man. Maybe we'll let you live."

"Um, let me think about it. No." Cy cocked his gun and the man covered in gang tattoos just laughed.

"You think you can stop me? *You* think they can stop *me?* I'm the badass that runs this place." He held up his arms as his minions circled around him waiting to strike.

Cy didn't have time for this. He pulled the trigger and heard the scream as the man grabbed his knee, falling to the floor. His minions looked stunned. "Who else wants to find out if they're badasses?" They looked at each other and then to the advancing wall of guards and decided they weren't gods after all. With their hands up, they backed through the door and ran back into the mob.

"Hands up," a guard shouted.

Cy rolled his eyes. "CIA," he said as he lifted his badge. "Now will someone be kind enough to escort us out?"

Gemma sat on the couch in Mo's plane. She was worn out. Her adrenaline was now depleted and all she wanted was to sleep for days. Cy took the seat between her and Cole as Ahmed chose a chair across the aisle from them.

They started talking about the night and the criminal network, but it was almost three in the morning and she was too tired to participate. Her body shook with exhaustion and Cy put his arm over her shoulder as he continued to talk. She knew she shouldn't, but she couldn't resist putting her head on his chest and snuggling closer to him. He was so warm and safe. She had finally done it; she'd gone and fallen for him. Oh, she knew he was trouble the second she crashed into him.

She had been trying to ignore the feelings, trying to tell herself that she wasn't his type, but it hadn't worked. When she saw him leap across the desk and put himself in danger, her heart had tripped and she couldn't imagine him not in her life anymore. Cy talked and gently rubbed her shoulder as Gemma felt her eyes flutter. Soon the low rumble of his voice and the warmth of his embrace had her fast asleep dreaming of what might be.

Cy never wanted to move. Gemma felt so perfect in his arms. He spent the short plane ride talking to Ahmed and Cole, all the while perfectly aware of every gentle breath she took. Halfway through the flight, she rested her hand on his stomach and he thought he'd never felt anything so sweet in his whole life.

"Honey, we're landing," he whispered into her ear.

"Mm-hmm," she mumbled and buried her head deeper into his chest. The plane landed with a bump and she tightened her hand on his shirt but didn't wake up.

"Man, she's out of it. Want my help getting her home?" Cole asked.

"Nah, I got it. Just make sure I don't fall down the stairs." Cy stood up and in one easy motion picked her up. Cole went ahead of him and told him where the steps were as he exited the plane.

"Sleep well. We'll talk tomorrow. Good night, Ahmed."

Ahmed nodded to Cole and Cy and took off in his car. Cole gave him one last wave and got into his truck.

"Come on, honey, it's time for me to get you into bed," Cy whispered as he put her into the truck.

"Okay," she mumbled.

Cy felt himself hold his breath. Okay to what? To helping her home or okay to getting into bed with her? Either idea had him pondering quietly as he drove back to Miss Lily's.

Cy balanced Gemma in his arms as he unlocked her door. He carried her to the large bed and again wondered at her invitation. No. He was a gentleman and gentlemen didn't take advantage of women. He would do the right thing and get her into bed. Then, tomorrow, he would properly try to earn his way into her bed.

He grinned as he took off her sandals and placed a blanket over her. Gemma's hair tumbled onto the pillow. She had curled up on her side and was hugging the other pillow when her eyes fluttered and she looked up at him.

"Good night, Gemma," Cy whispered as he rose to leave.

"Kiss me. Just once?"

Cy felt the invitation instantly. He looked down at her and knew he shouldn't, but when she smiled up at him and held out her hand, he was done for. He bent forward and brushed her bottom lip with his thumb gently before touching his lips to her. He ran his tongue along her lip as she opened for him. Cy knew it would be like this. He knew that once he got his first taste, he'd never be able to forget her. Now all he wanted to do was worship her.

Gemma hugged the pillow tight and responded instantly to the kiss by moaning into his mouth. Man, this dream was even better than the dream she'd had the night before. She opened her eyes and stared at Cy's soft face. She ran her hand over his stubble as she caressed him. She wondered if this was what he would look like if he dropped his guard. She sure hoped so because this man was gorgeous.

He ran his hand over her head and brushed back her hair. "You have no idea how badly I want you," her dream man said to her. Well, it was what she was longing to hear and her subconscious just gave it to her—who was she to deny it?

"Oh God, yes," she called out as his hands ran up her ribs to cup her breasts. This was definitely better than last night's dream, she thought as he gently massaged her while he brought his lips to her stomach. He traced a line of kisses from her belly button upward, and when his mouth closed onto her nipple, she decided right then and there she was never going to wake up.

Gemma gasped and ran her hand down his back. This was her dream and there were things she had been dreaming of doing to him since she first met him. She grabbed his shirt and ripped it off before pulling him onto the bed. Straddling him, she slowly raised her shirt over her head, teasingly. Next she stood on the bed and stepped out of her shorts and panties as she swayed above him. His hands tried desperately to reach for her as she playfully pushed them away.

"I've been wanting to do this since the night we met. To feel my body against yours," she confessed.

"By all means, you should do it then." His voice was different. Deeper, more gravelly as she straddled him again. His hands were on her instantly as she threw her head back and gave into the sensation of his hardness beneath her.

Cy sat up, cradling her in his lap. "But now it's time for me to show you what I've been thinking about since I met you."

"If you really want to." Gemma smiled before he flipped her beneath him.

"Oh, I do . . ." And with a ravenous glance at her body, he showed her just what he'd been thinking about.

CHAPTER THIRTEEN

emma knew she had woken up, but the soft breeze coming from the overhead fan and the perfect way her arm was wrapped around her pillow made it hard to open her eyes after such an exhausting day.

The day had been so long and filled with such emotion. She was glad to be back in the quiet of her room and left with the remembrances of her dream last night. Wow. It had been one hell of a dream. She had fallen asleep on the plane after the adrenaline wore off and remembered waking up when Cy carried her into her room. He had said good-night and she had fallen right back to sleep to have the be-all-and-end-all sex dream. In fact, just thinking about it brought a blush to her face.

She squeezed her pillow and then screamed when it turned to her and sleepily smiled. "Good morning."

Gemma leapt from the bed, kicking at the covers tangling up her feet. "Oh my God!" She panicked as she bounced from foot to foot breaking free of the sheets and moving to the end of the bed.

"Wow. You're even more beautiful in the daylight. Better than I could've ever imagined. How did I get so lucky?"

Gemma felt Cy's eyes traveling the length of her body and she looked down and automatically tried to cover her nakedness. "I . . . you . . . you were a dream," Gemma stuttered as her eyes focused on his bare chest. His lap was still covered, but the top of a tattoo close to the bulge under the sheet caught her eye. What was that?

"I'm very real, sweetheart. Want me to prove it to you again? I'm more than happy to accommodate you." Cy grinned and Gemma got that flip-flop feeling again. He was so handsome, so sexy when he showed his real self. He was playful but tender. Assertive but giving as she remembered her non-dream. He was everything she wanted and more . . . and completely unavailable.

"But you're dating every Hollywood bimbo around," Gemma moaned as she rolled her head up toward the ceiling in distress.

"And . . . you didn't like me. I think last night proved we were both wrong. In fact, I think we're pretty perfect together. I mean, that thing you did with your leg and then you moved—"

"I can't believe I did that." But Gemma's worry disappeared and her mouth went dry as Cy pushed aside the sheet and patted the bed next to him. The tattoo was uncovered to reveal a family crest and a very excited Cy.

Gemma ran her eyes over his broad chest, ripped abs, and narrow waist. His legs were long and muscled. Scars marked his body here and there, but somehow they only made him more masculine. And that tattoo. She got hot just looking at it. It was small, maybe only five inches in the crease of his thigh across his pelvic bone. She was drawn to it.

"I love your tattoo. It fits you," Gemma stepped forward and traced her fingers over the small red shield. A black lion was in the middle of the shield with a knight's helmet on top. Plumes cascaded from the helmet around the top of the shield.

Cy patted the bed and the nagging doubt disappeared. "Want to get a closer look?"

"Well," Gemma smiled as she dropped her arms to her side, "if you insist."

***

Cy couldn't keep the smile off his face as he clasped his hand around her smaller one. He absently rubbed his thumb over her knuckles as he felt more like his real self than he had in years.

Being with her, laughing with her, it was like seeing the light at the end of the dark undercover tunnel he was trying to escape.

"If you think the muffins Miss Lily has been giving you were good, you'll love the food at the café. You should try the biscuits and sausage gravy; they're my favorite." Cy felt a smile settle on his face as he looked down at her beautiful face. She wore no makeup and her hair was swept back into a sloppy ponytail. He didn't think he'd seen anything so sexy before in his life.

"Sounds good," Gemma smiled back.

Cy opened the door to the café and walked in behind her. The café went quiet and he felt Gemma stiffen.

"It's like they all know we slept together," Gemma whispered as she hesitantly smiled at the patrons.

"That's because they do, sweetheart." Cy placed a quick kiss on her forehead and the patrons groaned.

"Yee-haw." Noodle jumped up and pumped his fist in the air.

"I take it you won the bet?" Cy asked, smiling. No wonder he missed this town.

"I sure did. Today was my day. I gotta call Emma. We're upgrading to a suite for the honeymoon now." Noodle pumped his fist in the air and reached for his phone.

"They bet on us?" Gemma hissed incredulously.

"They bet on everything." Cy saw her shoot him a *yeah, right* look and decided to prove his point. "Miss Daisy, what's the line on Dani and Mo's baby?"

"Two to one that it's a girl. August third is the leading due date. Want in?" Miss Daisy asked as she set down a plate of bacon and eggs at the closest table.

"No thanks, but I do think we'll have two orders of biscuits and gravy." Cy pulled out a chair at an empty table for Gemma as she sat.

Gemma tasted the food and felt happy. A fluffy biscuit was smothered in gravy. It was the perfect comfort food. The conversation in the café had resumed to a normal level and she was surprised how easily she and Cy talked. For once, Hollywood wasn't interrupting and she enjoyed hearing about all the residents of Keeneston.

"Cy Davies?" a tall woman with strawberry-blonde hair asked as she stopped by the table. Gemma almost threw down her fork in frustration. Hollywood just interrupted. Gemma didn't know who she was, but she was striking even though she was wearing black cargo pants and a tight black scoop-neck shirt.

"Yes?" Cy was polite as he looked up into a face lightly sprinkled with freckles.

"Bridget Springer," she said with a sweet voice that held nothing but authority in its tone.

Gemma was suddenly jealous. She wished she had the confidence Bridget did. She seemed so secure in who she was and maybe that was Gemma's problem. She was suffering an identity crisis. She wasn't happy with her job, just lost her sister, and had no idea what direction her life was going in.

"And I'm Gemma Perry," Gemma said with a smile as she held out her hand.

"It's nice to meet you both. Mr. Davies hired me to train Marko for the sheriff and I ended up staying here. And, from what I've heard, I'm the reason you're at the bed-and-breakfast instead of Paige's. I was just going to offer to move out if you need the space."

"Nonsense," Gemma waved the idea away. This woman was a strange contradiction. While there was authority there, she seemed to be a genuinely kind person and Gemma definitely wanted to get to know her better.

"Thank you. Just know the offer stands." Bridget paused for a minute before looking back to Cy. "Forgive me if it's none of my business, but I also had some ideas about the case."

"Well, then, take a seat and tell us what you think." As Bridget sat, Cy filled Gemma in. "Bridget is an elite K-9 handler. She's worked the front lines of the War Against Terror, guarded the president, escorted ambassadors, and more. She's very well respected in the security world."

"Thank you," Bridget said with a slight nod before lacing her fingers together and turning serious. "I think the men Ahmed turned over to the police may be of some use to you. As you know, they were the ones charged with finding you. They could be able to tell you how they found you. If you have that information, then you can work your way back up the food chain, so to speak. Also, if they're personal security, for example, then they may have information on the boss they protect and run these kinds of errands for."

"That's a good point. I had just assumed they'd be hired henchmen, but you may be right. I wish I knew if they had a tattoo. That would tell me if they were hired or part of the security team."

"They had a small black tattoo on their wrist. It was a Roman numeral X." Gemma jumped back as she heard Ahmed answer from directly behind her. She hadn't heard the bell ring or even felt anyone standing behind her.

"Then we need to have a talk with them," Cy agreed.

"I thought the same thing. It's why I came to see you. Miss Springer," Ahmed acknowledged with a quick nod of his head.

"Ahmed," Bridget responded in kind. Gemma had to hide a smile behind her napkin. There was certainly a spark there, but it was strange. They were both so good at hiding their feelings, she couldn't tell if it was love or hate.

"Well then, what are we waiting for?" Cy asked as he placed some money on the table. "It's about time these guys meet who they were looking for."

Cy followed Ahmed into the Lexington police station. The old concrete building somehow looked like every other police station in the world. Overworked and underpaid people living off caffeine ran them all. The old tile floors somehow darkened the fluorescent light beating down as their steps echoed down the hall.

Ahmed stopped at the front desk and quietly spoke to the woman behind the plastic window. She nodded and then picked up the phone. Just as quickly as she dialed, she hung up. "Detective Basher will see you now. Through the doors and up to the third floor."

Gemma came and stood near Cy when a man in handcuffs was led down the hall by two uniforms. He liked the way she instinctively felt protected by him. She probably didn't even notice she did it.

"It's this way," Ahmed said, paying no attention to the man in cuffs now cursing and struggling as the officers tried to control him.

Cy slid his arm around Gemma's waist and urged her forward. After they passed through the doors, the environment turned more office-like. They pushed through a swinging door and into a large room filled with desks. An older man stood up solemnly on the far side of the room. His hands rested on his hips and Cy knew it wasn't good. The man's lips were pierced into a tight line as he waited for them to approach.

"I was just about to call you," he grumbled.

"Detective Basher, Cy Davies and Gemma Perry. Cy, Detective Basher arrested your brother." Ahmed looked somewhat amused, but it was hard for Cy to tell for certain.

"Jeez, how many of you are there?"

"He's the target our two friends were really after. That's why we're here. We need to have a quick word with them," Ahmed stated rather than asked.

"That's why I was going to call you. Seems they were sitting down to lunch and got shanked in a little disturbance between rival gangs."

Cy cursed. "This is a lot bigger than it seems and now our leads are dead." Cy continued to curse under his breath and fought the urge to slam his fist against the old metal desk.

"What does that mean?" Gemma asked from beside him.

"It means your sister's notebooks are our only lead now."

Gemma nodded and her eyes showed steely determination. "Then let's get back to Miss Lily's. I have work to do. There's no way I'm letting these guys get away with murdering my sister."

CHAPTER FOURTEEN

Cy paced his room at the bed-and-breakfast. An evening sportscaster was trying to get his attention, but the only thing keeping his attention was knowing that Gemma was right across the hall from him. After they got back to Miss Lily's yesterday, she'd locked herself up for the rest of the day and night. This morning when Miss Lily had brought her a breakfast tray, Gemma had told her that she didn't want to be bothered. When Cy heard that, he called Ahmed who sent a guy to watch her while he spent the day at the farm. He cleared brush, cut fence boards, and helped Pierce herd some cattle with the help of Cade's dog, Justin, and Miles's dog, Bill.

How could Cade let his dog run around with that bow? It was embarrassing. This week it was purple with white polka dots.

"You wouldn't wear that, would you?" Cy asked Fred who was curled up in his arms. Fred looked up and stuck out his little pink tongue. "Exactly. You're a man's dog, aren't you?" Fred gave a little bark and then rested his head on his tiny feet.

"You're one to talk! You're holding a frou-frou dog, for crying out loud, and you're making fun of Justin?" Pierce had teased.

Cy had taken Fred with him to the farm where he had enjoyed running through the fields and leaping through the tall grass. When Pierce had asked for help, he hadn't really known what to do with Fred. He dug around the barn and found a backpack that Fred jumped into happily. Cy put it on and he and Fred enjoyed the horseback ride, although Cy was a little worried that Fred was starting to get a big head. He barked as if he were giving orders to Justin and Bill as they moved the herd.

The sportscast resumed and Cy looked at the clock. Another hour had gone by. It was eleven at night and he had been cut off for as long as he could stand. It was time to see Gemma again. And maybe, just maybe, he would get to see a whole lot of Gemma again. She was mesmerizing. He'd never been with a woman so passionate and free in bed before. He couldn't wait to find out what new things they'd try tonight. With a cocky grin, Cy opened the door to the hall.

Gemma rolled her neck from side to side to ease the cramping. She had gotten about four hours of sleep last night and was exhausted. While she had translated her sister's notebooks, there were still key questions to be answered. The trouble was she just didn't know how to answer them.

Gia had left clues she was sure made sense to her sister but ran Gemma in circles. She didn't know who the contacts were that Gia referred to only by code names. After finally giving up, Gemma had turned to the flash drive only to meet a dead end there, too.

It didn't help that every five minutes her thoughts ran back to Cy. The way he treated her as delicate china, always opening doors, helping her through crowded rooms, protecting her with his life during jailhouse riots. It wasn't something the average woman could say. However, she now totally understood her friends' fascinations with cowboys. The way his jeans fit, the way he looked wearing his cowboy hat, and the pure chivalry had her thinking relationship thoughts she wasn't sure he wanted to hear.

It was also hard to stop thinking about him with *the* bed right there next to her. No matter where she went in the room, as soon as she turned around she saw the bed and her mind instantly went to the other night and the following morning. Cy had proven that sometimes dreams can't live up to real life. She had never been so secure with someone before, and it left her both slightly embarrassed and wanting more at the same time. She couldn't believe she'd done that thing she'd only read about in magazines. She really should write them and tell them it worked. But then she would also think about the pictures sent to his phone and an imaginary bucket of ice water would hit her. Women were trying to claw their way into his bed and she not only fell into it, she literally leapt into it after a few nice words from him.

Stop thinking of it, Gemma scolded herself. She needed to focus on what was before her. The bed was literally right before her. Oh God, she was thinking about it again. Gemma turned and banged her head on the desk. *Focus,* she told herself as she tried to banish the image of Cy before her with his hands and mouth and . . . *Dammit.* Gemma jumped up from where she was sitting and headed straight for the windows. She needed air to clear her head.

Cy opened his door in eager anticipation and didn't see the white-haired woman sitting in one of the armchairs in the comfortable reading nook that filled the space between the two rooms.

"Good evening, Cyland. Is there something I can get for you?" Cy depended on years of training to not show his surprise. His roommate during training had thought Cy was joking when he told him about the three sisters from his hometown who could bring the whole government to their knees if they wanted. But he was serious. They had eyes in the back of their head and he was pretty sure they could read minds.

"Good evening, Miss Lily. I was just checking to see if Gemma needed anything before I went to bed," he said as he shot his most innocent look to Miss Lily.

"Humph. And I'm here because I like the view. Has anyone ever told you that you're a bad liar?" Miss Lily set down her knitting and drilled him with a knowing look as she picked up her broom and pretended to sweep the floor.

"Actually," Cy paused, "no. You're the first. Others thought I was so good the U.S. government put me undercover. You could say I'm a professional liar, so much so Cy Davies has ceased to exist for many years now."

Miss Lily swatted him on the bottom with her broom and glared at him. "Nonsense. You're a spy. It's a job. It's what you do, not who you are. You're the same boy who used to help my sisters unload their groceries and who rescued that poor cat that got stuck in the tree out front there. You just need to remember that and stop lying to yourself about who you are. Now," Miss Lily said with finality, "it's time for bed. Off with you."

Cy chanced a quick glance at Gemma's door that didn't go unnoticed. "Good night, Miss Lily." Cy may have lost the battle, but he hadn't lost the war. He shot Miss Lily a smile as she put her broom down and picked up her knitting. She had reminded him of the mighty cat rescue and now he had an idea.

Gemma took a deep breath of the night air and enjoyed the inspiration from the stars twinkling in the dark sky. What was she doing wrong?

"Mom . . . I don't want to wear the same thing as Gia." Gemma stomped her pre-teen foot on the ground and crossed her arms.

"You're twins. You're the only ones who can get away with wearing the same outfit. It's cute. Now put it on." Her mother handed her the matching floral dress.

"While we may be twins, we're not the same person. I hate flowers and Gia loves them. It's not fair."

Gemma felt her heart speed up. That was it. They aren't the same person. Gemma hurried back to her seat, pulled out her cell phone, and starting scrolling through her contacts.

She was sending texts when she suddenly felt as if she were not alone. A hand came down and suddenly covered her mouth before she could scream. A strong arm wrapped around her chest, pinning her to her chair. She felt the man press her body tight to his as he lowered his head to her ear.

Gemma tensed as she felt his warm breath on her neck. "You look so beautiful when you're concentrating." His hand left her mouth and Gemma whipped around and smacked Cy's stomach.

"You scared me to death!" she hissed. "How did you get in here? My door is locked."

"I came in through the window. You have a guard dog outside the door—about five feet, white curly hair, sensible shoes, and large knitting needles." Cy leaned against the table and pulled her from her chair to stand between his legs. "It's good to see you again."

Gemma snuggled into him as he wrapped his arms around her waist to pull her closer. He smiled down at her and she couldn't help but notice his eyes were darker tonight right before he brought his lips to hers. He kissed her softly but soon his hands were sliding downward as he deepened the kiss. His tongue swept into her mouth while his hands were busy pulling up the hemline of her jersey skirt.

They were combustible, Gemma decided. He made her feel as if she was the only woman in the world and he couldn't breathe unless he had her right then and there. That feeling gave her such a rush.

The knock at the door had her jumping back. "Miss Lily," she whispered as she looked around for a place to hide him.

"Gemma, dear? May I come in?" came the inquiry through the door. She turned back around and Cy was gone.

"Coming," she called out. "Cy?"

"Over here." Gemma looked and then saw the very edges of his fingers on the windowsill.

"Oh my God." Gemma rushed over to where Cy was hanging from the window.

"Sweetheart, can you please get the door and put your guard dog to bed?" he asked calmly as he dangled two stories from the ground.

"Don't fall in her azalea bush or she'll kill you," Gemma grinned before answering the door. "Yes?"

Miss Lily stepped into the room and looked around. "I was just going to bed. Is there anything I can get you before I retire?"

"No, thank you. You've done more than enough." The woman had kept her fed and undisturbed as she worked. For that she was grateful. But now she really wanted to get the man hanging from her window into her bed.

"Okay then, dear. Good night."

"Good night, Miss Lily." Gemma closed the door and quietly locked it.

"Now we have all night together," Cy whispered against her ear as he slid his hands under her shirt to gently cup her breasts.

"How . . ." but she was cut off from asking how he snuck back into her room when he whipped her around and kissed her again. She pushed him back to the desk and kissed him back.

Gemma ran her arms down his back, clinging to him as his hands slid up her legs and pushed her skirt up. *Dink, dink, dink.* Gemma pulled back. "Seriously? You couldn't turn off your cell phone? Who's begging to sleep with you now? Because it sure isn't going to be me." Gemma shoved down her skirt and crossed her arms over her chest. She was tired of all these women coming between them, and it was clear she shouldn't even be thinking of a future with him when he couldn't tell these women to back off.

"My phone is in my room," Cy snapped back as he stood up. "That's all you, sweetheart." He turned and walked to the window to look out and Gemma felt horrible. She had just hurt him and now she didn't know what to do to fix it.

"Cy, I'm so sorry. I guess I just don't know what we're doing. I'm not used to that. Usually there are dates, movies, and then comes the mind-blowing sex. And I'm certainly not used to competing for a man with America's Sweetheart and women who get paid to be beautiful. Please say you understand."

Cy turned around and she saw the frustration on his face. "But don't you see? There is no competition." *Dink, dink.*

"Are we okay?"

"Yes. And now we've had our first fight. Let's get to the make-up sex," Cy grinned. " *Dink, dink.* "But first why don't you get that. Once I get started, I don't want to stop."

Gemma nodded breathlessly and picked up her phone. "I found something." She scrolled through the text messages and quickly typed back. She felt Cy come and sit on the edge of the bed, waiting for her to finish typing. "See, I figured out why I couldn't get to the bottom of my sister's notes. I was trying too hard to be her. I needed to do what I'm good at."

"That thing last night where you put your leg . . ."

Gemma blushed. "No, I mean gossip. I'm good at finding out gossip," Gemma laughed as she answered her now ringing phone.

Cy leaned back and watched Gemma man the phone. She talked, texted, and emailed all at the same time as she worked to find the identity of some of the main players.

"I'll get you into the Pink Rose as a VIP as soon as I get back to L.A. if you can get this for me. Thanks." Gemma hung up and immediately took another call. "That's perfect. I'll get you Lakers tickets when I'm back."

Cy felt a knot in his stomach. It was crazy, but the idea of her going back to California didn't sit well with him. He was done with that life. The other night had meant more to him that he'd even admit to himself. Since then, he'd been thinking of starting a family here in Keeneston with her. But as she talked about getting home to L.A., he decided he must've read too much into it.

Gemma continued to work with her back toward him and he could tell she was in her element. He wasn't going to

distract her now. He quietly unlocked the door and made his way back to his room, hoping he could figure her out. How could he be a spy, a professional at reading people, and yet Gemma was a mystery to him?

***

The irate boss slammed his fist on the Brazilian wood table and cursed. His most trusted advisors were around him giving him an update on his enterprises. Sure, they were all going well and he was making money hand over fist on the black market, but his one mistake was still haunting him.

"I've had to kill two of my men and organize a riot in a prison to fix this Keeneston matter. I don't care about anything else. I want this fixed." With a satisfying crash, he threw his coffee mug into the wall and watched it shatter.

Sergei cleared his throat. "Sir, I think we should take him down before he digs any further."

"Oh? You think?" he spat. Luckily, that prison warden had contacted Sergei or he'd never have found Cy Davies's identity. He turned to his right-hand man, the only one he'd been able to depend on for all these years. "Get your ass to Keeneston and get a base set up. I'll be there by the end of the week."

***

"Come in," Gemma yelled as she hung up the phone. Cy walked through the door and into her room. "Hey. Where did you go last night?"

"I know how important this is to you and you were on such a roll I didn't want to interrupt. How is it going this morning?"

"Excellent. I have something big, but now I don't know what to do with it." Gemma jumped up and started pacing the room. "I tracked down the man with the goatee that Senator Bruce told us about. Then I had a buddy from the IRS pull his records. Guess what I found?" Gemma knew she was waving her hands around like a mad woman, but she was just too excited.

"What?"

"He has a huge house in the suburbs of D.C., but he also has a very nice condo downtown. I have a gut feeling his wife may not know about this second house because the taxes were filed separately, almost like he was hiding it from her. Do you know why I think that?"

"Why?"

"Because he writes it off as rental property he's owned for two years. Funny thing about it, though—he's never collected rent."

"A perfect place to hide a girlfriend," Cy stated with less excitement than she had hoped. "We just have to find a way to turn her. Shouldn't be hard. She probably doesn't know he's married."

"I might have already done that." That got his attention. Gemma almost laughed as Cy's head snapped up. "I kinda called and pretended to be his insurance adjuster and said someone filed a claim against him for hit and run. I told her he needed to come into the police station immediately as they were looking into criminal charges." Gemma paused and took a deep breath. They finally had a lead and she did it her way. She couldn't stop smiling.

"And?" Cy coaxed.

"And she told me he left for Kentucky this morning and gave me his cell phone number so I could call him."

Cy stood up and hurried to her desk. "Where's the number?" he asked.

"Here." Gemma handed him her notes with the number circled. "What are you going to do?"

"Track it. I guess they've found us out. Let's take the offensive and see what they're up to." Cy opened her laptop and started typing. Screens popped up and Gemma was lost as to what he was doing. Then all of a sudden a map appeared on the screen with a little dot on it. "Bingo."

"Where'd you learn to do that?"

"Spy school. I'm full of neat tricks." Gemma remembered some of those neat tricks and suddenly felt hot. "It looks like he's right outside of Keeneston. Let's see what he's been up to."

Cy's fingers flew over the keyboard as he typed away. "What are you doing now?" Gemma asked.

"Pulling up all his financials and all the information I can on that address. It's a private residence on a horse farm right outside town. It was for sale, but a cash offer was made today, probably by our guy. Oh, and look at this. He just purchased a ticket to the Mayor's Annual Charity Ball in Lexington tonight."

"Why would he do that? Fly into town, buy a house, and attend a ball?" Gemma wondered.

"He's laying the groundwork. His boss is very powerful and he may have connections here . . . or he will shortly."

"So, what are we going to do?"

"Dance. You need a gown, sweetheart."

CHAPTER FIFTEEN

$\mathcal{G}$emma stepped into the beautiful royal-blue silk dress and prayed it fit. Kenna gave her the nod and Gemma sucked in as the zipper made its way up.

"Oh, thank goodness." Gemma let out her breath. The dress fit. She had three hours to get ready for a formal ball. Cy had called Paige, who had called Kenna, who had called Dani, who had called Katelyn. Soon her room was filled with women, dresses, shoes, hair products, and things she couldn't identify.

"They give you cleavage, although in this dress I don't think you're going to need them," Katelyn said as she put away the boob enhancers that strangely resembled chicken cutlets.

"This dress is perfect for you." Kenna clapped as she took a step back and checked out the fit. "I wore this to a ball at Mo's, so it should be perfect for the charity event."

"I've got just the shoes for you, too," Katelyn dug around in her bag and pulled out a pair of silver heels. "I got these at a fashion show in Milan, but they're a size too small. I think they should fit you perfectly."

Gemma slid on the expensive designer shoes and got a tingly feeling. She'd never tell Cy, but these shoes were almost as hot as he was. Almost. "This is amazing. Thank you so much. I wouldn't have been able to do this without you."

"Wait, we're not done yet." Dani dug around in her purse and pulled out a velvet bag. "Sometimes less is more. Especially when less is a huge diamond."

Gemma gasped at the large diamond pendant. "I couldn't possibly wear that."

"Sure you can. It will make a statement and statements without words are the best way to get information. People will be clamoring to find out who you are and will gladly answer your questions."

Paige stepped over to fasten the necklace. "You look perfect. Remember, just smile."

"Oh no, it's time! Okay, purse, shoes, dress, hair, makeup, jewelry," Kenna checked off. "You're good to go. We can't wait to hear how it goes."

The ladies grabbed their things and headed downstairs with Gemma. Gemma was so caught up in talking that she was halfway down before she saw Cy standing by the door in his black tuxedo with a crisp white shirt and perfectly tied black bowtie. The tuxedo emphasized his broad shoulders, narrow waist, and hugged his muscled legs.

"I think I'm going to cry," Kenna whispered to Dani as she sniffled.

Crying wasn't what Gemma was thinking about. Roaring emotions flooded her as she felt happiness, fear, and guilt. Cy was fun to be with and she felt a closeness to him that she couldn't even describe. She just knew that no matter what, through the highs or the lows in life, he'd be there for her with a cocky smile and a gentle touch. But thinking of a future she badly wanted was scary, too. What if he didn't feel the same way? What if he really was the player that he seemed to be in California? And then there was the guilt. The loss of her sister was overwhelming at times and she felt horrible that Gia would never have these feelings. It was that feeling that was winning out. She shouldn't be engaging in an affair while her sister's killer was free.

Cy had been waiting for what seemed like forever when he finally heard the group of women emerge from Gemma's room. He was lucky he already owned a tux and was ready and waiting for Gemma as soon as he ironed the wrinkles out. One look at her, though, and the wait had been worth it. She looked breathtaking as she came down the stairs. It was going to be hard to remember tonight was a job.

"You're beautiful," Cy said as he took her hands in his and placed a soft kiss on her cheek.

"She is, isn't she?" Kenna blew her nose into a tissue and batted her teary eyes.

"What is the matter with you?" Dani whispered as she nudged her.

"It just reminds me of Will and me and this house and . . ." Cy didn't know what to do as Kenna wiped the tears from her eyes. She was all red in the face and teary-eyed and he felt a slight moment of panic.

"Oh, bless your heart," Miss Lily cried as she too grabbed a tissue and raced across the entranceway to embrace Kenna.

"What?" His sister seemed as confused as he was.

Dani smacked Paige and then joined Miss Lily in the hugs and tears. Cy almost laughed as Paige's eyes widened before squealing and leaping into the knot of friends.

"I think we're missing something," Cy whispered to Gemma. When she didn't answer, he looked down at her face and saw a single tear running down her face and a huge smile on her lips. "Okay, what's going on?"

"She's pregnant, you goof," Gemma said as if he were the stupidest man in the world. But it was the envious yet happy look on her face that had him picturing her carrying his child.

"I'm so sorry to ruin your moment. These pregnancy hormones kick in and won't stop until I've cried them out," Kenna apologized as she fanned her face with her hands.

"Don't worry. I'm very happy for you and Will. Now, if y'all will excuse me, I have a gorgeous woman to dance with.

It's a hard job, but someone's got to do it." Cy turned and held out his arm for Gemma before leading her down the stone path toward the truck.

Gemma looked up at the old colonial house where the ball was being held. A valet came and opened her door before taking the keys from Cy. A red carpet ran up the brick pathway lined with roses. She felt as if she were both in a fairy tale and a nightmare. She didn't know which to attribute to the nerves she was feeling.

"Relax. We're just here to have a good time," Cy whispered as he led her into the large open ballroom. Couples were dancing, drinking, and mingling as Cy led her straight onto the dance floor.

Cy put his arm around her waist and swept her into the dance. Gemma fumbled and cringed when she slammed her foot onto his toe. "I'm so sorry. I'm used to dancing in clubs, not like this."

She relaxed some when he just laughed. She didn't hear it, but she felt his shoulders bounce. "It's okay. We can go clubbing next. For now, just stop looking at your feet. Look at me and trust me to lead you safely around the dance floor."

Gemma looked up into his clean-shaven face and wanted to run a hand down his cheek. He exuded confidence as he navigated her through the crowded floor. She leaned forward and noticed the subtle smell of cologne—cedar dancing with fresh lemon. She drew in a deep breath, and Cy's arm tightened around her back, bringing her flush against him.

"You keep doing that and I may forget all about dancing," he whispered before pressing a kiss to the delicate skin beneath her ear.

Gemma warmed as he pulled slightly back and looked into her eyes. She felt such intimacy when he looked at her that her body started to hum with anticipation. She ran her tongue over her lips, closed her eyes, and leaned forward to kiss him.

"There he is," Cy stated as he turned her abruptly on the dance floor and started leading her toward the far side of the room.

"Huh?" Gemma tripped over her foot and stomped on Cy's toes again.

"Arthur Pinnelli. He's talking to the mayor and I think it's time to go say hi." Cy dropped the pretense of dancing and grabbed her hand.

"Wait. Shouldn't we have a game plan?"

"Where's the fun in that?" Cy's mask fell into place as he shot her a carefree smile. Gemma took a deep breath and ran through everything her improv teacher taught her back in school.

"Mayor Austin, it's a pleasure to see you again," Cy interrupted as he came to stand next to the tall mayor across from the goateed man.

"Cy Davies, you son of a bitch. I didn't know you were back in town." The mayor slapped Cy on the back and Gemma didn't know who was more surprised—she or Pinnelli.

"Just got back a couple days ago. And don't forget you owe me twenty dollars from that pick-up game last year. Oh, I'm sorry. I didn't mean to interrupt." Cy shot Pinnelli a look that said he was definitely anything but sorry.

"Nonsense. Meet Arthur Pinnelli. He's just moved here and is looking to open..." the mayor turned to Pinnelli questioningly. "What kind of business were you looking to open again?"

"Art gallery. I'm so very sorry, but I just received a text that a painting I want to buy is about to go up for auction. I need to call my buyer and make sure he knows what to bid. Excuse me." Pinnelli gave a brief smile to the mayor and shook his hand before making a quick departure toward the valet.

Gemma wanted to race after him, but Cy started talking guy-talk with the mayor and squeezing her hand as she watched Pinnelli wind his way through the crowd. Finally

Cy squeezed so hard she realized he was talking to her.

"This is my girlfriend, Gemma Perry. Gemma, meet one of my old buddies, Dan Austin."

"It's nice to meet you," Gemma forced out as she tried to keep an eye on Pinnelli.

"It's nice to meet you, too. I didn't know you had settled down, Cy,"

"She hasn't agreed to yet. Maybe after one more dance I can convince her. Excuse us, Dan. Give Janie my best and let's meet up next week for a pick-up game," Cy said as he started directing Gemma to the dance floor.

"Sounds good. Enjoy your night. It was nice meeting you, Miss Perry."

Gemma shot him a quick smile as Cy whisked her onto the dance floor and danced her right toward the entrance. "I had the valet keep the truck handy. I told him we wouldn't be long."

"You could've told me you knew the mayor. And what good did it do to let Pinnelli know we knew who he was?"

"People do stupid things when they get panicked. He didn't have time to prepare a response or think how to act. If I lose him now, though, it'll be bad." Cy hurried her from the floor and through the crowd.

Gemma felt her stomach drop at the sight of the red convertible zipping out of the circular drive. Cy gave a sharp whistle as they ran down the red carpet. The valet looked up and with a nod grabbed a set of keys and tossed them to Cy.

"Right there, sir." The young man pointed to the truck sitting just fifteen feet away.

"Oh thank goodness," Gemma said with a sigh of relief as she hiked up her dress and sprinted toward the truck—well, as fast as one could sprint in four-inch heels.

"You know, you really should have more faith in me. I do this stuff for a living, after all," Cy shot back to her as he reached the truck and started it.

Gemma didn't have time to respond before the large V8 engine hurled the truck forward. She scrambled to put on her seatbelt and hang on for dear life as he took turns faster than she thought possible in such a big vehicle.

"It looks like he's going to the house he's rented," Cy told her as he ran red light after red light through downtown Lexington. Horns sounded and tires skidded as cars were forced to yield to the larger truck.

The busy streets of downtown quickly turned to country roads as Cy came up behind Pinnelli's car. "Gemma, I need you to unbuckle your seatbelt and get ready to slide behind the wheel," Cy ordered as he unlocked and opened the sliding rear window leading to the truck bed with one hand.

"What are you doing?" Gemma yelled over the sound of the wind rushing in through the open window.

"I'm just going to pop over and have a word with our friend there, but I need you to drive so I can do that."

"You're insane."

"Don't worry, I've done this countless times," Cy shot her his amused smile and pulled the truck into the opposite lane and sped up. He set the cruise control and looked over at her. "Take the wheel and keep it in this lane. As soon as I'm in the back, speed up so I can jump into the car."

"You better not die. If you do, I'll kill you again," Gemma yelled as she unhooked her seatbelt and grabbed hold of the steering wheel.

She tried to keep her eyes on the road as Cy angled his shoulders and shimmied his way through the small window. "Okay, speed up and pass him a bit," Cy shouted into the cab.

Gemma only nodded as she watched Pinnelli turn his head to see what they were doing. He stepped on the pedal and his sports car shot forward. Gemma floored the pedal as the big V8 ate up the road and closed in on the little red car. "No cars, no cars," Gemma chanted as she sped over a hill in the wrong lane.

She glanced back and saw Cy resting his hand against the top of the cab with one leg on the side of the truck bed. As soon as he saw there were no cars coming at them, he pounded the top of the cab. Gemma swerved toward the red car and forced Pinnelli to hit the brake. She pressed hard on the gas and started nosing in front of the car.

Cy hung on as Gemma flew over the hilltop. He had fifteen seconds to make the jump before they rounded a sharp turn. He pounded the top of the cab and Gemma accelerated in return and then turned sharply at Pinnelli's car.

"Crap." Cy went flying forward and was then flung backward as Gemma swerved back into the opposite lane and pressed the gas once again.

Cy scrambled to his feet and without hesitation launched himself off the side of the truck. He aimed for the windshield and, with momentum working against him, was happy when he landed in the tiny backseat of the sports car. Pinnelli started swerving, causing Cy to slam around in the back seat.

Cy pulled his foot from where it was stuck behind the driver's seat and used the passenger headrest to pull himself forward. "Hello, Arthur. Fancy meeting you here. Out for a drive? How about we pull over and have a little chat?"

Cy looked up and saw headlights coming at them. Gemma slammed on the brakes and fishtailed as she battled to gain control of the truck before sliding in behind Pinnelli. Cy almost laughed at the pissed-off look on her cute face.

"You'll be dead in a minute, so I don't think we have much to talk about except deciding how I should kill that bitch of yours. I wonder if Sergei will make her scream like her sister did."

Cy propelled himself over the center console and grabbed the wheel, turning it sharply. The car careened off the road and headed straight for a line of trees. He heard Gemma's tires lock up as she slammed on the brakes back on the road. Cy shot an elbow backward and connected with Pinnelli's face as he fought for control of the steering wheel. Pinnelli let go of the wheel with one hand and grabbed his eye. It was enough to allow Cy control of the wheel as he steered between the trees and into the field.

Pinnelli clenched his fist and slammed it into the back of Cy's neck. His head shot forward and smashed into the steering wheel. Dropping his hands from the wheel, Cy rolled to the side and grabbed the palm of Pinnelli's hand. With a quick twist, he felt it snap. Pinnelli howled in pain and slammed on the brakes. As the car spun in the field of grass, Cy was tossed into the passenger seat. He lashed out with his leg and hit Pinnelli right in his head. The man's eyes rolled back and his arms dropped from the wheel as his body slumped forward in unconsciousness.

"Cy! Oh my God, are you okay?" Gemma yelled as she ran to the stopped car.

"It was a piece of cake. Didn't you believe me when I told you I'd done this before?" He enjoyed the way her face scrunched in annoyance at his nonchalant tone.

"Jumping from a truck at over seventy miles per hour, barely missing a tree line, and fighting for control of a car as you spin uncontrollably through a field is *not* something you've done before and which you will *never* do again. Do you understand me?" Gemma yelled as she put her hand on her hips and glared at him.

"Yes, dear. And you're right. I haven't done it exactly like that before. Last time it was on an ice road in Siberia so there were no trees."

"Oh, you stupid man." Gemma swatted him and huffed past him to the man now groaning as he regained consciousness. "Hello, Arthur. Can you please tell me why my sister was killed?"

Cy choked on his laugh and then sprinted around the car when Gemma reached into it. She grabbed Pinnelli by the lapels and brought her face to his. "You don't have Sergei here to protect you, you piece of crap."

"Yet," Pinnelli smiled through the blood trickling down the side of his face. "Five minutes from now is a different story. Then you'll experience what your sister did. Tell me, will you beg for your life, too?"

Gemma pulled back her fist and rammed it into his face right as Cy reached her. Cy placed his hand over Gemma's left hand that was still gripping Pinnelli's lapel. "You've done well. Wait in the truck a minute, sweetheart," Cy told her as calmly as possible.

"Forget that. I have an idea what I want to do with these high heels," Gemma stared at Pinnelli with such hatred that he started to look a little less sure of himself.

Cy was beginning to think he wasn't needed. She was taking care of this all by herself. "Sounds interesting, doesn't it, Artie?" Cy gave a low whistle as he looked down at Gemma's shoes. "Four-inch spiked heels. I can't wait to see what she has in mind." Cy yanked hard on Pinnelli's lapel and dragged him over the door and let him fall to the ground. "Now, if you don't want to find out what she has in mind, you tell me what you meant about Sergei."

"I already told you. You'll find out in three minutes."

"He's here? Is your boss with him?"

"Of course he is. He's here to make sure you two never see morning."

"If we're not going to see morning, then tell me why your boss had my sister murdered?" Gemma asked as it looked like she was getting ready to hit him with her heel if he didn't answer.

"Because she somehow connected the dots. She was only one dot away from identifying our boss. But don't worry, honey, you'll see your sister in about two minutes."

Cy beat Gemma to the punch, literally, with a solid punch to his jaw. Pinnelli's mouth pinched and he spit out a tooth.

"Who's your boss?" Cy demanded.

"Like I'd tell you. He'd kill me."

"I'll kill you myself if you don't." Gemma quickly reached behind Cy and pulled out his gun.

"Gemma, do you know how to use that?" Cy asked quietly.

"No, I don't. But from this distance it doesn't really matter." Gemma placed the gun to Pinnelli's head and flipped the safety off.

"I'd start talking if I were you. That woman is madder than an old wet hen and is prone to fly off the handle at any moment." Cy rocked back on his heels and gave Pinnelli a silly little grin.

He looked at Gemma and decided that maybe Cy was right. "Fine. You're going to die anyway. Your sister found his . . ." Pinnelli's head slammed back and a tiny round trickle of blood fell from between his eyes.

Cy leaped forward and grabbed the gun from Gemma's still outstretched hand.

"What?" she stammered as he pulled her away and returned fire in the direction of the gunshot.

"Looks like Sergei got here early. Get in the truck." Cy pushed Gemma and laid down cover fire while she ran the short distance to the truck. When she dove into the cab, Cy took off at a run as he dodged the bullets now flying past him.

"Come on," Gemma yelled as she scooted over to the passenger seat. He dove behind the wheel and slammed his foot on the gas.

As Cy tore through the field heading for the tree line, a black SUV came to a stop on the road in front of him. "Well, shit. I never liked this truck that much anyway. Hang on."

Cy drove through the tree line and bounced up onto the road as the men with guns jumped out of the way. Cy plowed his driver's side headlights right above the front wheel of the SUV. The SUV spun as the men had to leap again to avoid being hit. He threw the truck into reverse and ran over one of the men as he drove backward into the field. Slamming on the brakes, he did a controlled spin and then drove off through the field and away from the road.

"Where are you going?"

"Home court advantage. I know every farm around here. I cut through this field and go around the cornfield where I can come out onto a road I can take back to Keeneston."

"But we know the boss is here. Why aren't we calling the police and storming our way into that house?"

"Do you know how many guns they have there? If they pick up anything on the police lines, he'll be in the wind so fast you'll never have a chance to find him again. It's personal now and he knows it. No cops. No CIA. Just him and me, and only one of us will make it."

Gemma finally stopped shaking by the time Cy drove into Keeneston. As soon as he had bounced his way out of the fields, he had placed his hand over hers and was still holding it. He absently brushed his thumb over the soft skin of her wrist during the short trip into town. The small action had her pulse slowing and the shaking anger fading away.

"Thank you. That was sweet of you." Gemma looked out at the sleepy town and wondered when she'd hear sirens or bullets. "It really helped calmed me down."

"I know how the adrenaline dump can affect you. I'm glad I could help some." Cy paused as if searching for the right words

147

to say. "Gemma, you were excellent tonight. With the emotions he was triggering, you kept your cool and really helped get as much information as possible from him."

"But, what do we do now? Mr. X is here and he's coming after us."

"Not tonight he won't. Tonight was our first run-in. He's going to evaluate us. It takes time to gather that intelligence. But it will be soon." Cy parked the car and helped her from her seat. She felt total relief when he put his arm around her, and she leaned into him as they made their way up the path.

"What's that?" Gemma asked quietly as they both stopped and listened to the night. Whispers were coming from the darkened porch. "They found us already."

Then she felt Cy shake with laughter, "I don't think so." He laced his fingers with hers and pulled her toward the porch.

She heard a giggle then and a deep chuckle. She smelled brownies. "Miss Lily," Gemma gasped at the sight of the sweet woman on the swing with her white hair messed and her lips puffy from kissing.

"John, how are you tonight?" Cy asked with barely controlled laughter ready to explode.

"Um, fine. Fine. Just replacing some light bulbs for Lily Rae here." John stood and Gemma snickered at his shirt pulled from his suspenders and the way a piece of his thinning hair was sticking straight out.

"Well, that was so sweet of you. We'll let you get back to it. Good night." Gemma didn't have a chance to say anything else as Cy pulled her inside and slammed the door before he lost control of the laughter. One look at him bent over had Gemma losing it. She started laughing so hard tears streamed down her face.

"Did you see his hair?" she gasped.

"Or the way her red lipstick was smeared and her eyes were so wide at being busted? Oh God, I don't know if I can stand this—it hurts." Cy grabbed his side as he tried to stop laughing. "Oh, I know." Cy turned and ran back to the front door and flipped the switch beside it. Light poured through the windows as the porch was bathed in light.

"Cyland Davies," Miss Lily shouted from outside.

"Uh-oh." Cy grabbed her hand and raced upstairs as the front door opened and a large hand slid through the crack of the door and flipped off the light.

Cy didn't stop laughing all the way upstairs. They stopped in the sitting area between rooms and he tried to figure out what to do. Let her go to bed? Alone? He'd been getting mixed signals. At the dance it had seemed they were of the same mind. That made up his mind: thinking of the way she fit in his arms, the way her legs brushed against his, the way her breasts pressed against his chest.

"Well, um. I guess . . ." Gemma stammered as she looked from Cy to the door. He held his breath as he waited to see what she was going to do. When she didn't move, he took it as a sign.

"Come here," Cy said with a gravelly voice. He stood still as Gemma looked up at him and took a step forward. He pulled her to him and closed his mouth over hers. He felt her grasp at his tuxedo as he deepened the kiss, pushing her against his door and leaning into her.

She moaned as he released her mouth to bury his head in the crook of her neck. Her hand raked his hair and she grabbed a fistful when he worked his lips over her delicate collarbone.

"I've wanted to do this all night," Cy murmured as he shoved the strap of the gown off one shoulder, exposing a breast. He looked into her eyes, dark with excitement. With one hand he grabbed her ass and squeezed. With the other, he raised her breast to his lips and with a flick of his tongue had her squirming.

Gemma's head fell back as he pulled the other strap down. He pushed the dress down, baring her to him. "Cy, don't stop," Gemma panted.

"I was planning on a lot of things, but stopping anytime soon is not one of them." Cy kissed his way up to capture her lips again. He turned the doorknob as he ravished her mouth with his tongue. He picked her up and carried her through the door, kicking it shut.

CHAPTER SIXTEEN

Gemma took a sip of the sweet tea Miss Lily had brought up and looked at the pictures and notes spread out across her desk. She had scoured the news this morning, but there was no report of a man found dead in a field, so she had turned back to her notes to find out what her sister had discovered that had gotten her killed.

"Knock, knock. Am I interrupting anything?" Cade asked as he came into the room.

"Only your brother's pacing," Gemma quipped as she pulled out a picture of a striking blonde. "What's going on?"

"You were right yesterday. Those words that seemed out of place were the key. I got the flash drive open." Cade dropped a huge stack of papers in front of her and Gemma felt like groaning. "And I can't read a single one of them. They're all in that language of yours. However, there were a couple of photographs and you're holding one of them. I may not know what's on these pages, but I'm guessing that woman is important. Do you know who she is?"

Cade and Cy came to stand beside her as they looked at the woman with the blonde hair and oversized sunglasses. "She looks familiar, but I just can't place her," Cy said as he examined the photograph.

"Me too. It's nagging at me. Hopefully, my sister will have her name somewhere in this pile."

"If you work with me, I may be able to build a program to translate it. It'll take a couple of hours up front but could save you a lot of time," Cade suggested.

"You could do that?" Cy asked. Cade just gave him a look and Cy nodded. "I shouldn't have asked. But I need a favor. I want to think over some things and I do that better moving around. I don't want to be in Gemma's hair, but I don't want to leave her alone either."

"I got it. It'll take us a while to get this program written and then I can help her go through it."

"Thanks, Cade. Is that okay with you, sweetheart?"

"Sure. You were about to drive me crazy with your pacing, so it works out perfectly. We'll just meet up for lunch."

Gemma raised her lips for Cy as he gave her a quick kiss before heading out. She turned to see Cade grinning like an idiot and just shook her head. "You ready to get started?"

"Sure am. Let's see that alphabet you have."

***

Cy found his brother at a peewee football game. Marshall stood by the sidelines between two tables filled with sweets. The Bearcats' mothers had pies in hand while Pam Gilbert and some other mothers from the Keeneston Cougars team held stacks of cookies as if they intended to toss them like throwing stars at the opposing mothers.

"Arrest them, Sheriff!"

"For what, Pam? Selling baked goods?"

"This is our fund-raiser for our team. They've been doing this all through the league and we've had enough. It's in the league rules that the home team is allowed to have a bake sale to raise funds for equipment and uniforms. Not away teams. They've been purposely bringing in baking ringers to have better goods so they make all the money and the other teams suffer for it."

"And why would they do that?" Marshall asked as he held up his arm to keep the opposing mother from cutting in.

"Because, bless their little hearts, they suck. They're the worst team in the league. But by outselling us, they'll have all new equipment and we'll have nothing. They're baking us out of competition."

"Is this true, Ginny?" Marshall asked the huffing mother.

"It's not my fault we're better bakers. I hope you choke on that overly dry cookie, Pam."

"Enough. Where are these league rules you were talking about?" Marshall asked as he intercepted a cookie that was launched at Ginny.

"Here." Pam thrust a book at him. "Page thirty-six, paragraph B, section two." Marshall opened the book and read the cited area.

"Sorry, Ginny, but Pam's right. Now while it's not illegal and I can't arrest you for violating league rules, they could kick you out of the league if I were to turn this incident in. So let's pack up those tasty pies and sell them only at your home games. Got it?"

"This isn't over, Pam," Ginny snarled before turning to Marshall. "Thank you for your discretion, Sheriff. Have a pie as our thank-you." Ginny handed Marshall a pie and the women grudgingly packed up their table.

"Yes, thank you. Have some cookies, Sheriff. Maybe your brother would want some, too," Shelly Duffy, Katelyn's secretary, said as she batted her eyes at Cy.

"You do know your husband is ten feet away on the field coaching, right?" Marshall asked as Cy sent her a dazzling smile.

"It would be rude not to acknowledge him standing right there and if southern women are one thing, it's not rude," Shelly said she handed Cy some cookies.

"That's right. Try my cookies, Cy."

"Mine are double chocolate, Cy."

"Mine won first place at the county fair."

"Ladies," Cy smiled as he held up his hands. "I'll try them all as I'm sure each will be perfect, just like their bakers."

Cy gave them a wink and saw Marshall roll his eyes. He pulled out his wallet and tossed down a fifty before holding out his arms for the pile of cookies he had just bought.

"Way to make me look bad," Marshall mumbled to Cy as he took out his wallet too. "Good luck at the game, ladies."

Cy walked with his brother back to where he parked his now slightly banged-up truck next to Marshall's cruiser.

"So, what's up?" Marshall asked as he took a bite of one of the cookies.

"Something happened last night that I need to talk over. But I'm antsy. I was hoping we could get a little training in while I bounce some ideas off you."

"Sure. Let's go to my place."

Cy threw a punch and Marshall blocked it with his forearm. Sweat poured off Cy as he and Marshall lobbed punches and kicks at each other on the soft grass in front of the house. Bob, Marshall's Vizsla, sat perched on a low-hanging limb of a tree watching them. Marshall had shed his uniform and put on a pair of athletic shorts similar to the ones Cy wore. Shirts had long ago been tossed to the side as they battled each other.

"So the body just disappeared?" Marshall asked as he delivered a strong kick to Cy's midsection.

"It makes me think they went back and cleaned it up. When they didn't follow us into Keeneston and now this, I'm sure they're waiting for their moment. I just don't know why."

"Seems to me they don't want attention drawn to it. It's going to be man-to-man. And, by not calling the cops, you've accepted those terms."

"Honor among thieves," Cy swept Marshall's legs and shot him a smug look as Marshall landed on the grass.

"Exactly," Marshall said before tackling Cy to the ground. "Now, while you've recounted what happened last night, you said Gemma's name no less than thirty times. Want to talk about it?" Marshall asked as they stood up and faced off once again.

"When we're together, it's amazing. We click and the chemistry . . . but I feel sometimes she's hiding who she is. She won't just let go."

"You're one to be talking," Marshall said and he ducked a punch.

"What do you mean by that?" Cy asked as he dropped his arms and stared at his brother. It cost him as his brother landed a punch to the jaw.

"It means you're hiding who you are, too. You're still Mr. Hollywood and that's not you. Well, not all you. You've always been a little cocky," Marshall grinned as he rested his hands on his hips.

"True. But, when I'm with her, I'm me again."

"You've got it bad. Why don't you invite her to Dani and Mo's going away/baby shower tomorrow? Katelyn says we're going. It's some picnic thingy."

"I don't think I'm invited," Cy said. It was a good idea, though. Try to bring some normalcy to his life. Give him a chance to unwind and try to forget about Mr. Hollywood, as his brother called him.

"I think you're about to be." Marshall pointed to the black Mercedes making its way up the drive.

"Who's that?" Cy asked. "He looks like a small version of Ahmed."

"Ah, that's mini-Ahmed. His real name is Nabi . . . well, Nabi is good enough."

"Mr. Cy Davies?" Mini-Ahmed asked.

"Yep, that's me." Cy held out his hand and accepted an envelope. "So you're Nabi."

"Nabi Ulmalhamsh Mosteghanemi," he said with a slight bow of his head.

"Right." Cy knew his limits on language and that was it. "So you're working for Ahmed."

"Yes. I'm very privileged," Nabi said while looking back and forth between the brothers. "Were you training?"

"Yes, we were. Would you like to go a round?" Cy asked as Nabi looked around as if to see if he was being watched. "Don't worry, I won't tell anyone that you took some time off. I'm good at keeping secrets after all."

Gemma held her breath as she read the last page Cade had printed from the translated flash drive. She was having trouble seeing through the tears rolling silently down her cheeks as she read the letter her sister had left for her. Gia had known she was in danger and had left this note the morning she was killed, just in case. She said she had a feeling something was wrong.

"*I never told you how proud I am of you,*" her sister wrote among the meaningful stories, the special moments, and the hopes for the future. Gemma sucked in a ragged breath as she finished the letter. "*Live life to the fullest for us both. I'll be checking in on you to make sure you do. I'm your big sister, after all.*"

The heartbreak was complete. The feeling of being ripped in two was so overwhelming that Gemma curled into a ball and sobbed.

"Gemma? What is it?" Cade asked quietly as he put a gentle hand on her shoulder.

"My sister left me a note. I should be with her now. It should've been me. I was running in circles, but she was going places. She was making a difference in the world with her reporting."

"Gemma, you can't do this to yourself," Cade reassured her. "Your sister loved you and there is no way she would want you to blame yourself. I've only known you a short time, but it's clear to me that you have great things ahead. Your sister would be very proud of you. I know my brother is."

Fresh tears started and Gemma couldn't stop them. She knew she looked a mess. She was an ugly crier, but right now she didn't care. Although Cade's slightly nervous look caused her some comic relief.

"What the hell did you do to her?" Cy yelled. She looked up and found him shooting daggers at his brother.

"Oh, Cy." Gemma jumped up, pushing Cade out of the way, and leaped onto Cy. Gemma pressed herself against him as she hugged him tight.

"I'll come back," Cade said as he started for the door.

"No. I'm okay. Tell him what we found." Gemma laughed as she dried her tears. Cy's confused expression was just as funny as Cade's had been.

"We read through all the notes on the flash drive and there was this one phrase toward the end that read *Sarah is the key*. Gemma thinks this blonde woman is Sarah. The question remains—who is she?"

"Wait," Gemma said, "that club in the background. I know that club. It's in L.A. and I happen to know the bouncer."

"Do you think he'll know her?" Cy asked as he looked at the picture again.

"I bet he does. She looks wealthy and if you and I both think she looks familiar, she has to be on the party scene. I'll call him tonight before the club opens. With the time difference, he's probably sleeping and waking him will not entice him to help. But we did it. We have our first real lead."

Gemma sat down in the chair Cy held out for her at the café and picked up the menu. This time the moment of silence when they entered only lasted a couple of seconds. She was growing on them. And they were growing on her, too. The town was cute and the gossip that was being traded at every table was friendly. Not the career-or-relationship-ending kind she normally dealt with.

"I'll have the chicken salad. Thank you, Miss Daisy." Gemma waited for Cy to place his order before she talked to him. "This is a good idea. If we hadn't come, I would've been pacing while I waited to call Joe at the club."

"Any time I get to spend with you is good. Actually, I was wondering if you wanted to go to a party tomorrow with me."

Gemma looked at him skeptically. "Will it end with high-speed chases and someone dying?"

"No. It'll end with eating cake and opening baby gifts."

"Then it sounds perfect."

The café went quiet and then started whispering again when the newest couple came in. "This is big. That's Henry Rooney; he's our town's only defense attorney. He's been dating Neely Grace for a while now."

"Why is that big?" Gemma asked.

"Because Henry is famous for his bad pick-up lines. I heard they fell in love over a battle of bad one-liners at my parents' house one night. That and Neely Grace is smart, good-looking, and also a lawyer. We all thought Henry would end up marrying someone he met on the Internet who didn't speak English."

Henry and Neely Grace stopped at the table on the way to theirs. "Cy. It's good to see you again. Have you met Neely Grace?"

"Of course I have. It's been a long time, though, Neely Grace."

"Since high school," Neely Grace told them.

"And this is my girlfriend, Gemma Perry. Gemma, Neely Grace and Henry Rooney."

"Nice to meet you," Henry said during a full body scan. Neely Grace rolled her eyes and smacked Henry prompting him to say, "What?"

"He's learning," Neely Grace said with an apologetic grin that told Gemma she was enjoying teaching him. Gemma giggled and gave Neely Grace an understanding look. She'd dated a couple of guys like that, too.

Gemma and Cy enjoyed dinner and he told her about the fight at the peewee football game, which had her laughing so hard a couple people turned to look at them. She met some more of the townsfolk and before long she looked at her watch and jumped up.

"It's time to call Joe. I almost missed it because I was having such a nice time."

"Come on. You can call him while we walk back to Miss Lily's."

Cy paid the check and Gemma went outside to call the club. She waited impatiently as the phone rang over and over again. "Hello. Can I talk to Joe?" she asked when the phone was picked up.

It took a couple minutes, but Joe finally came to the phone. "This is Joe."

"Joe, Gemma Perry."

"Hey, Gemma. What can I do for you? Do you need to be on the VIP list tonight?"

"No, I need to send you a picture and have you identify a woman for me. It's really important."

"Sure." Joe rattled off his cell number and Gemma sent the picture to him. "Okay, I got it. Damn, this is bothering me. She looks so familiar, but I can't place her. There are just too many bottle blondes with big tits to keep them straight. But Nick at the bar should know. Tonight's his night off. Can I give you a call tomorrow?"

"That would be great. Thanks, Joe." Gemma hung up the phone and turned to Cy. "Tomorrow. We'll know tomorrow."

CHAPTER SEVENTEEN

$\mathcal{G}$ emma stood proudly at Cy's arm as they followed the pink and blue balloons to the back of the biggest mansion she'd ever seen. A large white silk tent was in the backyard, filled with tables. Each table had a huge arrangement of pink and blue hydrangeas and little wooden alphabet blocks as napkin holders.

"This is amazing. Do they do this for every party?" Gemma asked as they nodded their hellos to some people standing in a group near the tent.

"I don't think so. I'm not here much, but from what I understand they're very laid back. All of this is because the King and Queen of Rahmi are here. And here are our hosts. Hi, Mo. Dani, you're glowing," Cy said as he gave Dani a kiss on the cheek.

"It's called sweat, but I like the way you say it much better," Dani laughed. "But now I'm going to steal Gemma away and introduce her around so you men can complain about being dragged to a baby shower."

Gemma waved goodbye as Dani linked her arm in hers and started walking toward their friends. "I wanted a small party with my girlfriends and this is the compromise we came to with my father-in-law. I need to get better at negotiating," Dani teased.

"Gemma, I'm so glad you're here. Tell us everything about the ball," Paige practically screamed. Gemma tried hard not to blush. While many things happened that night, it was what happened after she got home that she remembered the most.

"It was wonderful. Even if I'm not a great dancer."

"Was it romantic?" Tammy asked, her eyes big with anticipation.

"It was. Until we had to chase down the bad guy."

"If it's one thing I know, it's action. That can be the best kind of foreplay," Annie said with her eyes twinkling with mischief.

"You know a lot about action, huh?" Morgan teased.

"Not that kind of action."

"Poor Cade," Katelyn laughed.

"Y'all suck," Annie joked.

"Oh no," Dani said sadly.

"Are you okay?" Kenna asked, concerned.

"Yes, it's just my brother and sister-in-law are here, too, and no one is talking to them." Gemma glanced to the elegantly dressed couple standing uncomfortably alone a short distance away. "I'm going to bring her over here. She needs some girl time."

A couple minutes later Dani returned with a regal, yet somewhat shy, woman. Her dark hair was hidden under a beautiful scarf that complemented her suit to perfection.

"Girls, this is my sister-in-law, Ameera." Ameera's brown eyes widened and Dani patted her hand. "When *he's* not around, we go by our first names," she said with a wink.

Gemma smiled at the woman when they were introduced and saw she was concerned for her husband. "Don't worry. The guys sneaked him out. I'm sure they're doing something manly," Gemma said, trying to comfort her.

"Oh good," Ameera said with relief. "He has not left my side in the month we have been in the United States. Don't eat this, don't drink that—it's not good for the baby."

"You're pregnant?" they all asked at once.

"No, that is the problem. We are undergoing treatments to try to get pregnant." Ameera then looked nervously to Dani's rounded belly.

"I certainly hope that it works. You find out in a couple weeks if the first treatment works, right?" Dani asked.

"Yes. But, did you say you hope it works?"

"Of course I want it to work. I want to raise any children I have in Keeneston. I give His Highness enough problems just as a princess. Can you imagine me having to be the mother of the future king if we have a boy? It would be horrible."

Ameera smiled. "Yes, it would be very trying for His Highness. See, I've been raised since birth to be a queen and to raise the future king. I feel like such a failure that I cannot do the job I was raised to perform."

"Oh, sweetie. I understand. You know it wasn't easy for Mo and me either, but we're both here for you."

"And so are we. You're always welcome to Keeneston if you all need a place to relax," Paige offered.

"Thank you, that is so kind. We have really enjoyed our time here and I hope we have time to meet again before we all leave to go to Rahmi. Look, here come the men."

Gemma looked toward the entrance of the tent and saw the Davies brothers along with Mo, his brother, Will, and Cole all walking into the tent. They were all smiling and fixing their ties. If she were a betting woman, she would say they had a couple of drinks and tossed a football around behind the tent.

A mousy woman stopped Cy and when he looked up, he signaled Gemma to come join them. She made her excuses and headed his way.

"Sweetheart, this is Marianne. She owns the *Keeneston Journal*, our local weekly paper."

"It's such a pleasure to meet you, Miss Perry. Cy was just telling me you worked for *Inside Peek*. I love that magazine," Marianne pushed up her glasses and looked slightly embarrassed.

"Thank you. I'm surprised it's even sold out here."

"There's not a whole lot of news to report in a town this size, but we do have gossip. The magazine and articles really guide me on how to run the *Keeneston Journal*. It's so exciting to meet you. I must talk with you sometime about what you do there."

Gemma beamed at the compliment. She'd been yelled at, cursed at, spit at, and threatened for stories she'd run before. She'd never been praised. She was just about to ask Marianne if she wanted the scoop of her life—the memory card with Ginger and Tatum was back in her room—when she felt her cell phone vibrate. She never had a chance to turn it in. In fact, she had all the stories deemed too "feel good" about Hollywood celebrities on her computer that her boss refused to run.

"I'd love to talk more, but I have a call I need to take," she said, giving Cy a meaningful look. She answered her phone and hurried out of the tent as Cy gave his excuses to Marianne. He was beside her before she even had a chance to say hello.

"Joe?" Gemma asked as she stopped under the wide branches of a maple tree.

"Hey, Gem. I feel real stupid, you know. As soon as Nick said her name it hit me. Sarah Elizabeth Flannery."

"The socialite?"

"The very one. Not only that, but the boss man had me put her on tonight's VIP list. Should I add your name, too?" he asked with a smile to his voice.

"Looks like I'll be seeing you soon. Thanks a lot, Joe, I owe you."

"Can you get me an audition with Doug Mac for his next action movie?" Joe teased.

"Ha, I'll see what I can do. See you tonight." Gemma hung up the phone and turned to see half the town behind her.

"Just tell us all. John probably has your phone tapped, dear," Miss Lily said matter-of-factly.

Gemma looked past the Rose sisters to where Dani and Mo stood with the rest of the Davies family. "I have a little favor to ask," Gemma said sweetly. "We need to get to L.A. right now."

"I will have the plane ready in thirty minutes." Mo sent a quick message on his phone and then gave her a little nod. "Now tell us why."

"All the clues point to this one woman, Sarah Elizabeth Flannery. I don't know what a twenty-one-year-old socialite has to do with this mess."

"Isn't she the one with that sex tape out right now? She's supposedly horribly upset that someone got their hands on it. But as you pointed out in your exclusives section last month, there's a rumor she's the one who leaked it," a tiny woman with her hair permed within an inch of its life said from the crowd. "Oh, and it's nice to meet you. I'm Edna."

"Hi, Edna. How did you know that was me? I write under a pen name with a fake picture." Edna just smiled innocently and Gemma was starting to think it was *Inside Peek* that could learn a thing or two from Keeneston. "Yes, that's right. She ended up selling the rights and has made a fortune off it. Now she's trying to be taken seriously and wants to go into acting."

"But who is she?" Miss Lily asked.

"All I know is her mother was some Las Vegas showgirl who got pregnant and nine months later delivered a baby girl with a huge trust fund. She used the money to get a spot on some soap opera. Mama wasted no time getting Sarah in the spotlight, either. She was modeling by the time she was thirteen, dating the hottest teenage actors soon after, and even tried her hand at becoming a rock star. All failed and then suddenly this sex tape comes out with one of Hollywood's most talked about up-and-coming actors. And the sex tape is superior quality. Very fishy," Gemma told the group.

"What could she have to do with this criminal y'all are after?" Marcy asked from where she stood next to Jake and some of the local farmers.

"I don't know. Do you have any ideas?" Gemma asked Cy.

"No, but I do have an idea how to find out." Cy grinned as if he were the cat that swallowed the canary.

Cy almost laughed at Gemma's large eyes. They opened wide when they entered the ornate lobby of the luxurious hotel he booked for their stay. They grew even more at the sight of the suite they were sharing. A huge king-sized bed draped in rich material adorned a separate bedroom. A mahogany table lined with matching chairs offset the plush living room space.

"We could've just stayed at a friend's house or at your apartment. This must've cost a fortune."

"It did, but I heard that Sarah not only stays at this hotel occasionally for the privacy, but it sets up my cover story perfectly."

"What cover story?" Gemma asked as she looked out the window to the lush landscape below.

"That I'm a producer. I'm looking for the next big show about an up-and-coming celebrity and her challenge to make it big," Cy said proudly. It was a darn good idea. He knew women in Hollywood, and this was the perfect way to get her talking.

"Right. You were a stuntman, not a producer. There's no way she'll believe you. We need to come up with something else." Gemma turned and saw him on his phone. "What are you doing?"

"I just sent a tweet out that I'm looking to cast a reality show and am excited about this next phase of my life. Then I sent a couple texts to some people I know that I'm back in town and will be at a certain club tonight."

"And you think that's going to work?" *Dink, dink, dink, dink.* "Oh, shut up." Gemma turned and went into the bathroom as he tried not to gloat.

"What?" *Dink.* "I didn't say a thing." *Dink.* And with that, he failed to not gloat.

***

Cy had a hard time keeping his eyes off Gemma. Now he knew how she got into the VIP sections of clubs so easily. She was a knockout. She wore a black dress with a plunging neckline. A wide red belt showed off a narrow waist while the tight skirt emphasized her amazing curves and long legs. She finished the outfit with red spiked heels.

Her hair cascaded down her back in soft waves as she greeted Joe, the doorman. He was the perfect doorman: handsome, athletic, and had enough dings and dents to show overzealous patrons that he wasn't afraid to get his hands dirty if they got out of line.

"Joe, this is my friend Cy. We both really appreciate your help on this."

"Cy? Cy Davidson, the producer who's looking to cast a reality show about trying to break into the industry?"

Cy shot a triumphant grin to Gemma as he held out his hand to Joe. "That's me. From what I hear, you'll want this more," Cy said as he handed Joe a card.

"Doug Mac's private number," Joe said reverently as the looked at the business card.

"Tell him Cy told you to call. I have a feeling working with him will be more suited for you."

"Thank you. Oh my God, Gem, I totally owe you. And you, too, of course, Mr. Davidson. "

"You could call it even by letting Sarah Flannery know I'm here. Just don't let her know I was asking about her."

"You got it." Joe took out his wallet and looked at the card once more before safely tucking it away.

Cy followed Gemma into the club. The loud music coursed through his body as the lights bounced off the people dancing. They passed the bar and Gemma gave the bartender a quick wave before another club employee unhooked a velvet rope and allowed them up a set of stairs to the VIP area overlooking the dance floor.

Before they even sat down, the first expensively perfumed starlet enveloped Cy. Gemma rolled her eyes and sat down before she lost a seat. Cy smiled and laughed and played his part. It was something he was good at. While he wanted to be himself, Cy Davidson was a part of him, too, after all these years, and it felt good slipping back into character.

"Ladies—I've missed you all so much that I decided to come back for a bit," Cy laughed at Gemma sticking her finger down her throat as she sat on the couch behind the gaggle of fawning women.

"Here's my card."

"Here's my number."

"I'd be perfect for your show."

"I'm sure y'all would be perfect. But give all your information to my assistant over there so it'll be safe. You never know where I'll end up tonight and I'd sure hate to lose your card." Cy sent Gemma a wink just before all heads whipped around to look at her.

Cy used the time to cast a quick glance around the club. It was almost full as night turned into early morning. He caught sight of the very tall and leggy blonde as she strode into the club with her posse. Cy headed back into the pack of women before Sarah could reach the VIP area and was totally engrossed in conversation by the time she arrived and took her seat.

Gemma could only imagine this was what hell looked like. Her eyes were watering with perfume, her ears were ringing with their twittering, and two of them had "accidentally" stabbed her foot with their heels. Then there was *him*. Just sitting in the middle of the pack. She could see his head getting bigger and bigger as they flattered and flirted with him. Maybe she'd take her heel and pop his ego with it.

She also didn't know what to think of the quick transformation back to the man she met here just a short while ago. He'd been this carefree, hot-to-trot kind of guy her mother had warned her about. But after arriving in Keeneston, he seemed to drop the fakeness. He had actually seemed a little lost at times, but when they were together she felt as if they were both free. They both dropped all defenses and just enjoyed being together.

Gemma was knocked out of her reflections when Cy caught her eye and gave a slight nod toward a sitting area next to them. Sarah Elizabeth Flannery was draped across a chair and surveying her domain, which currently included Cy. Her two friends, both slightly less attractive and completely doting, were whispering in her ears.

"I'm sorry, I have to get a drink for Mr. Davidson, " Gemma said to the small crowd trying to hand her cards and headshots. She made her way to the private bar and took a seat to wait after ordering two drinks.

She didn't have to wait long for Sarah to take a seat next to her at the bar. "Hi. I'm Sarah."

"Gemma, nice to meet you."

"Same. So who's your boss over there? Seems pretty popular."

"Cy Davidson. He was a stuntman, but now he's gone into producing."

"Oh, that's Cy Davidson. I've heard a lot about him. I see the talk is true. Yummy! What's he producing?"

"A new reality series. He's trying to find someone young and new to follow around as they audition for major roles. Basically, he wants to document them becoming an A-list actor." Hook, line, and sinker, Gemma thought as she saw the excitement in Sarah's eyes.

"Really? What does *new* mean?"

"Well, they need a little family history in Hollywood so they may actually get their foot in the door, you know?"

"Of course. I completely agree with that. Oh, here," Sarah said as she winked at the bartender in the VIP section. "Let me get those. You sit here and take a minute to recover from those vultures. I'll take this to your boss."

Gemma sighed with relief. "Really? Thank you so much, Sarah."

Cy saw the second Sarah picked up his drink. Gemma had pulled it off. He turned to the women around him and asked for a couple minutes to relax. His assistant had their numbers and headshots and he'd look over them soon.

"I guess I have good timing," Sarah purred as she handed him his bourbon.

"I guess you do," Cy responded as he blatantly checked her out. "For bringing me my drink, I'll give you five minutes."

Sarah smiled, thinking she had succeeded. "I'm Sarah Flannery. My mother, Cashmere Flannery is a soap opera star. I'm twenty-one and looking to make it big in the industry. I have almost six million followers on Twitter and have a lot of buzz around me right now after that horrid sex tape was leaked."

"Horrid. Too bad. If it were a good sex tape, then you'd be interesting." Cy took a sip of his drink and turned away from Sarah.

"Oh, it's good. It was just horrible that it was leaked. Someone hacked my phone and stole it."

"I guess that means they want more of you. My assistant has a list of questions with her that we use during interviews. Why don't we sit down and go over them. If I'm interested, I'll get back to you in a couple days and you can come back for an audition." Cy led Sarah over to their couch and waved for Gemma who came looking very professional with her tablet.

"Miss Flannery has captured my interest. Now let's see if she can keep it."

"Oh," Gemma said, feigning surprise. "Let me pull up our background questions. Okay, here we go. Tell us about your immediate family, including any acting experience, how much money you had growing up, and where that money came from." Gemma looked up. "You know, old money from

Granddad's oil days, new money from your mother's technology company, stuff like that. And then what your family does now. Jobs, hobbies, and how close they are to you."

"Well, my mother is so talented. She's on *Summer Heat*, the soap opera. Before that she was a Vegas showgirl in town. She would be perfect for the show. I'm an only child, but I have two super-close girlfriends from prep school that add the sisterly feel. I don't know my dad, though. Is that a problem?"

"You don't know him? Surely you know a name," Gemma asked as she typed all of Sarah's responses onto her tablet even though it was recording the conversation.

"Nope. Mom said there was some massive party in the Hills one night and she was too drunk to remember what happened. See, her parents, my grandparents, were big in casinos and they passed away leaving a huge fortune to my mother. She said it was too painful to stay in Vegas because it reminded her of her parents. She hasn't been back once in twenty-two years. Anyway, she picked up and moved to Hollywood. She was celebrating getting her role on *Summer Heat* when she went to this party and got knocked up. Doesn't have a clue who my father is."

"That could be an interesting line for filming . . ." Cy murmured.

"Oh. That would be so cool. We could find my dad and interview a whole bunch of famous actors to see if I'm their daughter. Although, I'm super close to my mom and she wouldn't like it. But if I'm on the show, maybe she'll help out, too. It would be a real family bonding episode." Sarah's hands were gently crossed over her heart as she played up the show.

"Good point. Now, how is this sex tape going to play in? Are your lawyers getting it removed? Can we mention it or is it a no-go?" Cy asked.

"No, you can mention it. I decided to sell my rights to it so I can at least make money off it. As I said, it's very good."

"We'll need to talk to the man who starred in it with Sarah. Get his permission to be on the show as a guest a couple of times," Cy told Gemma.

"You can't do that," Sarah said as her voice cracked.

"Why not? This show is about your life and this is a big part of it," Cy reminded her.

"I know. It's just that Seth was killed. He was murdered right after the tape came out. They haven't caught the guy yet. Hey, could that be used on the show? A big shot investigative reporter is going to write a story on it, too, so I bet it would be really interesting to have it featured on the show. Very emotional and all. Hey, she kinda looked a lot like you. Ha! You have a twin out there and you didn't even know it."

Cy saw Gemma freeze and knew he needed to get her out of there fast. But he had an idea and he needed Gemma to play along one last time. "Gemma, let's take a picture of all of us." Gemma snapped out of it and handed the tablet to a waiter before joining them.

"Thanks for the picture, Sarah. We'll be in touch with you." He shook her hand and hurried Gemma from the club.

He opened the door of the limo the hotel provided and ushered Gemma into it before tossing one last glance at the club. Sarah was by the door with her cell phone out, no doubt checking him out. She saw the name of the hotel on the limo and smiled. He had a feeling he'd be hearing from her soon.

Cy closed the door and pulled Gemma close. She was shaking even though the club had been hot. "It's okay, sweetheart. You did it. We got all the information we needed."

"Was the picture really necessary? The thought of my sister talking with her just . . . I had this really weird feeling this is what got my sister killed."

"The picture was definitely necessary. Didn't you find it weird what she said about her father and her grandparents? And then her sex tape partner being murdered. Too many coincidences for me."

"That is strange. And strange that her mom got all that money just a couple days before getting pregnant."

"Yep. I think Mr. X is Sarah's father. Got a Vegas dancer knocked up, pays her off, and she moves away from Vegas with all this new money to try to become a star."

"And the picture?"

"I'm going to put the photo on the Internet with a caption about my great talk with Sarah. I'll have Cade work his magic so he can capture the IP addresses of whoever looks at it. I bet one of those addresses will belong to Mr. X. I also bet it's going to make him very nervous to see us both with her. So nervous that he'll make a move he's not prepared for."

"Are we heading home then?" Gemma asked.

"Not yet," he smiled. "I have plans that involve the marble soaking tub. Plans that will take most of the night and morning."

"Who needs sleep?" she asked as Cy slid his hand up her legs. "Totally overrated."

"What's not overrated? You in that dress. Now take it off."

CHAPTER EIGHTEEN

$\mathcal{D}$ ani looked at her husband and gave him a smile. She felt a little useless as the house was in chaos this morning while they were getting ready to take the king's plane to Rahmi for the birth of her child. Mo was directing what needed to be put on the plane versus what needed to be shipped when Bridget came in.

"I swept the limo and the plane. No explosives, and Marko and I are ready for the flight. Just let me know if you need me to help with anything else," Bridget said as she gave Marko, her explosive-sniffing Belgian Malinois, a scratch behind his ear.

"Thanks, Bridget. It really means a lot that you'll take time off to come to Rahmi with us. I feel safer just having you there."

Dani stood up from the table as Ahmed came in, looking serious as always. "The last of the bags have been sent to the airport. Your parents are waiting outside with the royal family. Nabi and Bridget will escort you while I lock the house down and instruct the remaining staff. My brother has all your security covered for your arrival and I will be in Rahmi as soon as Cy's back with your plane."

"Thank you, Ahmed. I don't know what we'd do without you, my dear friend." Dani clasped his hand and screamed.

Mo caught her as she fell to the ground and Marko barked as the tension in the room escalated. Dani blinked her eyes and took some deep breaths as her parents and four royal in-laws came running into the room along with most of the security force and staff.

"What is it?" Tony De Luca cried. She tried to give her dad a reassuring smile, but oh my God, she was in pain.

"I'm in labor," Dani said between clenched teeth.

Her mom pried her hand from Ahmed's and placed it in hers as Mo gathered her in his arms. "That's right, dear. Breathe." Her mom's confident voice soothed her.

"No!"

Dani's head shot up as the king loomed over her with a panicked expression on his regal face. "What do you mean, no?" Dani groaned.

"You can't have the heir to Rahmi in the United States. You must simply cross your legs and wait." Dani choked and sputtered, but nothing came but another contraction.

"Father."

"What? I'm giving her an order and she needs to obey, umph." The king stared in utter shock at his wife. "You hit me? You hit the king?"

"Well, dear. Someone had to knock some sense into you. It's better me than your son or, heaven forbid, Danielle. Now shut up and support your daughter as she gives you an heir." Fatima smiled at Dani. "But shouldn't we be going to the doctor's?"

"Oh no. The doctor is in Rahmi waiting for you," her father said.

"Don't worry, I know what to do," Ahmed said calmly.

"What? Pass out on me?" Dani snapped as she started to sweat.

"That only happened once. I have sawn off limbs in the battlefield," Ahmed defended. He shook his head and held up a hand. "I'm getting the limo ready and calling Dr. Francis to meet us at the hospital."

Dani grabbed her mother's hands as Mo and Ahmed helped her up. She had a death grip on Mo's hand as he led her to the limo. She was so worried about the baby coming early that she didn't care when her parents, in-laws, Bridget, and even Marko got into the limo first. Nabi and seven other security guards came running and leapt into two black SUVs, one in front and one behind the limo.

"Dr. Francis is going to meet us there. She's in a fitting for her wedding dress but started taking it off as we talked," Ahmed told her as he opened the driver's door. "Oh no."

"What?" Dani and Mo asked as the same time. Ahmed pointed to the large white car pulling into the drive.

"Good Lord, what is going on?" Miss Lily asked as she came out with a basket of baked goods. "Oh, now I see what all the runnin' about is for. How exciting!"

"Please excuse us, we need to get going," Mo said as politely as possible.

"Does she have a chocolate chip muffin in there?" the king asked as he leaned out the door.

"Father!"

"What? A king does not eat hospital food and this may take a while. Enough time to fly to Rahmi, I daresay," he muttered before a delicate, bejeweled hand appeared and thwacked him in the head.

"Here ya go," Miss Lily handed the basket over to him. "Well, get going. You'll do wonderfully, Dani." Miss Lily gave her a kiss on the cheek and Dani suddenly wasn't as annoyed. In fact, now she felt like crying.

"Okay, Ahmed, get us to the hospital," Mo called as he gently helped her into the limo.

The first security team was already in front of the hospital along with two nurses when Mo helped her out of the limo. The busy hospital seemed peaceful compared to the limo ride. Marko had whined the whole time. Ameera had been kind, but her silent looks of longing were making Dani feel horrible. Her mother sat on the other side of her calmly stroking her hair as her father and the king debated over going to the hospital versus trying to make the plane trip to Rahmi. She had managed to text Kenna and knew her girls would be there soon to support her. In the meantime, avoiding arrest for killing someone would be a good day.

"Stop right there. You can't bring that dog in here. And you, you need to get in line and register before you're admitted," the nurse shouted. Bridget stood with Marko and three men from her security team ready to do a sweep but an irate nurse stood in their way. Damn. There goes not killing someone today.

"I am King of Rahmi and you will get out of our way or deal with the queen. While you do that, my security detail will sweep this hospital along with your security personnel." The king pushed past the pissed-off lady and with a quick smile, Bridget followed.

"Well, I guess he is good for some things," Dani whispered to Mo as a wheelchair approached her. She took some deep breaths as she felt another contraction coming soon.

"I'm so sorry. Nurse Shelton is just getting off a twelve-hour shift, Your Highnesses. I'm Dr. Forge, the head of obstetrics, and will be assisting Dr. Francis. She just arrived and is preparing everything. Please, come this way," the man in green scrubs said as he offered Dani a wheelchair and led them to the elevator.

Dani felt as if she were leading a carnival procession as the whole royal family, her parents, and a team of security all stepped onto the elevator. Mo and the doctor were squeezed in beside her as they rode to the sixth floor.

"So what do we have in there?" the doctor asked.

"We don't know," Mo answered for her.

"It's against our customs for the royal family to be told anything. We don't even like ultrasound. But we are trying to embrace technology in our country so I allowed them to have one to determine if my heir is healthy, provided the doctor tell no one the results," the king explained.

"Yes. See, we don't want to accidentally say he or she in an interview. There are strict customs for when an heir is born, so it's best we don't know a thing," Mo finished.

"Lots of couples do it that way. It'll be a nice surprise for us all then. Here we go," Dr. Forge said as the elevator opened and Dani made her push for fresh air.

"This is the lobby for family. Through those doors are the patient rooms. So if you'd like to say your goodbyes to the group, I'll take you back along with anyone else you may want."

"Ahmed, you'll come with us and guard the delivery room. Nabi, stand guard here at these doors," Mo directed.

"Guard from whom?" Nabi asked as he took his post in front of the two doors.

"The entire town of Keeneston," Mo said ominously. Nabi's face blanched and a look of fear shot through his eyes before he squared his shoulders and nodded his head.

"Mom, can you get me registered?" Dani asked as her brother-in-law and sister-in-law took a seat in the waiting area and two of the security men made their way to the opposing stairwells to stand guard.

"Sure. You'll do wonderfully. Just call me if you need me, okay?" Her mother gave her a kiss on the cheek and a quick pat on her head that made her think her mother was remembering when she was born.

"When it's all over, I'll make stuffed shells that will make you forget all about pain. You just think about those shells." Her father kissed her gently, and with tears in his eyes, gave the king a pat on the back. "Let's go wait to become grandfathers."

"Wait, I'm going with them."

"Father." Mo rolled his eyes and Dani almost laughed.

"What? I need to verify my heir is brought into this world correctly."

"If he gets to go, I get to go." Dani's father almost stomped his foot and she felt like crying again.

"That's it," Mo said in his scary calm voice. "This is my wife. I will verify anything that needs verification. You will *all* stay here. As a courtesy to you, Father, we will notify you first of the birth. Until then, stay here." Dani smiled and squeezed Mo's hand as he wheeled her around and through the doors into the labor and delivery floor.

"That was really sexy," Dani said as she beamed up at her husband. He was her hero right now.

"Well, just try to remember that in six weeks," Mo joked before softening his voice, "How are you doing, my love. Can I get you anything?"

Dani heard a thump and turned to see Nabi plastered against the window of the doors. "It looks like the town got here. I hope Edna didn't bring her gun."

Six hours later, Dr. Emma Francis rolled back in her chair and looked up at Dani and Mo. Emma was getting married in two days to Noodle and she'd had a test run on her hair and makeup with her dress today. Her makeup was flawless. Her hair was in a beautiful up-do and the amazing flowered and feathered fascinator was still in her hair. The prettiest doctor around would deliver her child. The pictures would look fantastic.

"Okay, you're nine centimeters and ready to go. By the way, you should see the waiting room. Here, I had a nurse take a picture. I'll show it to you after your next contraction," Emma said as she put on new gloves.

The contraction hit hard and Dani tried to remember to breathe, but all she could do was push through the pain. "You're doing great, my love. You are the most amazing woman I have ever seen," Mo whispered to her as he wiped the sweat from her brow.

"Jane, show her that picture," Emma said as she organized the equipment down by Dani's feet. The nurse took the phone to Dani, and as she panted, she couldn't help but be encouraged by the picture of the waiting room completely full of her friends. The Rose sisters, Edna, and John were giving Nabi a hard time. The king and her father actually looked like excited grandparents. The picture also showed her friends, her mother, and the queen smiling as they talked in a tight circle.

And there were flowers everywhere. "Yeah, Neely Grace has whipped those Belles into shape. The flowers are from them along with baskets of food. Okay, push." Emma said easily as she sat back down.

Dani pushed hard for what seemed like forever. But then she finally felt her baby's head crowning. She gripped Mo's hand hard as he calmly gave her encouragement, but his excitement was clear. She took a deep breath and pushed again.

"Congratulations! You have a son." Emma called out as she held up the screaming infant.

"Oh, he's perfect. I love you so much, Danielle," Mo kissed her forehead and leaned down for a closer look at his small son. "Is he going to be okay?"

"Here, you can cut the cord and then the NICU doctors will look him over. He'll probably have to stay here for a couple days. He looks about five pounds or a little less, so they'll want to make sure he's gaining weight and can breathe on his own before he goes home," Emma told them as she showed Mo where to cut the cord.

Dani nodded; she knew he'd be fine. She felt it in her heart. Tears came to her eyes as Mo cut the cord and the nurse snapped some pictures for them. "Emma," Dani gasped. "Something's not right."

The pain started again and Dani just knew this wasn't normal. Fear flooded her as the pain came again. Emma pulled on a new pair of gloves and examined her. "Did you say you had an ultrasound and that everything was clear?" Emma asked.

"That's what the doctor said. He's not allowed to tell us anything," Dani panted as Mo ran to her side after turning their son over to the doctors.

"Well, then I guess you wouldn't have known you were having twins. Now push," Emma ordered.

"Twins?" Mo said in awe as he stared at her. Dani didn't know what to think; her body had just taken over as she pushed. Relief came and she fell back to the sound of more cries.

"It's another boy," Emma laughed as Mo cut one more cord before she handed the squirming bundle to Dani.

"Two sons. My father may forgive you for not crossing your legs until we flew to Rahmi," Mo laughed. Dani felt the laughter start in her belly and then was laughing so hard she could hardly catch her breath.

"You better go tell him," Dani said as she watched in amazement as the doctors examined not one, but two babies. Her babies. Hers and Mo's. She looked up at her husband and felt like crying again. She was so happy she didn't think she could stand it.

Mo looked upon his wife holding their two sons and thought he'd never seen a more beautiful sight. He called in his best friend and celebrated with hugs before handing his camera over for him to take pictures. Ahmed snapped the first family photo and some of each of his sons before he left to get the king.

He was holding his sons, the heirs, in the bed with Dani when he heard the king practically running down the hall. It was hard to miss with him shouting to Ahmed about which room they were in.

His father burst through the door and looked from one bundle to the other and tears welled in his eyes. "Father, may I present my two sons and your heirs." He'd never seen his father so overwhelmed with emotion. Dani sat beside him puffed up with pride and filled with the calm of a mother he never could've guessed she possessed. She was so sure of herself and he was just scared he'd drop the small bundle.

"Two babies," the king whispered reverently as he approached the bed. "I am deeply indebted to you, my dearest daughter. You have given me a gift I will never be able to thank you for. To be surrounded by grandchildren in my old age is all I have ever wanted. Thank you."

"You're welcome, grandfather." Mo looked to Dani and saw the tears in her eyes as she proudly handed one of their sons to him.

Mo rapped on the door to the waiting room and Nabi moved aside. The rush of feet was deafening as the townspeople all pushed forward to hear the news. His parents and Dani's parents were back in the NICU watching their grandsons being examined and cleaned up. They were both five pounds and only slightly premature. They'd be in the NICU for the next week, but both were perfectly healthy, happy, and hungry boys.

"Thank you all for coming out and showing your love for Dani and me. Emma showed us a picture of your support during the delivery. Dani and I really appreciate it. We are very blessed. Everyone is doing and feeling great. Mom and her two sons." Mo smiled into the sea of stunned faces.

"YES!" Dinky leaped up into the air next to his girlfriend, Chrystal. "I can't believe it. I bet that she'd have twin boys. I won. I can't believe it. I won."

"You were the only one with that bet, too," Miss Daisy said with a huge smile. "The entire pot is yours. It was our biggest yet."

Dinky suddenly dropped to the ground and everyone gasped as he took Chrystal's hand into his. "I can now give you the ring and the wedding you deserve because you deserve only the best. How I got you, I don't know. But I don't care if I'm not the best. I'm holding on tight and loving you every day for the rest of my life. Will you marry me?"

"Yes. Yes, Darrel Dinkler, I'll marry you." Dinky leapt up and kissed Chrystal as all the town and nurses and staff started clapping.

Neely Grace turned to Henry. "Are you crying?"

"Just thinking," Henry said wistfully.

"About what?"

"I want this," Henry told her as he looked around the happy room.

Mo knew what bet he'd be placing next time he was in the café.

CHAPTER NINETEEN

$\mathcal{C}$y drove his truck from the airport into Keeneston. It was evening by the time they touched down and he felt invigorated after their night and morning together in Los Angles. They had relaxed, laughed, played, and made love. It had brought them closer together than he ever thought two people could be.

"This is strange. Where is everyone?" Gemma asked as they pulled to a stop in front of the café.

"Something's happened. There's a note on the window." Cy and Gemma got out of the truck and walked with dread to read the hastily scribbled note.

Dani's gone into labor. No more bets can be placed at this time.

Cy let out a breath. It was a good something. "You know what this means?"

"We don't have dinner?"

"It means we'll have to fend for ourselves. Luckily I'm good at fending, among other things." He got a laugh out of Gemma and felt invincible.

Cy drove her back to Miss Lily's and took her to the kitchen at the back of the house. He'd make her dinner. He'd never made a woman dinner before, but he had an urge to do so now. He scrounged around the cabinets and found a box of pasta, some tomato sauce, and some sausage and hamburger in the refrigerator.

"How does penne with meat sauce sound?"

"Great. I love a man who can cook," she teased. Only Cy wished it were the truth. He'd woken up this morning knowing without a shadow of a doubt that he loved the woman he had been holding in his arms. He only hoped she loved him, too.

Gemma set the napkin down and leaned back on the kitchen chair. Dinner had been fabulous. Cy hadn't struck her as the cooking kind but had proved her wrong. He moved confidently through the kitchen and she had to admit it was a major turn-on. The only problem was, she got tired of trying to guess which Cy would show up. In public it was Cy Davidson, CIA superspy and Hollywood playboy. But alone it was just Cy Davies. Her Cy.

"Now, about that other idea I had," Cy grinned as he finished putting the plates in the dishwasher.

"Hmm? What could that be?" Gemma pretended to ponder as Cy leaned over her.

"Here, I'll show you." Gemma felt the butterflies in her stomach as his lips met hers. Soon she was lost to his mouth and hands. But then suddenly he froze with his mouth still against hers. One of his hands was on the back of the chair and the other was cupping her breast. "Someone is coming up the back walkway," he whispered into her mouth before quietly standing up and sliding a large knife from the block sitting on the counter.

She looked around and the closest weapon was Miss Lily's broom. She tiptoed to the wall and grabbed the broom. Cy directed her to move behind the door as he quietly unlocked it. He slowly turned the handle and opened it just a crack, making the voices clearer.

"Oh, John," Miss Lily giggled. Cy put down the knife and his body relaxed as Gemma slumped against the wall and let out a breath. They'd just busted another senior make-out session.

"Psst. Gemma. Hand me that broom, will ya? It's payback time."

Gemma handed him the broom. And in one quick action, he flipped the switch for the yard light and opened the door. He feigned total shock at finding Miss Lily in John's arms as he casually swept around the door.

"Oh, I'm so sorry. There's this leaf right there," he said as he gave Miss Lily a light swat. "I just wanted to help clean up to show you how thankful I am that you've let us stay here." Cy continued to sweep around Miss Lily and Gemma tried hard not to laugh as Miss Lily stewed at being caught.

Gemma decided she wanted in, too. She looked at her watch. "Gee, Mr. Wolfe, it sure is getting late. How nice of you to escort Miss Lily back home. You better scoot, as Miss Lily likes to say. Because what would the neighbors say?"

"Traitor," Miss Lily said under her breath as she stomped past Cy and Gemma like an angry teenager.

"You know, Kenna and Dani told me the funniest stories about you swatting their husbands when they stayed here."

"Well, you can't believe a word they say. They're Yankees." And in a huff Miss Lily slammed her door.

Gemma handed the tablet to Cade who looked at the picture they had taken at the club the other night. She and Cy had met with Cade and Cole this morning to tell them what happened in L.A. and give them their theory on Sarah Flannery.

"Mr. X's daughter, huh?" Cade said as he pulled up the photo with one hand and scratched Fred with the other. Fred and Justin had become big buddies and were currently resting their furry heads on Cade's lap. "Oh, yeah, this will piss him off big time."

"So you can do it?" Gemma asked.

"Of course I can. Cole, what do you think?"

"I think it's going to be a lot of numbers coming in. She has a ton of followers. But I have an idea," Cole said as he put down his Smartphone. "You set up the links. Have the data sent to the Lexington FBI office. I'll have a classified team running the numbers as they come in. We'll be able to see names and addresses of the IP addresses and weed out her friends or fans pretty easily. Then we'll be left with a manageable list of candidates."

"I can have this ready for upload by this afternoon. What kind of time frame are you looking at?" Cade asked as he sent the image to his computer.

"We'll be ready by then. I'll let you get to it and will start picking my team. We'll call you as soon as we have something." Cole grabbed his black cowboy hat and left with a nod.

When he opened the door, he found Paige and Pierce walking up the steps. "Hey!" Paige greeted. "It's just a big party over here, isn't it?"

"Hi, honey. They did a great job out in California. I'll probably be home late tonight," Cole told her as he bent down and gave her a quick kiss.

"No problem. I was actually coming here to steal Gemma for lunch. I'll see you whenever you get home." Paige waved her husband off and turned her attention to Gemma. "So, what do you say? Girls' lunch?"

"Sure. I think I've done all I can here," Gemma said as she grabbed her purse. Fred jumped into the bag. His little black nose twitched in anticipation of the treats Miss Daisy would sneak to him.

"I'll pick you up from the café. Pierce wants to show me his Cropbot at work on my fields. I think he's trying to get me to buy one," Cy teased his brother who was covered in straw and not looking anything like the multimillionaire Cy told her he was.

"You boys have fun," Paige yelled as she linked her arm with Gemma's and led her to her truck. Gemma gave a quick glance over her shoulder and smiled as Cy watched her leave. He gave her a wink in return and Gemma felt the click, felt the connection of an actual relationship. Now, if only she could convince him to get a new phone number.

Cy leaned forward in the saddle and watched the Cropbot move up and down the rows of corn. It tested water levels and directed irrigation, tilled the soil to keep it weed-free, and even had a way to spray organic-friendly pesticides to keep the bugs from snacking on the stalks.

"This is amazing, Pierce. I'll take one. With this helping me, the transition to farmer will be much easier."

"I still won't believe you as a farmer until I see it."

"What? You already forgot how I took care of the farm with Dad until you were in college? I'm hurt."

"I don't know too many farmers with a Jaguar F-Type."

"How do you know about my car?"

"Marshall told me it was delivered to his house today. He also told me to tell you he appreciates your kind donation and will be using it as the sheriff's car for the rest of the week. Between you and me, you may not get it back. Katelyn was thinking of reasons to get Marshall to go into the house so she could steal it."

"Well, I do have my eye on a new truck. Maybe Gemma would want to use it."

"Gemma, huh? Is she thinking of sticking around after this is all over?" Pierce asked as he programmed the Cropbot to finish its task and return to the barn.

"I guess. I haven't really asked her, but I just assumed."

"You're assuming? Not a good move, bro. Women liked to be asked. I made the mistake of assuming Tammy would want to go on a romantic camping weekend. Yep, should've asked. She hates hiking, hates sleeping on the ground, and basically everything else camping. Let's just say the weekend wasn't what I had thought in my head."

"Fair point. I'll talk to her now. It's about time to pick her up from lunch anyway." Cy turned his horse around and started trotting back to the barn. "Pierce, you've done a damn good job here and I'm very proud of you."

Pierce smiled and puffed up with the compliment. And maybe Cy's little brother was right about women, too. He'd talk to Gemma right now and let her know he'd love for her to stay in Keeneston as long as she wanted. However, the question going through his mind was would he ever be able to let her leave? Keeneston wouldn't be the same without her now.

Tears slid down Kenna's face as she gasped for air. Paige had her hand over her heart trying to calm herself down and Annie was still snorting with laughter. Morgan was leaning on Katelyn for support as they giggled and Tammy stared at her wide-eyed. "Shut the front door."

Gemma paused in her relaying the story of catching Miss Lily and John to stare at Tammy in utter confusion. "It is shut," Gemma said slowly, only bringing more laughter from the table.

"It's just a saying of surprise. I don't know if I can breathe yet," Paige said between deep breaths.

"Broom!" Kenna barked and the peals of laughter started all over again. "I can't wait to tell Will." Kenna used a napkin to try to dry her tears but gave up in the end.

"And I'm sure you and Cy were completely innocent in this situation," Morgan said mischievously.

"Oh, do tell." Katelyn sat forward in her chair. "We all want to know about Cy. He's so mysterious, even to us."

"That's not all he is," Tammy said as she started fanning herself.

"Listen to you talking like that. You're almost a married woman," Annie chided, "but not yet." The women laughed again and Gemma felt the warmth of sisterhood for the first time since she'd lost Gia. These women weren't even related by blood, but they had found a similar connection and Gemma wanted it again. It felt so natural being here with these amazing women. They were all so different, but equally strong.

"It's actually going well. When it's just the two of us, we're so relaxed and comfortable with each other. It's really quite strange, given the circumstances, isn't it?" Gemma asked the women who all shook their heads.

"Not at all. I think being in this kind of situation brings out the real person. There's no time for pretending. If you all are hitting it off now with all this going on around you, you'll be nauseatingly cute when you have time to slow down and enjoy each other," Annie said with fake disgust.

"I guess we'll see. Sometimes it's hard to get the real Cy to come out. He had become this Hollywood guy and sometimes he just falls back into it. And then there's his phone. I am not a violent person but I daydream of shooting it or beating it with a bat until it doesn't *dink* anymore."

"What's that all about?" Morgan asked as Gemma tried to relax her grip on her glass of special iced tea the girls told her she had to try.

"All these super-hot actresses," Gemma paused and took another sip of the drink, "models, and socialites. They just keep calling and texting and it always makes me stop and wonder why he is with me when these women want him. I guess it's giving me a little trust issue. Especially after seeing him in action at the club."

"You have nothing to worry about. I used to be self-conscious, too. But when the Davies men set their sights on you, they have a way of making you forget all about that," Tammy giggled before she started to fan herself again. "Is it getting hot in here?"

"Besides, those women are a thousand miles away. You're here and he's giving you his undivided attention," Katelyn said with a wiggle of her eyebrows.

"Cheers to that." Gemma took a sip and then stopped when she realized no one else was taking a drink. Tammy's eyes were wide. Katelyn's drink was paused in the air and Annie thumped her head with her hand. "What?" Gemma asked, but her question died in her throat as she turned in her chair.

A blonde knockout in cut-off jean shorts, sexy heeled boots, and a shirt that didn't quite cover her navel stood in the door of the café. "Excuse me. I'm looking for Cy Davidson. Can someone help me?" the young bombshell asked the stunned restaurant.

Gemma downed the rest of the glass of the ice tea. "Taylor freaking Jefferies." She turned and grabbed Tammy's glass and started drinking hers. The door tinkled again and Cy walked in with his little grin that she used to think was sexy.

"Cy," Taylor squealed as she leaped into his arms.

"You've got to be kidding me," Gemma groaned and she finished Tammy's drink. The only sound in the café was the clinking of the ice in her now empty glass.

"Taylor, what are you doing here? Is everything okay?" Cy asked with a grin Gemma realized as his real look. Apparently he didn't feel the need to be his undercover self with her.

"Oh, I'm fine. I just wanted to see you and you said I could come anytime," Taylor told him as she finally let go. Gemma grabbed the drink from where Katelyn still had it paused halfway to her mouth and downed it. They had told her it was special and she had to agree with the way the world was tilting around her. Maybe a couple more and the perfectly perky blonde would simply disappear.

As she set the glass down, Cy caught her eye and smiled. "Gemma, you have to meet Taylor."

Gemma smiled, raised her middle finger, and passed out.

CHAPTER TWENTY

$\mathcal{C}$y dropped his arm from around Taylor and stared at the woman he loved face down in a plate of peach cobbler. Katelyn's mouth was open, Tammy's eyes were wider than he knew possible, Paige looked ready to stab him with a fork, and Kenna would back Paige up. Morgan's look was so cold he practically shook where he stood and then heard the unmistakable sound of a gun being unholstered. Annie gave him a sweet little smile as she placed the gun on the table.

"What is wrong with you all?" Taylor gasped at the sight and hid behind Cy. Annie directed her gaze to the starlet and cocked the gun.

"I'll tell you what's wrong. Cyland, you should be ashamed of yourself." Miss Violet came at him with her wooden spoon in hand and thwacked him on the head before he knew what was happening. "You toy with a woman and make her fall in love with you and all the while you have some blonde tart in the background," Miss Violet berated before she lowered her voice and looked to Taylor, "Sorry, hon, I loved you in *Mountain Falls.*"

"Wait. Everyone calm down. There's been a misunderstanding." Cy held up his hands in self-defense. The table of women shot him a can't-wait-to-hear-this look so he knew he had to hurry. "Taylor and I aren't dating. We've never dated and we're never going to date."

"Eww, I couldn't date Uncle Cy. That would be totally weird," Taylor's voice said from behind him.

"I've known her since she was eight. I helped her out on the set and took care of her when she emancipated from her parents," Cy told the café.

"That's right. He taught me to cook, clean, and drive a car. He even made me get my GED." Taylor stuck her head out from behind Cy.

"So he was the perfect big brother?" Paige asked as tears welled up in her eyes.

"Yes," Taylor said, relieved that someone understood.

Cy grimaced as Paige calmly stood up, grabbed her purse, said goodbye to the table. She stopped before him and grabbed Miss Violet's spoon and cracked it over his head.

"Paige, wait." Cy grabbed his sister as she sailed by him. "I know you're upset. But you need to know that you and our family are the reason I decided to retire and come home. I missed everyone and I'm here now. I can't help but feel like such an outsider. You're married with a beautiful child. You've all moved on and it's like I was never even here. I know I was gone for a long time, but I'm trying, Paige. I'm trying to be part of the family again. Don't shut me out now."

"Shut you out? I called you every week for the past eight years; sometimes you answered and sometimes you didn't. And you think I'm shutting you out? You shut yourself out, Cy—you still are. Wake up and realize we all want to see you, be with you, and hear what you've been up to. But we can't. You won't talk to us. You won't be you, Cy Davies. You're still Cy Davidson. When you realize we don't give a crap who you were, just that you're here and we love you, then I'll talk to you again. Shoot, even Gemma realizes it."

Paige yanked her arm free and shoved the door to the café open. It slammed shut as the sound reverberated through the café. The only noise was the slight snore coming from Gemma as she unconsciously took a lick of the caramel sauce she was sleeping on.

192

He thought he was doing such a good job of being good ol' Cy. He guessed he was wrong. Now Paige was mad at him and Gemma thought he was having an affair all because he let his undercover work come home with him.

"Who's Cy Davies?" Taylor asked quietly.

"I am. Or at least I used to be."

Cy sat on the bench outside of the café with a quiet Taylor next to him. He had just told her the whole story and what she had unknowingly walked into. He had tried to carry Gemma home, but Annie had rested her hand on her gun again and ordered him to "fix this" before he saw her again. Even sweet Tammy narrowed her eyes at him.

He had disappointed them all when he had tried so hard not to. And that was the problem. He had been doing what he had been doing in Hollywood as a spy. Pretending to be someone else to make everyone happy and like him. Although this time he couldn't pull it off. They all knew him too well and instead were insulted. So rather than taking care of the woman he loved, he was forced to watch Annie and Katelyn maneuver her into the car and take her back to Miss Lily's.

"Let me make sure I got this." Taylor took a breath and looked up at the sky. "You're a spy. You've been pretending with your family and now because you aren't pretending with me, they're kinda mad at you. And your girlfriend, whom you just figured out you're in love with, thinks we're having an affair."

"Yep. That about wraps it up."

"Well, that's easy. Just go talk to them while Gemma sleeps it off. If they're as great as you've said, they'll understand and help you with this transition. Sometimes just talking helps. Or so says my therapist of ten years." Taylor gave him a nudge and Cy realized she was right.

He'd wanted to be like his brothers. Wanted to prove he was tough enough to handle undercover work and just bounce right back to who he was before, but that person didn't exist anymore.

A new Cy Davies did; he just needed to discover him. The door to the café opened and Trey Everett walked out. He saw the open curiosity on Taylor's face and grinned. Maybe he wasn't the only one discovering who they were. "Trey," Cy called out.

"Yes, sir?" Trey stopped and politely took off his Vanderbilt football cap.

"Trey Everett, meet Taylor Jefferies. Taylor, this is Trey."

"It's nice to meet you," they both said at the same time and then blushed.

"Trey, would you mind doing me a favor?"

"Of course, sir. What is it?"

"I need some time to talk with my family. Could you spare an hour or so and show Taylor around Keeneston?"

"I'd be happy to. I can drop Miss Jefferies off at the bed-and-breakfast before practice."

"Practice?" Taylor asked as she stood up.

"Yes, I play football. I'm working out this summer with some coaches. I just transferred to Vanderbilt."

"Vanderbilt? I'm starting my freshman year there. It's so wonderful to meet someone who's going to the same college. And you're already a sophomore? What is college like? Tell me all about it." Taylor hit him with rapid-fire questions as the two started walking down the street. Well, at least he did something right today.

Cy hugged his mother as his father stood proudly by. Paige even managed to give him a little smile. He had sat the family down, all except Cade, and told them the trouble he was having adapting. He felt stuck between L.A.'s Cy Davidson and Keeneston's Cy Davies. Surprisingly, he was the last to know. Everyone had already figured it out. It was why his brothers were taking him around the farm and showing him what they had done. Not as an example of what he missed, but to remind him of what he was returning to.

"We love you and we're very proud of you," his mother said sweetly before letting him go.

"I don't know if it helps, but I had trouble readjusting
ian life, too. Why don't you come with Bill and me on some vis..
to the hospital? He's a great therapy dog. I think you'll like it."

"Thanks, Miles. That means a lot. Let me know next time you
go and I'll tag along." Cy's attention was drawn to the door as
Cade came hurrying in.

"You have a cell phone for a reason," Cade yelled impatiently.
"I found something. Hey, where's Gemma?"

"At Miss Lily's. I'm surprised Annie didn't call you since she
almost shot me earlier," Cy informed him. When Cade grimaced
at his own cell phone, Cy just smirked.

"I'll ignore that. What did you do?"

"She may have misinterpreted a zealous hug from a friend,"
Cy hedged.

"From Taylor Jefferies to be specific." Paige smiled as she
happily filled in the blanks.

"I can't wait to hear the details, but now's the time for you to
kiss and make up. I found a thread, but now I need to figure out
how to pull on it. It's a company name. Happens to be the same
company name that rented the house Mr. Goatee Man was staying at."

"That's fantastic. What's the problem?" Cy asked as he stopped
to kiss his mother and sister goodbye.

"It's a legal game of hide and seek. There're so many shell
corporations and different names of officers that I'm having
trouble finding a real lead," Cade told him.

"What about asking Henry and Neely Grace if they can help.
As much as you get distracted by the shiny suits, Henry's pretty
smart. And from what I've heard about Neely Grace, she puts
him to shame."

"Good idea. I'll talk to them while you're begging Gemma to
believe you," Cade chuckled.

***

He paced the large office at his newest home in Kentucky.
He had homes all over the world, but never one in such a small,

out-of-the-way place like this. The quiet was getting to him. He heard things at night, things that he knew weren't real. Even though his team surrounded him, he felt more and more isolated. There was no one he could trust anymore.

"Sir. There's been activity on that account you wanted me to watch."

He nodded and the guard hurried from the room. Taking a breath, he made his way to the massive desk and turned on his computer. He pulled up his account and searched out Sarah Flannery's page. A picture was front and center that caused him to throw his glass of whiskey into the fireplace. In the middle of his screen sat a picture of his beautiful daughter with that son-of-a-bitch spy and no-good journalist determined to bring him down.

"Sergei!" he roared as he slammed his fist on his desk. He was going to take care of this himself.

***

Gemma opened her eyes to a room of women. The smell of coffee whiffed through the air along with a huge tray of brownies. And then she remembered what happened. Taylor Jefferies leaping into Cy's open arms.

"Oh no," Gemma groaned and rolled back into her pillow.

"Here, dear. Have some coffee. It'll help clear your head. Cyland is downstairs and needs to talk to you," Miss Lily told her.

"I don't want to see him."

"You really should. We might have misjudged the situation," Katelyn told her.

"Yeah. It turns out that Taylor really is just a friend. Trust me, I would've shot him if it were otherwise," Annie said reassuringly while patting her sidearm.

"Thanks. That's very nice of you." Gemma attempted to laugh but it hurt her head to do so.

"And I should tell you that little Miss Jefferies is staying in the room on the third floor," Miss Lily said hesitantly.

"No," Gemma squeaked as she hid her head in the pillow. "I made such a fool of myself."

"There, there. She's actually quite sweet. Poor dear, she's never been a teenager before. She acts as if she's already forty years old instead of eighteen," Miss Lily clucked as she shook her head.

"Thank you all for your help. Now if only I could get over the embarrassment of it all, I could leave this house again." Gemma sat up and took a sip of the strong coffee.

"Oh, we've all been there. It's nothing compared to that time I walked through school with my skirt tucked into my drawers," Miss Lily shrugged. "It happens."

Katelyn and Annie shook their heads as they grinned at Miss Lily. "It does happen. Especially when the Rose sisters' special iced tea is involved. We'll meet you downstairs." Katelyn smiled in a way that had Gemma thinking there was a story to be told there.

Gemma took another drink of coffee as the room cleared and finally stood up to take a quick shower. The hot water felt good as she began to wake up. Unfortunately, now the only thing she felt was foolishness for getting so upset over someone she didn't even have a well-defined relationship with. They were sleeping together and sometimes he called her his girlfriend. But she knew the real reason she was so upset. She loved the man.

Not the incredibly hot Hollywood stunt hero and international spy, but the kind, caring gentleman he was when they were alone together. The one who loved his family and wanted to take care of her. The one who told her corny jokes and helped Miss Lily carry in the groceries. The one who snuggled with her tiny fur ball of a dog and then took him to playdates with his brothers' dogs. That's the man she loved.

Gemma turned off the shower and slipped on a skirt and shirt before brushing out her hair and quickly braiding it. She knew she had kept him waiting. But quite honestly, she was scared to see him. What would she do if he looked at her with pity or worse, without that spark in his eyes?

Cy paced back and forth on the porch as his brother and sisters-in-law laughed in the parlor. He didn't see what was so funny. He had never been this nervous before. Waiting to see if the woman he loved with all his heart would even talk to him was worse than the time he had to lift a passkey from a warlord in the Sudan.

The screen door opened and Cy turned around to see a freshly washed and barefoot Gemma standing shyly by the door. "Gemma, please believe me. There's nothing going on with Taylor. I . . ."

Gemma cut him off. "I know. The girls told me. Can we forget it happened? I'm so embarrassed I don't think I can stand it."

"It's okay, sweetheart. I would've done the same thing had a man hugged you like that." Cy paused. "Well, after I punched him." Cy opened his arms and relief flooded him when she tucked her head under his and placed it against his chest. He closed his arms around her and never wanted to let her go.

"Good. Glad that's settled. Now we need to discuss something important," Cade said as he pushed open the door. "Ow." Annie and Katelyn both slapped Cade against the head at the same time while they shot Cy and Gemma an apologetic look.

"It's okay. What's going on?" Gemma asked from where Cy kept her tight against him.

"First, we discovered that Sarah is very popular. But, we found an IP address from Lexington. It's registered to the same company that rented the house for the Goatee Man. Someone in that house saw the picture."

"Mr. X?" Gemma asked.

"Someone did. I'm guessing you'll find out soon enough if Cy's plan works the way he thinks it will. Henry and Neely Grace are making progress, but it's slow work. Maybe they'll have something by Noodle's wedding tomorrow, but Neely Grace warned that it could take time. I'll let you know if we find anything else out."

"We'll see y'all there, won't we?" Katelyn asked, as she looked him right in the eyes, making it more of a statement than a question.

"Yes, of course. Noodle invited me the other day and I happily accepted. It's been a while since I've been to a Keeneston wedding." Cy looked down at Gemma and smiled. "They're a blast. The whole town is there and there's food galore, music, dancing, and more gossip than you can shake a stick at."

"Sounds fun. But what about Mr. X?"

"The whole town will be there. By the time the reception starts, we'll know all of Dr. Francis's family. It would be very difficult to slip in unnoticed. Hopefully, Mr. X will act before then." Cy gently ran his hand down her back and wished this were over. He couldn't move on with Gemma until it was.

***

Gemma stroked her fingers down the back of Cy's neck as they swayed to the music. His hand gently rested on the small of her back as he held her to him. The wedding had been beautiful and packed with every person in town, half the hospital, and all the bride's family. The reception, true to Noodle, was held outside in a field next to his favorite fishing spot. Trees surrounded the open area that had been decorated with beautiful lanterns casting a warm glow onto the happy group. Lanterns also lined the small waterway, causing the water to twinkle.

Gemma pressed herself against Cy's hard body and ran her other hand from his chest down his stomach.

"You're killing me," he whispered into her ear as he pressed her bottom toward him so she could feel just how much she was killing him.

Gemma slid her hand down and as she let it fall, her nails skimmed the bulge in his suit pants. She enjoyed the hiss he made as he slid his hand around her upper back and gently used his thumb to stroke the side of her breast.

"Let's get out of here. There's a little spot in the woods I know, if you're up for an adventure." Cy's suggestion had her heart pounding. It had been days since she'd been with him and it had seemed like an eternity.

After Cade and the girls left yesterday, she had met his friend Taylor. She couldn't wait to talk to Gemma about this nice boy she had just met. And, grudgingly, Gemma had to admit she liked Taylor a lot. But when night came, Cy hadn't come to her room. Instead he had woken up every so often throughout the night to do his shift watching the house along with one of Ahmed's men.

As they sat next to each other in church earlier listening to Noodle (known to the Rose sisters and his own mother as Eugene Miller) and Emma Francis exchange their vows, it had turned her into a romantic mess. Gemma had held his hand and watched the ceremony envisioning what it would be like to look Cy in the eyes and say those words. She decided then that life was unpredictable and she wasn't going to waste a second of it. She was going to tell him she loved him.

"Okay, let's go," Gemma giggled as Cy grabbed her hand and tried to casually walk to the tree line.

Cy quietly led her to the punch bowl and then slipped behind the trees when no one was looking. She had to smother her laughter with her hand as he hurried down a path to a little clearing deep within the woods. She could still barely hear the strings of bluegrass music coming from the band as Cy spread his suit coat onto the ground.

"Dance with me," Cy's voice rasped as he held out his hand. She placed hers in his and laughed as he pulled her tight against him. "Gemma, there's been something I've been meaning to tell you."

She nuzzled his neck with her lips and let him talk when in reality talking was the last thing she wanted to do. His hand slid down her back as they swayed to the music.

"I . . ."

"Well, isn't this cute? The spy and the reporter."

Gemma spun around as Cy shoved her behind him. She looked over his shoulder at a little man with big glasses and a crazed look in his eyes.

"Mr. Boss Man, I presume. To what do we owe this honor?" Cy asked casually as he rocked back on his heels.

"Honor, you have no honor. You and this bitch are the downfall of society. When a man can no longer earn a living because you're arresting his people or writing an exposé on my group, huh, Gia? I thought I had gotten rid of you once, but you know what they say about evil—it never dies. Now I'll make sure you die, Gia," he spat.

"I feel introductions need to be made. I'm Cy and this is Gemma. And you are?" Cy's casual voice turned hard and she felt him pushing her away. She looked down and saw him frantically motioning for her to run. But she couldn't. She had to find out his name.

"Stop playing games. Just ask Gia who I am. She figured it out, just as you did when you found my daughter. But I'll make sure you're both dead this time."

Cy shoved her and she started to run only to run straight into a solid wall of muscle. Gemma gulped as large hands clamped around her arms and she screamed in pain.

"Ah, there you are, Sergei. Bring her to me. Don't even think about it, Cy. Sergei will snap her neck if you move from that spot."

Gemma smashed her foot onto Sergei's and fought with all she had. But Sergei just squeezed tighter; she thought her arms would snap under the pressure. Sergei shoved her into the outstretched arms of the mastermind behind her sister's death and without thinking, she pulled back her arm and punched him in the face.

"Bastard!" she screamed but all too soon the back of his hand connected with her face so hard that she fell to her knees. She felt him grab her and haul her up as Cy ran forward.

"Sergei. Take care of him."

"No." Gemma fought against the man's grip. She twisted, kicked, and screamed against the hand that muffled her, but she couldn't stop this fight to the death. She kicked out once more, and screamed when the hand was removed from her mouth. But this time her scream was cut short as a cold metal object was pressed against her neck. Electricity from the stun gun stopped her fighting instantly. Her body cramped and her legs gave out as he caught her and started dragging her deeper into the woods.

Cy heard Gemma squeak and then drop to the ground. Sergei took advantage of the distraction and landed a solid punch to Cy's face. His head snapped back and he lost the advantage in a split second.

Ducking another punch, Cy leaped forward and tackled Sergei to the ground. There was no sound except the breaking of tiny branches and the occasional grunt as they rolled on the grass grappling for position. Cy managed to pin Sergei's arm, but Sergei raised his legs and clamped them around Cy's neck. Cy's fingers slipped from the hold he had on Sergei and Sergei tossed him to the ground. Before Cy could catch his breath, Sergei had him in a chokehold.

"I'll enjoy killing your girlfriend, but I won't be so kind. I'm going to take my time," Sergei hissed.

Cy felt his world darkening. He knew he couldn't break the hold and that left only one choice left if he wanted to save Gemma. He dug out his cell phone and pressed Speed Dial.

Miles had his arms around his wife and enjoyed feeling her tiny belly growing. Her small bump pressed against his stomach as he danced with her. "Did the baby kick?" he asked, jumping back.

Morgan giggled. "No. That's your cell phone. The baby will kick but not for about eight more weeks."

With great reluctance, Miles pulled out his phone and looked with confusion at his brother's number. "It's Cy." He answered the phone and listened to sounds he knew too well. "And he's in trouble."

"What?" Morgan asked, but he was already running.

"Where's Cy?" Miles shouted to the crowd.

"He went into the woods with Gemma," Miss Violet told him as she wiggled her eyebrows. "Behind the punch bowl."

"Miles?" Marshall called out, but Miles didn't stop to answer him. He knew his brothers would follow. He had heard the unmistakable sound of fighting and then the collapse of a body, followed by footsteps.

Miles ran through the woods, following the small trail Cy and Gemma had taken. He burst into the small clearing and found Cy on his stomach. Evidence of a fight was all around and Gemma was missing. He put the pieces together before he even got to Cy. As he rolled him over and felt for a pulse, he heard his brothers crashing through the woods. There was still a faint pulse as Miles started CPR.

Cy felt life flood back into him. The world had gone dark and he was sure he was dead except for the fact that he refused to leave Gemma. He felt as if he were struggling between life and death until that rush of air entered his lungs. He opened his eyes and saw Miles and Marshall over him with relief on their faces.

"Gemma," he choked out.

"We know. I can follow the trail, but I think we all know where it leads. It was Sergei, wasn't it?" Ahmed asked from the spot Cy had last seen Gemma as she was dragged away.

"And the boss. I still couldn't get a name. But they have her. They have Gemma and he's crazy. He kept calling her Gia." Cy struggled to stand up as his brothers helped him to his feet.

"Come on. Let's get you some water and we'll develop a plan. We'll get her back." Miles led his brothers from the woods and right into the heart of a very worried town.

CHAPTER
TWENTY-ONE

Gemma felt the plastic ties cutting into her wrists as she struggled against them. She sat in the back of the limousine with a gag in her mouth and the plastic zip-ties holding her hands and feet behind her back.

"Stop struggling, Gia. It won't be over for some time. I'm going to let Sergei have his way with you this time. Last time I told him to kill you quickly, but that obviously didn't work. You went to my daughter again. You're getting bolder and so must I. Sergei will take his time torturing you so you'll spill every secret you've learned about my organization. You'll be made an example."

Gemma cringed at the almost gleeful look of anticipation on his face. The only thing stopping her from utter panic was the anger she felt. She didn't know if Cy was alive or not. Sergei came back, which couldn't be good. This man killed her sister and may have killed the man she loved. She wasn't about to give him the satisfaction of freaking out. Instead she turned her body so he could see her hands and held up both middle fingers before calmly turning back around in her seat. When the look of excitement died from his eyes, replaced with shock and then hatred, Gemma felt strangely triumphant. She wasn't going down easy. She was ready for the fight to come.

***

Neely Grace and Henry sat discussing what they had found with Cy, as the town discussed the current situation. "I'm waiting for one last name from a court in India, but they're not giving it to me," Henry told him.

"Give me your phone." Neely Grace held out her hand and waited for Henry to put the phone in it.

She scrolled through the numbers and hit the one for the court in India. She waited for the phone to be answered and introduced herself. Cy shook his head. The waiting was killing him. He wanted to barge in right then and kill them. He knew they could be hurting her right now, but his brothers had been right. They needed a plan.

"I don't give a rat's ass if the judge is eating lunch." Neely's normally calm voice rose. "You go in there right now and get him on the phone or I'll send the embassy down on you so fast you'll wish you were never born." Neely Grace paused and then smiled. "Why, thank you so much for your help. Yes. I'll hold," she said with her best southern charm.

"She's so hot," Henry said with a grin.

"Cy, can I have a word?" Cole asked.

"Sure, you have a plan? Is the FBI on their way?"

"That's what this is about. I got a call from internal affairs. I had them run an audit on all the financials of my agents. I got a ping. One of my guys just cashed a very large check from a company connected to the one Henry and Neely Grace are investigating. My office is dirty and I need to clean house. I don't know who to trust enough to call them in. I thought this one guy was clean. They're digging deeper and fear there may be more."

Cy ran his hand through his hair. This was not good. "I can call in the DEA's office, but it may be the same. What do you want me to do?" Annie asked.

"Cy, I got it. I got a name," Neely Grace called from where she had stalked off to talk to the judge. The wedding reception quieted down as she hurried toward him. "Liam O'Flannigan."

"Got him," Cade said as he punched away on his Smartphone. "He was born in New Jersey and attended public school until he was suddenly admitted to the top private school in the state. When he was sixteen, he dropped out of school. Then reappeared at an Ivy League college where he earned a business degree and an art history degree. It says he owns an art studio in New York City now. No mention of a family with the exception of a mother— Eloise O'Flannigan, who died of a drug overdose when he was just sixteen."

"Wait. That name sounds familiar," Marcy Davies said as she snapped her fingers. "She was the Mistress of Politics. It was never proven and the news didn't make a big deal of it. They discounted it for gossip, if I recall. But when I was a young girl in college, I liked to read those gossip rags. Anyway, there was an article about a woman who had been a mistress to some of the most powerful men in politics. It was rumored she was even the mistress of the vice president."

"I see it," Cade said as he read something on his phone. "The magazine was sued and they took down the story and issued an apology. No one credited it as being truthful and the reporter even pled guilty to libel."

"But if that were true . . ." Kenna said.

"It would explain where he got his connections. Now, what do we do about it?" Cy asked. "My idea is to storm the place."

"I like that idea. But I was thinking of something with a little more finesse," Ahmed said as he stepped forward.

***

Tires squealed, a horn blared, and then the sound of metal hitting metal resonated through the night. The door to the beat-up Chevy Lumina creaked open as Trey Everett stepped out.

"Oh my God, are you okay? Someone call an ambulance! Babe, call an ambulance," Trey called to Taylor as he rushed to the large white boat-of-a-car with a smashed front end.

The doors opened as Miss Lily and John stepped out on wobbly legs. Miss Lily gently collapsed to the ground as Trey rushed to her side. "Look what you did. You teenagers are all willy-nilly out here like you own the place. You could've killed us."

"Yo, man. It wasn't me. You were the one swerving into the lane. You old people need to get your eyes checked. You're the hazard on the road," Trey shouted back.

"Hey! What's going on here?" a man in a suit asked as he walked down the driveway from the gated house.

"I'll tell you what's going on. This young whippersnapper and his lady were doing the hanky-panky in the car instead of paying attention to where they were going and crashed right into us."

"That's not true," said the cute woman in shorts so short the perfect globes of her derriere showed when she bent over . . . as she did for the guard. "These old geezers couldn't see the road in the dark and crossed the line and hit us." Taylor straightened back up, having picked up her purse from the ground.

"Oh sure, so says the tart," Miss Lily said prudishly from the ground.

In the distance, another set of car lights rounded the corner. "That ambulance must've gotten here fast," Taylor said as she ran the tip of her tongue over her bright red lips. "I like fast." She dropped her voice so only the guard could hear her as Trey and Miss Lily argued. "When the cops come, you'll say the old man hit us, right?" She ran a hand down his chest and he smiled as she gave him a clear shot of her pushed-up boobs.

"Sure, doll. What do I get for it?" the guard asked before more tires squealed.

"You hussy," Edna yelled as she hurried from the car. Out poured Miss Daisy and Miss Violet with her. "What are you doing with my man?"

"Your man? It's not my fault if you can't hang onto him. Maybe if you got that bunion fixed, he wouldn't have run off in terror for someone younger."

Edna gasped along with Miss Daisy and Miss Violet.

"And you called me a tart," Taylor said with full twang, really getting into her role. "And all the while you're a man stealer."

"As if you weren't just feeling up that young man over there," Miss Lily shot back.

"Babe?" Trey asked, wounded.

"I was doing no such thing. You're the home-wrecking hussy, not me." She slammed her foot down and crossed her arms, shoving her boobs up for the guard to see again.

"That's right, just because she dresses the part doesn't mean she's a slut. You, on the other hand . . ." Miss Violet sneered.

"Hey now, ladies. Calm down." John smiled and all the women harrumphed.

"Don't get me started on you, you hound dog." Miss Daisy wagged her finger at him.

"I'm just saying there's more than enough of me to go around. We can all get along."

"No, there ain't. I'm woman enough to keep my man satisfied. And so is my chicken and cheese casserole." Miss Lily threw down the figurative gloves and the other women gasped.

"You can steal my man, but don't you dare say your casserole is better than mine," Edna hissed as she dug around her purse and brought out "Ol' Magnum."

"Yeah, this is gate. I have a situation here. I need security—lots of it," the guard said into his phone as he pulled his gun. "Now, put it down slowly, ma'am."

"Stay out of it, sonny. This concerns me and the old woman." Edna pointed the large gun at Miss Lily.

"Who are you calling old? Why, you're so old you couldn't shoot me if you tried. You'd break a hip, for crying out loud. With your glaucoma, you'll probably shoot the tart over there instead of me."

"I'm not a tart!" Taylor stomped her foot and shouted.

Bam!

***

Bridget sent the text. *Go.* "Okay, everyone," she whispered into her microphone. "Be on the lookout. The crew just gave us one hell of a distraction. The gates are opening and I see . . . eight guards rushing out. Move forward now."

She gave Marko the command and they both moved silently toward the fence surrounding the large mansion. Cole, Dinky, Noodle, Jake, Miles, Marshall, Cade, Pierce, Paige, and Annie were all making their way toward their assigned positions. Jake and Paige were in sniper positions far enough away to be out of immediate danger, but the others were to advance to the fence. They would scale it when they got the signal from Cy.

Marko let out a low growl that Bridget felt on her leg as opposed to hearing it. She froze and Marko did, too. A tree provided her cover as she watched a guard walk the property. She waited until he passed and then grabbed him from behind. Using leverage, she placed him in a chokehold until he passed out. She quickly gagged and tied him to the tree in complete silence.

"One down on my perimeter," she whispered.

"One down on my side, too," Cade replied.

"Damn, why don't I get any fun," Annie complained. "Never mind. One down on my side," she said when she came back on a couple minutes later.

"The distraction out front is still working. Where's Cy?" Paige's voice asked over Bridget's earpiece. Good question. It shouldn't be long.

Cy strapped on the parachute and then checked over Ahmed's as the plane approached the mansion where Gemma was being held. His phone vibrated and he saw Bridget's message.

"Mission is a go," he said to Ahmed who was now checking his parachute.

"We'll be there in seventy-five seconds." Ahmed walked over to the open door and looked out into the night. "You love her."

"More than anything."

"How do you know?" Ahmed asked.

"I know because I can't stand the idea of living without her. I love the good and the bad and everything in between. She's my life. What about you, Ahmed? Ever been in love?"

"Yes," he answered so softly Cy barely heard.

"Does she know?"

"No, not until Sergei is dead will she ever know. Now jump." Ahmed disappeared from view and Cy looked out into the darkness. With a calm breath, he jumped out of the plane.

Gemma's head snapped back as pain blossomed around her cheek. She'd been dragged into the house through the garage and now sat in the middle of a large foyer with Sergei and his boss.

"Where is the evidence? How did you find me?"

"I think it was you who found me. I came to Keeneston first."

He nodded for Sergei to hit her again. Blood blossomed on her lip as she cringed in pain. "You shouldn't have gone after my daughter again. When I killed you the first time, they told me you begged for your life. So start begging, bitch. I want all the evidence you have and I want it now," he yelled, standing in front of her.

Gemma shook, not in pain, but in fright. The man was delusional and Sergei knew it. But it didn't stop Sergei from hitting her. Gemma refused to beg. She lifted her chin a notch and stared at him straight in the eyes. "Never." Gemma used all the energy she had left and launched herself at him. Her head connected with his chin and they fell to the floor in a heap. She managed to stay on top and was about to head-butt him when Sergei picked her up and slammed her into the chair.

His boss stood up, blood dripping from where he bit his lip. "Kill her."

Gemma watched in horror as Sergei pulled out a long knife from behind his back and smiled. She didn't think she was actually going to die until this moment. Anger had fueled her, but now it seemed death had caught up with her. She closed her eyes and pictured her sister. But it was Cy who was in her heart. A gun fired and Gemma looked to see where she was hit as the knife arced down to finish the job that the gun hadn't.

Cy and Ahmed landed quietly on the roof. They unhooked their parachutes and slid to the attic window. Ahmed jimmied it loose and pushed it up. Then it was just a matter of finding Gemma. Ahmed took the second floor while Cy headed for the first.

The diversion out front worked; he was able to make his way down the stairs, only having to disable two guards. He heard voices as he rounded his way down the steps. Gemma's voice sounded strong and he was able to breathe for the first time since she had been taken. But then he heard the order to kill and that relief fled.

Cy rushed down the stairs and into the large foyer. Gemma was sitting in a chair as Sergei had a knife raised above her. Cy didn't take the time to aim and fired off a shot that barely missed Sergei, but it threw off Sergei's attempt at Gemma's chest. He had cut her arm instead.

"No. Kill them, kill them!" Liam O'Flannigan screamed to the guards as gunfire erupted outside. It seemed the others had arrived right on time. The guards were forced to divide their numbers.

"You first," was Ahmed's cold response from behind them. Sergei turned slowly, forgetting Cy was there, to confront his oldest enemy.

"Ahmed. I've been waiting to see you again."

"Likewise." Ahmed pulled a large knife from his leg strap and the two started to circle each other. Cy took the opportunity and rushed to Gemma.

"Are you okay? You're bleeding." He sliced her restraints free but that was all he could do before two other guards rushed into the room. Cy turned and shot one before the other grabbed him from behind, sending Cy's gun sliding across the floor.

Gemma shrieked as the man pushed her aside and grabbed Cy from behind. She was about to leap on him when Liam ran from the room. Torn between helping Cy and chasing after the man who ordered her sister's death caused her to freeze in place. But then Cy flipped the man over his back and sent her a wink.

As she ran from the room, she passed a large fireplace and grabbed the poker, then gave chase to a back room. The chaos from the foyer was left behind as she stopped at the door to the study.

"I'm glad you followed. I'll kill you myself now," Liam said from behind his desk.

"Who are you that you needed to kill my sister because she found out about you?" Gemma asked as she walked slowly toward the massive desk.

"I am God. I rule the world. I overthrow governments, wage war, surround myself with the wonders of the world—Rembrandt, Klimt, Renoir, Picasso, and jewels bigger than your hand. That's who I am. Who are you?"

"I'm a woman who loved her sister." Gemma stalked forward raising the poker. She knew, even with her rage, she couldn't kill him but she sure could take out a knee or two.

"And did I mention I'm the man with all the guns?" Liam opened the top drawer and pulled out a gun. Gemma stopped in her tracks and swallowed hard.

"Move," Cy yelled.

Gemma didn't bother to ask why; she fell to the ground as two shots were fired and prayed that Cy was safe.

"Gemma, you scared me so much."

Cy's arms pulled her to him as she was lifted off the ground. She threw her arms around him and sobbed into his neck. She had almost died and he had come to her rescue. He had saved her.

"You came for me," she whispered.

"Of course I did. I could never leave you. Now let's get out of here." Cy scooped her up and held her close to him. Then he put his arm around her and hurried her to the foyer. As they approached, the only sound was the clinking of metal against metal.

Ahmed didn't notice the sounds of the gunfight quieting down outside. He only saw Sergei and his knife as they thrust and stabbed, trying to disable each other. Both had been militarily trained in the same techniques and therefore were matching move for move.

Ahmed tossed his elbow out as a distraction. When Sergei glanced, Ahmed sliced through the air and connected with the killer's side. The cut wasn't fatal, but it dropped Sergei's guard some. Ahmed could finish him off; he knew it. But then he heard the sound of people coming at him. In his peripheral vision, he saw Cy with his arm wrapped around a bruised and bleeding Gemma.

Cy stopped and bent to help Gemma sit down in the chair. He knew without a doubt Cy was coming to help, but then a figure emerged slumped against the wall. He was bleeding from the shoulder and had a trickle of blood streaming down his rounded head. Ahmed blocked a weak attack from Sergei and landed a solid punch to his face. Sergei staggered back. He had the kill shot to finish off his nemesis, but then the man behind Cy raised a gun and aimed it right at the couple.

Ahmed raised his arm and went for the kill. His knife flew through the air, tip over end, and sank into the chest of Liam O'Flannigan. Liam was knocked back and collapsed to the ground as Gemma and Cy spun around in surprise. When Ahmed looked back, Sergei was gone.

CHAPTER
TWENTY-TWO

*C*y looked down at the woman he loved and felt whole. She slept quietly on the pillow next to him, her white-bandaged arm lying on the quilt as her hair fanned out over the pillow. He pushed back a lock of hair and she turned her face into his hand, seeking him in her sleep. He cupped her cheek and lowered his lips to hers. He had almost lost her and he was determined that would never happen again.

The Keeneston Sheriff's Department and their citizens had been credited in this morning's paper as heroes for bringing down the world's largest black market dealer, arms trader, and terrorist. Dani didn't even get mad that Ahmed had loaned them her old car.

Shots had been fired, but those had come mostly from Annie. She had fired at the feet of the guards who were trying to rush back into the gate after they had confronted the group in the car crash out front. When they turned around to run back down the driveway, Paige fired off a couple of shots and they were met with the barrel of a large Magnum held by the surprisingly steady hands of Edna.

Cy had kept a tight hold on Gemma since he found her in the office with Liam. Ahmed had disappeared in search of Sergei as soon as Liam hit the ground with Ahmed's knife lodged in his heart. Ambulances and the rest of the FBI had been called. The Rose sisters clucked around Gemma even though Cy made sure to keep her in his arms. Ahmed had returned a short time later and, with a slight shake of his head, Cy knew that Sergei hadn't been found.

Still beautiful in her wedding dress, Dr. Francis had arrived before the ambulance and stitched up Gemma's arm as she gushed about how this was a wedding to remember. Noodle had stood beside his new wife beaming with pride as she gushed about her hero of a husband.

Cy answered the questions for Marshall's report and then for Cole's. When completed, he took Gemma back to her room. She looked so delicate with her face slightly swollen and her dress splattered with blood. He'd carried her upstairs against her protest and helped her undress. He made a warm bath for her and helped clean away the nastiness of the night. As soon as he had her tucked in bed, she had fallen asleep.

He had been awake all night watching her. She had rested with surprising peace. The night had given him the time and the perspective he needed to think. The conclusion he reached was that he didn't want to go another day without Gemma by his side. He loved her, his family, and his town. He realized he was genuinely happy. Now all he needed was Gemma to be his wife, if she would have him.

***

Henry Rooney handed the last of his and Neely Grace's research over in duplicate to the sheriff's office and the FBI. Neely Grace was still in the beautiful fitted dark green dress she had worn for the wedding. She sat on the edge of his desk with her legs crossed and one high heel dangling off her toe. Henry felt his heart pound along with something else. Suddenly, Henry cleared his throat, "Neely Grace, can I show you something out front?"

"Sure. Can you believe last night? It was crazy but it was such a rush, too. We worked really well together. Go us!"

Neely Grace beamed with pride and excitement.

"It was." Henry opened the front door and stopped in front of the plaque to his office. He took a deep breath and felt his hands shaking. He rubbed them on his pants and with one last breath dove in. "Neely. I've lost something to you. I've lost my heart."

Henry went down on one wobbly knee and tried to remember to keep breathing. Neely's face was full of shock.

"Neely Grace, will you marry me? Will you take my name and keep it with you forever? Will you make this place Rooney and Rooney Law Firm? I'll even let you be the first Rooney . . ."

"Henry, shut up." Neely laughed. "Yes! Yes, I'll marry you."

Henry stared at her in confusion. "Yes?"

"Yes," Neely smiled and nodded her head.

Henry leaped up and swung her around in his arms. He put her down and then kissed her with every ounce of love he had for her. "I love you."

"I love you, too," Neely rested her head against his shoulder and hugged him. "But I'm picking out your tux for the wedding."

"I'll let you pick out my clothes for the rest of our lives." Henry paused and then set her back a bit. "You see this shirt? Do you know what material it is? It's husband material." Henry laughed as Neely Grace rolled her eyes and tried her hardest not to laugh. He was going to enjoy every day of his marriage to this spectacular woman.

***

Gemma awoke slowly and reached over to feel for Cy but found the bed empty. There was a slight tug on her arm that reminded her of the night before, but it was finally over.

The man responsible for her sister's death was dead and the man who carried out the order was injured while fleeing for his life. Justice had been served. Now she could claim her sister and finally put her to rest in peace.

The thought brought her much relief. She felt like a new person, but just as quickly as that feeling came, it fled. This meant she had no more reason to stay in Keeneston. Her stomach knotted at the thought of leaving the town that seemed more like home than the city she'd lived in her whole life. And then the thought of leaving the man she loved hit her. The thought of going back to L.A. suddenly held no appeal.

Gemma pushed back the cover and slipped on a sundress and some flip-flops before hurrying from the room. She needed to see Cy, see what his reaction would be. She couldn't stay if he didn't want her to.

Gemma hadn't found Cy or anyone else in the house so she made her way down the street to the café. She knew she'd find people there. It was Gossip Central and she was sure those involved last night would be regaling the town with their story. If anyone knew where Cy was, it would be the Rose sisters.

Kenna laughed as her daughter stuffed her face with pancakes at the café. Will pulled one auburn ringlet and teased Sienna for looking like a chipmunk. Kenna placed a hand over her still-hidden bump and rubbed what she was positive was their son.

"Good morning, Mrs. Ashton." Tom Burns, the prosecutor for the county, took a seat next to Sienna. With a jovial laugh and bushy brows, he scooped their daughter up and started bouncing her on his knee.

"Good morning, Mr. Burns. How are you this fine morning?" Kenna asked as Will shook Tom's hand before Sienna reclaimed the "reins" to her horsey.

"I woke up this morning and decided today was a great day to retire. The missus and I booked a cruise and we leave tomorrow morning."

The people in the café stopped eating as they all turned to listen. "Retire? But you still have three years before the next election. Who? What?" Kenna for once was at a loss of words.

"That's right. And I'm asking you to be my replacement. Cases are on my, *your*, desk and Martha will get you up to speed. Dani's welcome back if she wishes. Martha wants to retire at the beginning of the year. So, have fun hiring people." Tom gave Sienna a kiss and then placed her into Will's lap when he stood up. "Bye y'all. See you in a month when we get back from Europe."

Gemma thanked the man with the hairy eyebrows who held open the door for her at the café. She walked in and immediately the volume rose to near-deafening levels. Questions were being thrown at her. People were hugging her. But she still couldn't see Cy. Although the celebratory atmosphere did cheer her up, she couldn't shake the feeling she had to find Cy.

"Kenna, have you seen Cy?" Gemma asked when she finally made it over to her table.

"No, I haven't. Have you, Will?"

"Yes. I passed him on his way out to the farm. You may want to check out there."

"Thank you." Gemma leaped up and smiled at Kenna and Will before trying to make her way to the door.

Finally breaking free of the happy crowd, she hurried through the door and out onto the street. She needed a car. Gemma turned to head back inside to ask Kenna and Will to give her a ride when she heard something. She looked up Main Street and there was a man on a horse coming down the center of the street. Cars pulled over to honk and wave. The rider waved back.

Gemma shielded her eyes from the sun and looked at the rider. He was in jeans and a button-down shirt with the long sleeves rolled up on his masculine arms. A dusky brown cowboy hat set low on the man's face, but she didn't need to see it. She knew Cy's body anywhere.

The café door opened and people started pouring out onto the sidewalk, but Gemma didn't even see them. She started walking down the street toward Cy. He slowed the horse in front of her and dismounted with an amazing amount of grace. The hat hid his face, except for the smile he was wearing. He turned back to the saddle and set Fred down on the ground. Gemma put her hand to her chest and laughed at her little dog with a black bandana around his neck.

"Fred and I have come to find you," Cy said as he swept off his hat. The sun shone on his face. His eyes danced with excitement as he smiled at her.

"Well, here I am." Gemma was overtaken by excitement. She belonged here, with him.

"He's turned into a good farmhand and doesn't want to leave. I don't want you to leave either." Cy's smile disappeared as he hung his hat on the horn of his saddle. He took her hands in his and looked into her eyes. "Gemma, this is me. The new me and the old me, all mixed into one. A former spy and stuntman turned farmer. I've had trouble coming to terms with my new life, but I've never had trouble coming to terms with how much you mean to me. I love you, Gemma. I loved you when I was a stuntman, when I was a spy, and now as a farmer. Do you think you love me for who I am now? A boring farmer living in a crazy small town in Kentucky with a huge family?"

Gemma reached up and ran her fingers along his jaw. "Oh, Cy. There's nothing boring about you. I love you so much—the real you. The one who loves his family and the one who embraces this town."

She raised her chin and pressed her lips to his. At first he was hesitant, but then his arms wrapped around her and he deepened the kiss. Cheers erupted from the patrons spilling from the café.

Cy smiled against her lips and stepped back. He dug into his pocket and Gemma couldn't stop staring as he pulled out a black box. She heard herself and all of Keeneston gasp when Cy went down onto one knee. Fred ran around him barking and wagging his tail as Cy opened the box, showing her a ring—a solitaire diamond between two emeralds.

"I love you for everything you are, have been, and will be. I am yours and the love we share will only grow throughout our lives. I look forward to each day when I wake up with you beside me. Gemma Perry, will you do me the honor of becoming my wife?"

"Someday we'll find the one we cannot live without. The perfect man who will love us both," Gia giggled as she wrapped Gemma in a hug.

"He'll make you smile and laugh and put up with you talking to me every day."

Gemma felt the tears streaming down her face as Gia's voice filled her head with the memory of their conversation when they were just sixteen. And she was right. Gemma had found the perfect man who made her smile and laugh. She looked down at Cy's nervous face and nodded. "Yes."

Cy fumbled the ring but managed to slip it onto her shaking finger before standing up and pulling her to him. He kissed her with such love and passion that Gemma forgot she was in front of other people. His tongue caressed her mouth as she flung her arms around him urging him on. The sharp sound of catcalls and whistles broke the spell as Gemma felt her face flush with embarrassment.

"Come on. I know the perfect place to celebrate," Cy whispered in her ear before grabbing his hat and mounting his horse. "Thank y'all. Miss Lily, would you mind watching Fred for a bit?"

"Not at all."

Congratulations broke out from the crowd. Gemma smiled and waved, but looked up at Cy, wondering what he was planning.

He held out his hand. "Grab my hand and put your foot here." He withdrew his foot from the stirrup and when she put her foot in it, he swung her up and into his lap. His arm wrapped securely around her waist as he turned the horse and trotted back up the road.

"Where are we going?" Gemma asked as she tossed her head back in the air and soaked up the moment.

"Home."

Cy sat down next to Gemma on the blanket and tossed his hat on the ground. He looked out at the flat field surrounded by large trees like the one they were sitting under. "I thought we'd put the house right here. What do you think?"

"Oh, it's lovely." Gemma glowed with excitement. He leaned over and kissed her. He had a romantic picnic planned, but right now all he wanted was her.

As he deepened the kiss, Gemma arched forward, pressing her breasts against his chest. Cy fought for control as his hand slid up her side, caressing the outside of her breast before reaching her shoulder. He slipped her dress straps down, freeing her to him. His hand cupped her as his thumb traced a nipple.

His heart pounded as he eased her down on the large blanket. Soon all pretenses of slow and romantic faded as she tore his shirt off and tossed it on the ground. When words weren't enough, action was. And he was going to show her just how much he loved her.

CHAPTER
TWENTY-THREE

Four months later...

$\mathcal{G}$emma heard her new sisters in the room next to her laughing while they got dressed. Her hair was finally pinned up and the fingertip veil floated around her as she grabbed a replica of the maid of honor's bouquet and put it in a basket. Without saying a word, she went down the large staircase of Miss Lily's bed-and-breakfast. She picked up the front of her A-line gown and hurried down the street. The smell of fall was strong in the air. The trees were radiant shades of red, orange, and yellow as she ran past them.

It only took five minutes to make it to the Keeneston Cemetery where she stopped in front of her sister's grave. After her engagement to Cy was announced, Gemma sent notice to her magazine and had movers pack up her house while she and Cy went to Gia's apartment to pack. They arrived back in Keeneston the next day and buried her sister next to Morgan's mother. The whole town came out to support her and to honor Gia, who was laid to rest with honor befitting an American hero.

The next day Tammy and Pierce announced they didn't want to wait to get married. They got married the following weekend in a beautiful ceremony at the church. Tammy looked fantastic in her tea-length dress with sky-blue high heels. The Rose sisters had been hired to cater and were in a state of frenzy and pure delight to have been asked.

Gemma had needed an outlet and had started writing her and Gia's story. It was a story of a sister's love and determination and the downfall of an international criminal. Marianne from the *Keeneston Journal* had run the first chapter, and before Gemma knew it, she had become an author and the small newspaper's articles were being picked up around the world.

Gemma opened the basket she had brought with her and pulled out the book she had placed inside. "This is the first copy of our book, Gia. I found my passion finally. You led me to it. It's writing.

"Yesterday Cy gave me my wedding present, the *Keeneston Journal*. I own a newspaper. Marianne wanted to write part-time and couldn't keep up with the demands now that other papers have picked up my articles. She's covering the court dockets and I'm writing hard-hitting and feel-good articles. Every now and then, I'll sneak in to host the weekly gossip column. It's actually a ton of fun. It's silly, but when done right, the gossip column can bring true joy and laughter."

Gemma set the book down and pulled out the bouquet of flowers. "Today I'm getting married. I wanted you to have this. You will be my maid of honor, just like we talked about. Katelyn has agreed to stand in for you and we're wearing the matching charm bracelets we made on spring break our senior year of high school. It's actually quite a compliment to have a world-famous model wearing your design." Gemma laughed and wiped away a tear. The pain had lessened over the months, but it hadn't gone away yet. She didn't know if it ever would. But there were more good days and more happy memories than bad, so she took that as improvement.

"You were right, Gia. I did find the one perfect man I couldn't live without. And today I'm going to marry him. Hopefully we'll have a family of our own soon. I wonder if we'll have twins?" Gemma stood and smiled. She was ready to get married.

***

"Suck it in, Tammy," Annie ordered when Gemma entered the room full of bridesmaids getting ready.

"I am."

"Well, try harder."

"Tammy, raise your arms above your head and then suck it in," Katelyn calmly instructed. Tammy followed her instructions and the zipper slid up.

"Thank goodness," Tammy sighed.

"Well, I know Katelyn and I had that same scare, but we couldn't suck it in." Morgan joked at she rubbed her baby bump.

"No kidding. I'm about to burst." Katelyn slowly lowered herself into the chair and put her feet up.

"There you are. Oh, you look beautiful." Paige clapped her hands just the way Gemma noticed Marcy did.

Gemma blushed and did a little twirl for them. "Thank you. I feel beautiful. And anxious. But I'm really looking forward to the reception."

"Right. That's the part you want to get to," Tammy giggled.

"Ladies, it's time to go. Oh . . . don't you look lovely?" Miss Lily twittered as she kissed each lady on the cheek. "Now, we don't want to be late."

Cy stood at the altar and waited for the doors to open. His sister and sisters-in-law had all made their appearance and now he was waiting for his bride to make hers. The months had flown by and they'd only fallen deeper in love. Their house would be done by the time they returned from

their honeymoon. He hoped they'd be filling that house with children soon.

The music changed and the doors opened. His father stood proud as he escorted Gemma down the aisle. Cy never saw the huge smile on Jake's face or the joyful tears from his mother in the front row. No, he only saw his glowing bride as she floated down the aisle.

He took a step down and offered her his arm as they stepped in front of Father James. "You're breathtaking," he whispered to her as she grinned up at him.

"And I love you," Gemma said as she squeezed his hand.

Cy mouthed the words back to her as Father James started the ceremony. He happily pledged his love and life to Gemma. When the priest pronounced them husband and wife, Cy grabbed his bride and kissed her with all the love he had.

Laughter and cheers erupted as Cy scooped Gemma into his arms and ran down the aisle. She wrapped her arm around his neck, tossed her head back and laughed with such joy that he knew their life would be filled with nothing but happiness.

The bridal couple took a seat at the head table as the town sat around them talking gleefully and eating dinner. Gemma leaned over to Cy and rested her head on his shoulder.

"I wanted to give you your wedding present tonight, but I'm too excited to wait," Gemma whispered.

"Sure. I won't turn down gifts. Does it involve that thing you do with your leg and then you bend . . ."

"I've learned a new trick. Think we can escape?"

"A new trick? Let's go," he winked.

"You think they'll notice?"

"Have some faith in your husband, Mrs. Davies. I was a spy after all. They'll never even miss us."

Cy casually stood up and offered his hand to his wife. He led her around the perimeter of the reception, talking to

friends, before leading her toward the small break in the white curtains hanging from the tent. Now he understood the goofy little grins his brothers always wore, because he knew he had the same look as he looked down at Gemma.

"So, what's the plan, super spy?"

"We're going to walk right out of here and no one will notice." Cy stopped her near the hidden exit and looked around. When he was sure no one was looking, they slipped through the curtains and into the moonlit night. "Now, about that new trick?"

"Come right this way, husband."

"I'd follow you anywhere, wife." And he would.

Marcy Davies smiled to herself as her family talked around her. Cy thought he was so sneaky, but she always knew when he had slipped out of the house as a boy and tonight was no different. She had seen the look in her son's and new daughter-in-law's eyes. And definitely didn't miss them sneaking out of the tent.

Marcy nudged her husband of forty years and nodded to where Cy and Gemma had just been standing, "It looks as if your son couldn't wait to begin the honeymoon. Oh, Jake! I just know there'll be more grandbabies on the way soon," she whispered as she wiped a tear from her eye. Her family gave her so much happiness.

"Just make sure you don't die of happiness too soon," he whispered back with a grin on his face that Marcy still found sexy. Oh no, she was very much alive tonight and if her husband kept smiling at her like that, Cy and Gemma wouldn't be the only ones sneaking out of the tent.

"You're right, honey. I can't die happy until I have all my grandbabies. Tammy and Pierce . . ." Marcy's eyes narrowed on Tammy and Pierce and the rest of the Davies family gathered around Gemma and Cy. "Tammy? Is that apple juice?"

"Um . . ." Tammy stuttered.

"And your dress looks different than it did last month." Marcy paused as she looked Tammy over. Tammy fidgeted under the examination. "Oh my gosh. You're pregnant!"

"We are, but we wanted Gemma and Cy to have their day before we announced it. So, thanks for blowing the surprise, Ma," Pierce tried to chide.

"Well, bless y'all's hearts," Marcy cried as she wrapped her dear daughter-in-law up in a hug.

Miss Lily and a group of townspeople came over to offer their congratulations. "Keeneston will be in full bloom by spring," Miss Lily said as she and her sisters dabbed their eyes.

Ahmed stood by the door and watched his love dance. She was beautiful. But the man dancing with her didn't deserve her. He had to remind himself he couldn't claim her by punching the guy out. She couldn't know his feelings until Sergei was dead. Until then, he had to love from afar. It was starting to hurt, but Ahmed tried to keep the hope alive that someday he would be where Cy was today—married to the love of his life.

"Sir," Nabi said as the serious young man approached him with a piece of paper, "this popped up in a Pakistani newspaper. One hundred people and counting are dead in a train explosion."

"He's back," Ahmed said as he glanced at the picture of destruction.

"You're sure it's Sergei?"

"I'm sure. He must've found a new employer. See, the minister of energy was on the train. Instead of just killing the minister, he blew the whole thing up. The high body count hides the assassination. It's one of his old tricks."

"What are you going to do?"

Ahmed thought about his deceased wife and child before looking up from the newspaper. His eyes automatically fell on the woman he had to love in secret as she danced around. "End this."

Cy swung his wife around the dance floor as the crowd cheered. No one seemed to notice when they slipped back into the tent thirty minutes later. The music was fast and the floor was full of couples laughing and talking the night away. He couldn't imagine a better night—marriage to the woman he loved more than life itself.

He pulled Gemma to him and kissed her enthusiastically before spinning her away again. "Hey, Cy," Gemma called as she lifted her skirt and twirled.

"Yes, my love?"

"I love you."

"I love you, too." He pulled Gemma back to him and leaned down. "I think it's time to go and let me show you how much I love you. Maybe if I'm a real good boy, you'll do that thing you just did with your . . ."

Gemma blushed. "So soon? We just got back," she giggled. "Well, if you're a real good boy and dance with me some more, then I might show you what I can do when I bend my back like . . ."

Cy feigned shock. "You've been keeping secrets."

"Not anymore. No more secrets. Just us and our new family."

The sound of clinking caught their attention as Jake raised his glass. "A toast . . . I want to welcome Gemma to our family. Over the past couple of years, our family has more than doubled in size. By the end of next year, I'll be bouncing more babies than I can hold and my wife will be able to die happy." The crowd laughed and Marcy smacked him even though she was smiling from ear to ear. "But our family wouldn't be who we are today without the help, matchmaking, gossiping, and happy trigger-fingers y'all have. So, from my family to y'all—please raise your glasses to Keeneston!"

###

ABOUT THE AUTHOR

Kathleen Brooks is the bestselling author of the Bluegrass Series. She has garnered attention as a new voice in romance with a warm Southern feel. Her books feature quirky small town characters you'll feel like you've known forever, romance, humor, and mystery all mixed into one perfect glass of sweet tea.

Kathleen is an animal lover who supports rescue organizations and other non-profit organizations whose goals are to protect and save our four-legged family members.

Kathleen lives in Central Kentucky with her husband, daughter, two dogs, and a cat who thinks he's a dog. She loves to hear from readers and can be reached at Kathleen@Kathleen-Brooks.com

Check out the **Website** for updates on all of Kathleen's series. You can also "Like" Kathleen on **Facebook** and follow her on Twitter **@BluegrassBrooks**.

Other Books by Kathleen Brooks

Keeneston Continues!

The Bluegrass Brothers Series will have one last installment. The Davies brothers' stories may be told, but their brother-in-arms waits. Ahmed's book will be released in early 2014. Be sure to like me on **Facebook** or follow my **Blog** to get updates on the release date!

Bluegrass Series

Bluegrass State of Mind

McKenna Mason, a New York City attorney with a love of all things Prada, is on the run from a group of powerful, dangerous men. McKenna turns to a teenage crush, Will Ashton, for help in starting a new life in beautiful horse country. She finds that Will is now a handsome, successful race horse farm owner. As the old flame is ignited, complications are aplenty in the form of a nasty ex-wife, an ex-boyfriend intent on killing her, and a feisty race horse who refuses to race without a kiss. Can Will and McKenna cross the finish line together, and more importantly, alive?

Risky Shot

Danielle De Luca, an ex-beauty queen who is not at all what she seems, leaves the streets of New York after tracking the criminals out to destroy her. She travels to Keeneston, Kentucky, to make her final stand by the side of her best friend McKenna Mason. While in Keeneston, Danielle meets the quiet and mysterious Mohtadi Ali Rahmen, a modern day prince. Can Mo protect Dani from the group of powerful men in New York? Or will Dani save the prince from his rigid, loveless destiny?

Dead Heat

In the third book of the Bluegrass Series, Paige Davies finds her world turned upside down as she becomes involved in her best friend's nightmare. The strong-willed Paige doesn't know which is worse: someone trying to kill her, or losing her dog to the man she loves to hate.

FBI Agent Cole Parker can't decide whether he should strangle or kiss this infuriating woman of his dreams. As he works the case of his career, he finds that love can be tougher than bringing down some of the most powerful men in America.

Bluegrass Brothers Series

Bluegrass Undercover

Cade Davies had too much on his plate to pay attention to newest resident of Keeneston. He was too busy avoiding the Davies Brothers marriage trap set by half the town. But when a curvy redhead lands in Keeneston, the retired Army Ranger finds himself drawn to her. These feelings are only fueled by her apparent indifference and lack of faith in his ability to defend himself.

DEA Agent Annie Blake was undercover to bust a drug ring hiding in the adorable Southern town that preyed on high school athletes. She had thought to keep her head down and listen to the local gossip to find the maker of this deadly drug. What Annie didn't count on was becoming the local gossip. With marriage bets being placed, and an entire town aiming to win the pot, Annie looks to Cade for help in bringing down the drug ring before another kid is killed. But can she deal with the feelings that follow?

Rising Storm

Katelyn Jacks was used to being front and center as a model. But she never had to confront the Keeneston Grapevine! After retiring from the runway and returning to town to open a new animal clinic, Katelyn found that her life in the public eye was anything but over. While working hard to establish herself as the new veterinarian in town, Katelyn finds her life uprooted by a storm of love, gossip, and a vicious group of criminals.

Marshall Davies is the new Sheriff in Keeneston. He is also right at the top of the town's most eligible bachelor list. His affinity for teasing the hot new veterinarian in town has led to a rush of emotions that he wasn't ready for. Marshall finds his easy days of breaking up fights at the local PTA meetings are over when he and Katelyn discover that a dog-fighting ring has stormed into their normally idyllic town. As their love struggles to break through, they must battle to save the lives of the dogs and each other.

Secret Santa, A Bluegrass Series Novella

It wouldn't be Christmas in Keeneston without a party! Everyone's invited, even Santa...

Kenna's court docket is full, Dani's hiding from her in-laws, Paige and Annie are about to burst from pregnancy, and Marshall is breaking up fights at the PTA Christmas Concert. The sweet potato casserole is made, the ham and biscuits are on the table, and men are losing their shirts – and not because of bets placed with the Rose Sisters! All the while, the entire town is wondering one thing: who is the Secret Santa that showed up with special gifts for everyone?

Acquiring Trouble

As a natural born leader, Miles Davies accomplishes anything he puts his mind to. Upon returning home from his special forces duties, he has become the strong foundation of the Davies family and his company. But that strong foundation is about to get rocked in a big way by the one woman that always left him fascinated and infuriated.

Keeneston's notorious bad girl is back! Morgan Hamilton's life ended and began on her high school graduation night when she left Keeneston with no plan to ever return. As a self-made businesswoman, Morgan is always looking for her next victory. Little did she know that next victory would involve acquiring the company that belonged to the one man she always wanted for herself.

With their careers and lives on the line, will Miles and Morgan choose love or ambition?

Relentless Pursuit

Pierce Davies watched as his older siblings fell in love – something this bachelor was not ready for. After all, he was now the most eligible man in all of Keeneston! Though Pierce enjoys the playboy lifestyle, his life is his work and that hard work is set to pay off big time with the unveiling of a big secret. However, this work hard, play hard attitude may have also landed him in hot water as he finds himself arrested for a brutal murder with all evidence pointing to him.

Tammy Fields has been suffering from the crush to end all crushes. But her flirtations have fallen short as Pierce Davies always ended up in the arms of a Keeneston Belle. Having waited long enough, Tammy decides now is the time to grow up and move on. She has a good job as a paralegal and a hot new boyfriend. But everything changes quickly when Pierce is arrested and Tammy is called upon to help with his case. While working closely with Pierce to prove his innocence, she realizes her crush is something far more meaningful as she risks everything to save him.

Will they finally find love or will the increasing danger prevent their happily ever after?

Make sure you don't miss each new book as they are published. Sign up email notification of all new releases at **http://www.Kathleen-Brooks.com.**

29955832R00146

Made in the USA
Charleston, SC
30 May 2014